Light Journey

Light Journey

Anne Howard

iUniverse®

LIGHT JOURNEY

Author Credits: Anne Howard

This is a work of fiction. All of the characters, names, incidents, organizations, and dialogue in this novel are either the products of the author's imagination or are used fictitiously.

iUniverse books may be ordered through booksellers or by contacting:

iUniverse
1663 Liberty Drive
Bloomington, IN 47403
www.iuniverse.com
1-800-Authors (1-800-288-4677)

ISBN: 978-1-5320-0482-7 (sc)
ISBN: 978-1-5320-0481-0 (e)

Library of Congress Control Number: 2016914136

Print information available on the last page.

iUniverse rev. date: 09/27/2016

DEDICATION

In loving memory of
Junius and Velma Howard,
my creative and encouraging parents;
Francis (Frank) Howard, my brother,
whom I loved dearly;
and Bill and Marie Ising,
who were like parents to me.

ACKNOWLEDGEMENTS

My warmest thanks to the best sister in the world, Jeanne Howard, whose determination, dedication and loving devotion made this book possible. Besides her many hours of typing and formatting, Jeanne's creativity and spontaneity inspired the same in me. Her joy-filled affirmations and positive attitude kept alive the vision to share this story of Light.

My longtime friend, Donna Ising, gave the gift of her laughter, encouragement, support, patience and love. For her advice and inspiration over the years, I am deeply grateful and forever indebted.

A more recent friend, Sharon Bowers, has been like a sister to me. Her dedication in proofreading and research has been priceless. Her inspiration and cherished friendship have meant so much to me. More than anything, I deeply appreciate her humor and lightheartedness.

It is a privilege to have Charles Suddeth and Roberta Simpson Brown, both phenomenal authors, as treasured friends. They have inspired, reviewed, affirmed, encouraged, and challenged me to be a better author. Gratitude, for their giftedness and the gift they are to me, is beyond words.

The Louisville, Lexington and Nashville Critique Group, members of _Society of Children's Book Writers and Illustrators_ Midsouth (SCBWI), has been such a blessing to me. Charles Suddeth, Gail Noll, Amy Williamson, David Jarvis and Laura Stone have reviewed my manuscript and offered many energizing suggestions about character development and plot. Their insights have given me greater knowledge of the art of writing.

I wish to also articulate my gratefulness to my family and all of my friends who have been like kinfolk to me over the years, too many to mention. They have inspired and emboldened me during my own Light Journey.

To the Living and Triune God, who has gifted all of us with His Life, His Love, His Light, I give my praise, thanksgiving, love and worship. To God, be the glory.

You are the light of the world.
A city set on a mountain cannot be hidden.
Nor do they light a lamp and then put it under a bushel basket;
it is set on a lampstand, where it gives light to all in the house.
Just so, your light must shine before others,
that they may see your good deeds
and glorify your heavenly Father.

(Matthew 5: 14-16)

CHAPTER ONE
Nature's Pause

For a breathless moment, all creation seemed to wait for Jamie Travelstead to begin. She straddled her favorite oak, TimberWood. With each foot on a sturdy branch, she raised her arms and reached for the stars. As she pointed to TimberWood, the oak's branches and leaves became perfectly still.

By tapping her baton on the tree trunk, Jamie alerted the participants to get ready. Several oaks, maples, tulip poplars, and a Japanese red maple focused on Jamie. She waved her wand to the left, swirling it higher and lower. The trees obeyed Jamie's every direction. They knew when to come in and do their part.

She loved the role of a conductor, and drawing scenes in the air that went with the music. The tip of her wand drew sketches of teens playing soccer in the street. The kids scurried back and forth, keeping the ball in constant movement. The side kicking of the ball produced percussion sounds. One of the boys made a goal. The children's laughter and cheers permeated the air. Clarinets, French horns, oboes and saxophones reverberated.

Next, she drew an ice cream truck with its melodies created by bells, piccolos and triangles inviting all to come. The jingles of change, squeals of delight and the chatter of their parents added to the symphony.

"TimberWood, I'm doing it. I am giving sounds to nature, and it trusts me with its musical notes. I can create melody, harmony and rhythm. I do not have to pretend. I'm ready for my prince."

Jamie conducted another song. TimberWood's leaves danced in harmony with Jamie's feelings. Every tree joined in the dance while squirrels and rabbits frolicked around the base of the trees. The cardinals, blue birds, wrens and gold finches circled above like a kaleidoscope of colors. Sunlight flickered through the leaves, making silhouette patterns that tickled the sky with laughter. Jamie moved in rhythm, enchanted by the speckles of light on herself and TimberWood. She twirled her wand faster, staying in perfect sync with the music around her. All the trees' limbs swirled as they whistled and hummed her favorite music *Nature's Melodic Pause.*

TimberWood's leaves and branches swayed in festivity. "Your sounds match life," Jamie said. "We've touched each other's hearts. We've harmonized our music, drawing nature together in a rapture of one accord."

"We make beautiful music," TimberWood agreed. Jamie and TimberWood played together since she was a toddler.

Jamie hugged TimberWood. The middle section of the magical tree's trunk wrinkled up as his bark moved, twisted, and repositioned to form a mouth, nose, ears, and eyes.

He motioned to Jamie to move closer to his mouth. TimberWood stroked his bark covered chin. "My limbs act as arms and my leaves as hands. I have all the human senses and can use them to identify others' feelings." He whispered a warning. "Be careful. The witches' goal is to control you."

"What witches?"

"The witches who roam the universe from Black Eye Galaxy. I am very serious, Jamie, they are after you."

"Okay, I promise you. I will stay alert. Now can we just get back to happy stuff?" Climbing high into TimberWood, Jamie reached a stopping place where a larger branch split into two. She sat on one of the limbs and swung her feet. Jamie became reflective and watched the pathway of the sun.

TimberWood started up again. "I am concerned for you, Jamie. Watch out. The witches can cast spells and overtake you."

"My parents warned me against witches, but they also told me my powers increase as I get older. I will be able to defend myself. Besides why would they be interested in me? I am only twelve."

"That's true," TimberWood said, "but you have powers that you are not even aware of yet. You need to use extreme caution."

Jamie played with a leaf. "How bad can it get? My twin sister Kattie already steals my stuff. She tears up my room, and picks on me."

TimberWood cradled Jamie in his branches. "I'm sorry about your sister's behavior. Her meanness reminds me of the witches."

Jamie hoped to get the latest gossip. "Really."

"They are bullies just like your sister. You know how my roots extend under the yards in this neighborhood and beyond to the adjacent properties. They go under the lot owned by SpiderWood and SilverWorm. There are rumors these witches have joined forces to go after all the magical people on HallowWinds. Their hate for each other and other people propels them to target goodness. Havoc and destruction are the witches' mission. Kattie's aggravation is mild compared to the twin witch sisters. They are always threatening us. We must not fall into complacency. We must be prepared if they strike."

Jamie squeezed her tree. She preferred living in HallowWinds to any other place of magic, but her parents wanted to move elsewhere, some place safer.

The day's shadows deepened. It was almost time for Jamie to go in for the night, but she could not bring herself to do it. With the increased daylight hours of summer and the gorgeous sunsets, it was so hard to go inside before dark.

Jamie played one more game, pretending to have a fearless hero as a friend. Jumping from one branch to another, she felt like a fledgling springing off a launch pad to conquer the world.

She sang and swayed to the rhythm and words of another favorite song, *Your Winds Carry Me on High*. Jamie so wanted someone to be her superman and keep her safe.

Jamie's desires filled her mind with images so real she felt the prince's radiant smile warm her. His corn silk hair waved with the breeze. She saw his emerald green eyes blink at her, and heard his soft-spoken voice say *Hello there*.

Her mensch seemed so real. Jamie wanted him to scoop her up and take her to a castle with towers touching the sky. *Maybe he will come tomorrow and stay for a while.*

The sun finished its journey, forcing the light into darkness and heralding the night as a friend. Jamie watched the day disappear. Leaning her head against the center of TimberWood's trunk, she could feel his heartbeat. She stroked his bark. "I love you, my friend. Good night."

****

The next day, Jamie sat close to TimberWood's trunk with several branches cradling her. She propped her head on her knees. A ladybug landed on a nearby leaf. Jamie gently placed her finger in front of the bug. It crawled up her finger and settled into the palm of her hand. Jamie encouraged the bug to fly, but it didn't. The ladybug warmed its body, in no hurry to move on. Jamie knew that her destiny was worth the wait, but she could not help thinking that time crawls like a bug on a leaf. After replacing the bug to its leafy perch, Jamie climbed higher into the branches so she could see the images of the flickering sunlight.

Enchanted by the dancing light, Jamie stood up on a bulky branch. From behind the clouds, she could see strands of blonde hair sparkle and then flashes of shimmering green. *Has my leading man come calling today?* He seemed more real when she thought of him.

Absorbed in her imaginings, Jamie leaned forward and slipped. TimberWood tried to break her fall by gently moving his branches into the path of her descent. She caught hold of a branch and hung on for as long as she could.

Then Jamie lost her grasp on the limb. Mysteriously a teenage boy broke her fall, catching her in his muscular arms. Her hero had emerald green eyes, and shoulder-length blond hair reflecting the sunlight. His hair brushed against her face as she gazed into his eyes in disbelief.

Her heart pulsated, pumped, and added a beat. "Who are you?" Jamie gasped. "Am I dreaming about my prince?"

"Well, I've never thought of myself as royalty of any kind, and I am not a dream. My name is Griff Burton." The polite teen gently placed her feet on the ground. "Are you alright?"

Jamie rested on a tree stump to examine her hands and legs. "Yeah, except for a few bruises and scrapes. I am good. Thanks to you."

Griff switched from one foot to the other. "No problem. I'm glad to help."

"How did you know I needed help?"

"Your scream traveled the energy fields." Griff chuckled.

"What planet are you from? Are you sure that you are not a king or prince from some other place? You kind of look important."

"You ask a lot of questions. No, I am not a crowned anything. I am in Light Channel's Officer Training Corp. After high school, I will be an apprentice as a Light Keeper." He held himself up straight. "I just turned fourteen the last day of June. I'll be starting high school in late August."

"My birthday is on October 17 and I'll be in the eighth grade. I've never heard of Light Keepers."

Griff laughed. "Really? I thought you would know all about them. Your parents ...well I guess you are too young to know."

"Too young to know what? Some gentleman you are. And wait a minute, do you know my parents?"

"I'm sorry I didn't mean to imply anything. Let me explain myself. I live on the Light Channel with my uncle, Belcor Williams, who has been a Light Champion for many years and is now the Commander-in-Chief. Your parents have been his friends for a long, long time."

"Well, you know my last name is Travelstead. My first name is Jamie. I haven't met you before, have I?"

"No, but my uncle has a framed photo of your family on a bookshelf in his office. In fact, you are standing in front of this very same tree in the picture."

"Oh, this is my dearest and wisest friend, TimberWood. I spend a lot of time in his branches. Getting back to my falling from TimberWood's bough, you never really answered how you knew I needed help."

"I travel to Earth and HallowWinds with my uncle on some of his safer missions. He has fancy detectors that pick up signals from magical people or creation. I heard a call over his device that you needed help. As a Commander-in-Chief, my uncle protects the Light Channel and the whole Universe from Dark Particles. Occasionally, he sends me on a rescue assignment. Uncle Belcor allowed me to come by myself. So, here I am."

"Do you mean I'm your assignment?" Jamie asked sarcastically.

"I insulted you again. My uncle and I were close to HallowWinds, and he let me come. However, Jamie, I also came because I wanted to come.

I wanted to meet the girl under the tree for a long time. Besides, we don't rescue just anybody from a fall out of a tree – only special people like you."

"How sweet of you to say that." Jamie reached up to touch Griff's arm. The contact brought a brief insight. "I'm sorry you're having a rough time. You're sad over deaths in your family."

He fixed his eyes on Jamie. "I don't understand how you knew that."

"My parents told me that I have the gift of revelation," Jamie said. "I sense things about people. I feel you are grieving."

Griff sat on the stump next to Jamie. "I'm not handling the murders of my parents. The brutality still haunts me. When I close my eyes, I relive the events. Blood covered their clothes. I want the murderers to pay for their crimes, but my family and I have only a few clues to go on."

"I've had some bad experiences like yours."

"What happened? If you don't mind me asking," Griff whispered.

"Jaden was brutally murdered. I was the one who found him," Jamie sniffled. "I was really close to my cousin. I hung around him after school. We were best friends. I could not deal with his death so I tried to shove it out of my mind. It doesn't work."

Griff touched Jamie's face. "So that's why your heart is full of tears. I didn't want to pry."

"No, that's ok. It is good for me to talk about it. I have had this gift of revelation since I was three years old. It was fun then. When I was eight, I sensed Jaden's murder but I dismissed it. I did not know how to tell anyone. It took me a long time to talk about the death of my cousin. I blamed myself and couldn't face my emotions. I have enough anger to last a lifetime. Everyone thinks I am happy-go-lucky, and I can be."

"I'm like you. I am full of rage about dark and evil things happening. It is not fair. There's hope in knowing our gifts grow as we do and these powers will help us to fight the rage within us." Griff shifted and smiled awkwardly. Griff's royal blue cape whipped in the breeze. He wore a gold medallion on a glittering chain.

Jamie noticed the gem's beautiful swirling colors. "May I touch it?"

"Sure. Look at the inscription inside too."

Jamie ran her finger over the words, carved at the bottom of the rim, *Protector of the Light*. "Tell me about your gem," Jamie said. "It looks amazing, and I know it must be special to you."

"It is unique and distinctive. I inherited it from my father. He gave it the name, LightStone. It is an offspring of Genesis, which is a stone capable of greatest light. LightStone is one of my defenses."

"Defenses? You mean as a future Light Keeper?"

"Yes for the future and the present. Someday, after college, I will be a Light Champion. This tradition is important in my family. Actually, it is highly valued in your family also. There is unbelievable evil and darkness in the universe. We have to stay alert at all times – not just to protect ourselves but all those who are harmed by the Dark Particles."

"TimberWood told me yesterday that I need to stay alert, and now you. Maybe I really do need to be more serious." Jamie said as she handed the medallion back to Griff.

"Yes, please do. No matter how young we are, when we have magical power, the witches will target us. Would you like to see the LightStone in action?"

"Oh yes. I was hoping you'd ask me."

Griff touched his medallion. "Sun Particles. Come now."

Bright spheres filtered through the sky. They floated, exuding light that flooded the backyard. They passed close to Jamie.

"How exciting. I adore the rainbow colors created when they shine through each other." Jamie showed him the colors reflected on her arms.

Griff smiled as he held a crystal sphere, spinning it on his right index finger. He bounced it like a basketball. "They illuminate our Channel, which belongs to a galaxy without a separate sun or moon."

Jamie studied their delicate appearance. "It must take a billion of these spheres to get enough light for the Light Channel."

"You're right," Griff said. "Or maybe zillions."

Jamie relaxed even though she talked to such an impressive young man. She surprised herself.

Griff glanced at his medallion. "Hold on—my gem is turning orange."

"Is everything okay?"

"I don't know. The color is a sign of caution. The Sun Particles and I must go for our assignment with Uncle Belcor. I need to get back to his ship. We are requested to report to the command center of Light Channel."

"Will I see you again?" Jamie asked.

"Oh, yes, you will definitely see me. I want to see you soon." Griff patted Jamie on the shoulder.

Jamie touched his arm as energy flowed between them.

"Look up to the northeast for a message." Griff created a gust of wind that transported himself and the Sun Particles back to his uncle's spaceship.

Jamie watched the sky as multicolored banner spelled out *I enjoyed our time together. See you soon.* She touched the bark on TimberWood and rubbed her hand over the designs and textures of his trunk. In her heart, Jamie anticipated seeing Griff again. *We will be friends. I just know it. He is a trainee now, but he will be my prince.* Jamie was startled when she heard the back door open.

"Jamie, your sister and I are home. Come in and try on your new school clothes." Her mother and identical twin sister, Kattie, had gone to lunch and shopping together. Once a month, she took them out separately for mother and daughter time.

"Okay, I'm coming." *Good timing. Glad Griff had left. I do not want Kattie to know about him.* Bounding in the door, Jamie exclaimed, "What did you get for me?"

"We found the best back-to-school sale," Mom replied as she held up a yellow tuck pleated blouse. "This looks like it would be perfect for you, Jamie."

The trio had a wonderful time going through all the packages while Dad sat in his favorite chair watching them with such pleasure. Jamie caught her father's eye. They exchanged knowing smiles. *I wish it were always this peaceful with Kattie around. Today is a good day. A good way to begin eighth grade tomorrow. A prince and a peaceful home.*

CHAPTER TWO

Darkness

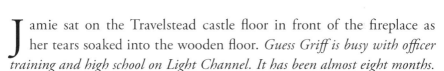

J amie sat on the Travelstead castle floor in front of the fireplace as her tears soaked into the wooden floor. *Guess Griff is busy with officer training and high school on Light Channel. It has been almost eight months. No time? I thought we had the beginnings of a great friendship. I know we connected.* Jamie brushed her hair away from her face.

Another tear fell and landed on her hand. She was astonished when it turned into a miniature dove. Then several more tears speckled the floor. They too became doves. The snow-white birds flitted and fluttered around Jamie, doing various tricks like an air show. Jamie laughed and the doves disappeared in the upstairs rafters.

After finishing all of her homework assignments, Jamie spread her drawing pencils in front of her and chose a dark red to make the final touches. With fluid lines, she sketched her mother's knitting basket with numerous colors of yarn. The family's black cat, with a ruby collar, had playfully pulled out a ball of variegated yarn, making colorful designs on the floor near the fireplace hearth. Jamie titled her drawing as *Rubie's Yarn Art*.

Eager to work on Griff's portrait, Jamie put the cat drawing aside and picked up her sketch of Griff. The drawing, with its vivid hues, showed a strong resemblance to him. It reflected what she thought was Griff's inner self and strength. Jamie had a supernatural adeptness to create a phenomenon of light in her art.

Jamie's dad was working on a small woodcarving of a bear. He glanced toward Jamie and caught her looking at him, "Are you drawing me?"

She perked up and placed the drawing of Griff at the bottom of her stack along with one of her dad. "These are surprises so don't peek," Jamie said.

Dad winked at her.

Jamie stared out into the room, picked a gray paper and a deep blue pencil, and sketched her mom who sat near the fireplace. Mom, curled up in a baby blue throw blanket, held an opened book titled, *Family Connections.*

Dad leaned against the wall close to the stairs as he whittled away on his woodcarving, making a few final changes. The bear carving took center place with a set of three-dimensional animals that already graced a two by twelve foot long plaque. The panel fastened on the wall from the first step up to the landing.

"What kind of wood are you using for the bear, honey?" Mom asked.

"Ironwood. It is very difficult to carve," he responded.

Jamie laughed, "Guess that is why it's called ironwood."

"I learned to use this wood from my Lakota friends. And, yes, smarty." Dad chuckled. "I found this piece in the Appalachians on our last vacation. It feels and looks a lot like petrified wood. Once I sand and polish it, the wood will have a dark, rich quality. He will look like a black bear in the middle of all my lions, tigers, monkeys, zebras and elephants."

The animals magically came alive and played with each other, running up and sliding down the banister. One of the monkeys hollered "Wheee" as he whizzed by the other creatures on his way down. "Wheee."

Jamie's parents gazed at each other affectionately. Not watching what he was doing, Dad sliced into his finger below the knuckle. Blood oozed onto his hand and dripped on the floor. "Blast it. I cut my finger."

Jamie jumped up. Her mouth flew open. "Dad, are you ok?" She ran to him.

"It's just a small cut, but I might need stitches." Dad winked at his daughter, "Maybe it is this tough ironwood."

Jamie's mom threw her book on the chair and rushed to assist him. She applied pressure to the cut and bound his wound to stop the bleeding.

"Mercy, it looked like half of your finger was cut off." She laid her hand on his shoulders. "Don't worry, honey. I think you will live."

Jamie's identical twin sister, Kattie, strutted into the family room and plopped on a chaise lounge in front of the fireplace. She watched the fire consume the wood and let out a shrill sarcastic laugh. "What happened to your finger Dad? This is the second time in a week. Is life so boring you're trying to get attention for the fun of it?"

Mom glared at Kattie. "Your dad just cut himself. Show a little sympathy." She turned her attention back to her husband. "Honey, go on upstairs and change your shirt. I need to spray stain remover on the one you are wearing to get the blood out."

Kattie got into her mom's face. "You baby that stupid man. He just piddles around doing those stupid carvings and we are supposed to respect him? You got to be kidding."

"Yes. Respect," Mom said. She swept her arm in a circle. "Your father works very hard in his consulting business to pay for all of this."

"Yeah right, and for my so-called boarding school. I am not the one who is crazy. Let me show you how crazy people act." Kattie knocked Mom to the floor.

Jamie shrieked, slapping Kattie. "Don't you dare hit Mom, you ugly little witch." The twins went at each other like two cats fighting over a mouse.

"Girls, stop it," Mom scolded as she struggled to get up off the floor.

Kattie grabbed Jamie's artwork and cackled as she ripped up the drawing of Dad into tiny pieces. "I can't believe you would waste your time sketching that old man."

Jamie sobbed as she picked up the bits of art paper. "You're so cruel."

"And who's this? Your knight in shining armor? What a daydreamer. No one that handsome would have anything to do with you." Kattie squealed with laughter while skipping around the large family room with Jamie chasing her.

Dad ran down the stairs from the master bathroom. "Kattie, stop your nonsense right now. I mean it."

"It's none of your business, old man. Look at Jamie crying like a baby," Kattie roared.

"Give it back." Jamie whined. "Mom, Dad, make Kattie give it back."

Mrs. Travelstead grabbed Kattie's arm. "Stop this instant. Go to your room and stay there until I come up to talk to you."

Kattie ran halfway up the stairs and tossed the drawing like a flying disc. It sailed through the great room.

Dad pointed at Kattie. "Do as your mother says. Go to your room. Immediately, if not sooner."

With lightning speed, Kattie ran down the steps, kicked her mom's legs several times with uncanny strength and scratched her fingernails across her parent's neck.

Dad pulled Kattie off Mom. Throwing punches uncontrollably, Kattie hissed and bit his arms painfully hard. In anger, he shoved her down into a chair, but she got up. Dad forced her down again.

As Kattie and her parents wrestled, Jamie quickly collected the remnants of her artwork including the one of Griff, which remained intact. Clutching her drawings, Jamie slid behind the couch to hide from Kattie. Jamie barely fit, but the snugness made her feel safe. She huddled there in fear remembering the last fight. *I will just make it worse like I did the last time Kattie went crazy. Mom will use her medallion, and force Kattie to leave again. Best to let Mom take care of it. Glad I can see everything from here. Maybe I can sneak upstairs. No, I want to help my parents. The whole family suffers when Kattie goes berserk.*

A sharp knock at the door interrupted the scene.

"Let's act civilized," Dad said with his face turning red. He breathed hard and buried one fist into the other hand. "We'll talk about this later." His jaw tightened. "We must resolve this and make peace with each other as a family."

Making a snarling noise, Kattie ran to the door. SpiderWood pushed her way into the Travelstead's foyer. "I didn't invite you in," Kattie hollered. She whirled around to deliver a hard karate kick in the stomach of this ugly pockmarked face woman dressed in black.

The witch pulled out her wand. "You are so agitating. Take this, you insane brat." SpiderWood blasted Kattie with electrical currents from her wand. Kattie screamed and slumped to the floor in a mound of bones and ashes.

Jamie gasped in horror. *How can this be happening? My sister! What can I do? I need magic now.* She started to come out of hiding when she saw her mother dash to the door.

Mom screamed, "What have you done to my child?" Jamie could see tears streaming down her mother's face as she stabbed the witch with a knitting needle.

The witch's words crackled. "That nasty little brat kicked me hard. I got even with her by reducing her to ash. Now I am going to entrap you in my web. You will need more than that ridiculous little needle."

SpiderWood touched the dull medallion with a black gem hanging around her neck. The jewel held spiders weaving their webs. She commanded the spiders, "Encase the adults this minute."

Mom sprung toward her husband as the black spiders spun out of the jewel growing in size with their every step. *Jamie, stay where you are. Do not try to help.*

Dad grabbed both of their gems from the coffee table, and quickly handed one to Mom. However, the black spiders swiftly entangled her in their web. They wrapped their strands around Jamie's mother, and pulled their threads tight, very tight.

The scarred face witch crowed as she watched Mom trying to twist herself free on the family room floor, "You can't get out of this one."

Dad demanded "Commando …" SpiderWood's magic proved more powerful. The spiders encircled Dad and his medallion, preventing him from defending his family. Breathing became difficult. He collapsed to the floor near his wife.

SpiderWood yanked Mom's blue medallion from her fist. Mom, laying immobile on the floor, commanded her gem, "Commando fierro Luna azul."

The gem stunned the witch's hands so she slung it across the room. It slid under the couch near Jamie, who grabbed it and held it tight. The gem connected Jamie with her mother. As long as her mother still lived, she controlled the gem.

Jamie heard her mother's cries coming through her medallion. "Jamie, this is Mom. Do not move. You are the future of HallowWinds. You must follow my directions so that the ultimate victory is ours, and you achieve your destiny. Say with your mind, Commando medallionia, so your father's power will come to you."

Jamie bit her lip. Shaking from grief, she commanded the stone to come to her. The rock made itself invisible, left her father's hand, and flew to Jamie.

"Good, Jamie, mine and your father's medallion are yours now. Stay concealed no matter what happens. Your father and I love you very much. Promise me, you will stay hidden," Mom insisted. "Be brave, my daughter."

Jamie obeyed her mom and remained hidden. She slipped her parents' medallions in her pocket. *Oh my, how I wish I knew how to use these to protect my parents. Mom, Dad, tell me how to save you.*

SpiderWood licked her burned hand and then indignantly whipped out her wand that had a serpent carved into its wood. The wand blasted the webs that bound Jamie's parents. The flames circled their way around the webs, stinging and burning the captives on their arms, legs, face, and torso. The smell of burned flesh filled the room. SpiderWood squawked as the tortured victims twitched. Their screams filled the large family room, but the silence was even more deafening. The necromancer gloated over their twisted and lifeless bodies. "No power surpasses mine."

Jamie crammed her face into the crook of her arm to muffle her sobs. *No, please, do not let them be gone. Mom. Dad. No. It cannot be.*

The double doors to the home swung open, permitting a woman riding her broom to enter. SpiderWood snarled at her. "SilverWorm, what are you doing here?"

"I'm checking up on you. I see you have gotten rid of the competition. I want my share of the spoils." SilverWorm walked briskly in her knee-high boots, laced with silvery wiggly worms, through the large room and halted near the couch. "I smell a girl. Where is she?"

Startled by the worms, Jamie put her hands over her mouth to keep herself from puking. *Oh God, please don't let them find me.* SilverWorm's floor-length dress displayed people she captured and tormented. Jamie gagged from the horrendous scenes of men, women and children with missing limbs and covered with bloody worms.

"Oh, look at the beautiful cut glass crystal." SilverWorm picked up the goblet from the coffee table next to the couch and pings the glass with a fingernail. "It's authentic. I want all of these glasses for myself," she stated as she moved away from the couch toward the china cabinet.

Horrified at their callousness, tears rolled down Jamie's cheeks as she watched the two witch sisters carelessly bag silverware, fine china, crystal glassware, jewelry, ancient coins, anything of value. *What do they want with these things?*

"They must have a vault," SpiderWood pronounced as she banged on every wall and turned every painting around leaving them skewed. They searched every drawer and closet, scattering the contents about the house. Everything overturned or broken and the sofa and chair cushions ripped apart. She felt the punctures into the cushions of the couch and the padding as it landed on her face and arms.

Stifling a sneeze with both hands, Jamie prayed her hiding place stayed secret. With fainting feelings, she fought to stay conscious.

Then SpiderWood stuffed Mom's spinning wheel into her bag, and the book Mom had just been reading. *Oh, Mom. I cannot take this. Not the book. Not the wheel you loved so much.*

"Is that the book with the information that we need?" SilverWorm quizzed.

"There should be a lot more than this, but this has her name as the author."

"Well, if you get the book," SpiderWood said as she headed toward the foyer, "I get Kattie's ghost. Where is her sister?"

SpiderWood shoved SilverWorm. "Kattie is mine. I am the one who electrocuted her. I am going to find Jamie and take her too. Where are you little girl?" SpiderWood baby-talked, "I have a gift for you."

SilverWorm, while SpiderWood looked for Jamie, dangled her metallic gray medallion in front of Kattie's ashes to coax her ghost to come with her.

Kattie's ghost formed an ashy hand and attempted to grab SilverWorm's medallion. "I love it and want one like yours. I will go with you. Nothing better to do anyway. Who cares about my parents? They were always on my case. I need a place to stay. I want my body back!"

"Selfish, aren't you? I like it. We will get along just fine. You're not getting my medallion, but I'll give you a place to stay and maybe the ability of embodiment." SilverWorm said. She climbed onto her broom, and Kattie's specter got behind her.

SpiderWood hollered at her sister. "What are you doing? You can't take her."

"Let's go, you old stick, or I'll set you on fire." SilverWorm and Kattie disappeared into the night.

SpiderWood expanded her own broom like a retractable umbrella, mounted it, and flew into the sky after them. Bags tied to the end of the broom carried the loot ransacked from the Travelstead castle. "I'm coming after you, you old witch!"

Jamie's insides screamed in longing for her parents and in anger over the cruelty of the deaths of her family. In spite of her intense feelings, she obeyed her mother's wishes and stayed hidden so that her heritage would live forever.

A loud noise jolted Jamie. Her heart skipped. A dragon's nose poked around the foyer doors. Her grandfather rushed into the room right behind him with his sword drawn. Rowdy, her grandfather's dragon abruptly stopped. Grandpa stared in shock.

"Ohhh, Grandpa. I am so glad to see you. This is a nightmare," Jamie sobbed as she left her hiding place and tearfully hugged him. "The witches . . . they killed Mom, Dad and Kattie. It looked like SilverWorm took Kattie's ghost. I didn't know how to stop it," she gasped, trying to catch her breath. "Mom told me to stay hidden."

"Rowdy, stand guard at the door. Central, Commanders Travelstead are both gone. Kattie down, but spirit theft. Jamie unharmed. Emergency Guards requested." Her grandfather clung to Jamie, wiping away tears from his own eyes. "Help is on the way, sweetie. Your Mom was right in telling you to stay hidden."

The charred, twisted bodies and agonized faces with open eyes branded themselves in Jamie's mind. Grandpa extended his hand over Mom and Dad. "Reangelo corporis." The two bodies changed. They became untwisted. Their wounds, cuts, and slashes disappeared, and charred flesh became renewed. Webs lying on the floor shriveled into foam and evaporated.

Jamie knelt next to her parents. Looking up at Grandpa, Jamie exclaimed, "They are so beautiful and peaceful looking. There is no sign of the horrible torture or pain." She touched Dad's arm and then her Mom's face. "I love you Mom and Dad."

Mom and Dad's spirits embraced her. Their white robes glowed with a brilliant light. Jamie bowed her head in a moment of prayer. She looked up in sadness. "What about Kattie, Grandpa? Can you change her?"

Grandpa Zack raised his hand over Kattie's fragments. "Cinderos collecto et entré urnos." Jamie's eyes followed the stream of powder as it collected and processed toward the mantle. Magically a slender black urn appeared there and all the dust gracefully went into the container.

"Sealios urnos." Grandpa commanded. "I am sorry, Jamie, until her spirit returns to her body this is the best that I can do."

"Will she be at peace like Mom and Dad?"

"Someday, Jamie. You and others will help her to have peace."

Using his forest green medallion, Grandpa Zack called for Light Keepers to escort the parents' spirits to a place of contentment, called Paradise. The Light Keepers transported their embodied spirits through the energy fields. "We'll watch after you," Mom and Dad said, waving goodbye.

Jamie stared at her grandpa. Words and feelings collided. Tears, speech ceased.

Grandpa took Jamie by the hand and led her to her mother's chair. He tuned it upright and motioned for her to sit down. Grandpa tenderly covered her with her mother's throw. "Jamie, I sent a message to your Aunt Esther and Uncle Jonathan about your parents and Kattie. I asked them if you could stay with them. We will hear from them soon. When we do, we must leave HallowWinds and go to Earth."

"Okay, Grandpa. I trust you," Jamie bawled.

Grandpa Zack Glosomore knelt beside his granddaughter and held her. When he felt her trembling body become calm, he began. "I don't like saying this to you now, but you need to understand the immense importance of your safety and survival. The witches came here for three reasons according to our intelligence agency. They wanted to confiscate your parents' records, kill your parents since both had amazing powers, and kidnap their children. The dark forces are trying to amass power from those not developed enough to stop them. The witches and others will keep following you to steal your gifts before you can fully advance them. Your parents were a threat to them, and you are a potential threat. I know you may not be able to hear all of this now, so we will have a long talk, you,

Grandma, and me later. With you as a witness to the events today, you are in more danger. I need to ask you two very serious questions. Do you know where your parents' medallions are? Did you see them take any papers or files? It looks like they ransacked every room."

"Here are their stones." Jamie pulled them out of her pocket. "*Family Connections.* They took Mom's book. I did not see any files." Jamie coughed.

"Whew! Keep the gems close to you at all times. Rowdy, take my place here next to Jamie." The huge red and yellow dragon stood guard at Jamie's side.

Grandpa, using his own stone, summoned armored men and women to guard every doorway and window on all three floors of the castle.

Jamie felt her body give way to exhaustion and to the comforting feeling of Rowdy and Grandpa's closeness. It was night. Darkness covered HallowWinds.

CHAPTER THREE

Wordless

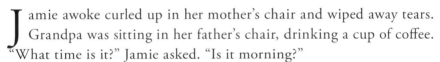

J amie awoke curled up in her mother's chair and wiped away tears. Grandpa was sitting in her father's chair, drinking a cup of coffee. "What time is it?" Jamie asked. "Is it morning?"

"It's about 3:00 a.m. I still have not heard from your aunt and uncle."

"Grandpa, their faces, their bodies … I am trying to remember Mom and Dad as they looked when they were escorted by the guardians … it is so hard. When Jaden died, I felt intense sadness. This is worse. It is too much to bear."

Grandpa Zack reached across a lamp table and patted Jamie on her hand. "Your aunt and uncle experienced great loss of a son. Judd knows what it is like to lose a sibling, and I know Jaden's death was very hard on you. All of your family will help and support you. Your grandmother and I will be here for you." A gold light swirled in Grandpa Zack's gem. "O good, your aunt and uncle want you to come tonight to live with them. Is that ok with you?"

"Everything is happening so fast. I won't be able to be myself."

Grandpa Zack teared up. "They won't either, Jamie. None of us will."

"Oh my, I'm sorry, Grandpa. Overwhelming grief causes me to be less aware of others. I am being insensitive."

"Shhh … you are not insensitive, child. You witnessed their horrific murders. It's alright," comforted Grandpa. "Light Keepers will take care of arranging your parents' burial, and will keep the house secure. They will also take care of Kattie's urn."

"Last summer, I met a boy named Griff. He said he is in officer training and lives on the planet called Light Channel. Do you know him?"

Grandpa Zack winked at Jamie. "I know Griff's uncle, Commander-in-Chief Belcor Williams. His uncle is very proud of Griff. He talks about him all the time."

"Do Light Keepers and Champions live on Light Channel too?"

"We'll see that you have the opportunity to travel to Light Channel, where you will meet Keepers and Champions. For now, your aunt and uncle are expecting you. You may want to pack a few of your things, toiletries, and clothes — enough for a few days. We need to head for Earth, okay?"

Jamie got up from her chair not remembering she had her mother's MoonCrystal medallion in her lap. The crystal pinged when it hit the floor, emitting brilliant colors. The gem rose in the air and hung itself around Jamie's neck, claiming her as its owner. The warmth of the medallion flowed into Jamie. She touched the gem. "It's Mom's. It is dispersing her energy into me. The gem chose me, so Mom wants me to start my journey with my inherited medallions from her and my Dad," Jamie declared.

"That's right. As you grow older, the bond becomes stronger between you, your gems, and the loved ones who communicate with you through the stones' energy."

Wiping tears from her face, Jamie sadly left for her bedroom leaving Grandpa in the living room drinking more coffee. Since her own energy wavered, she placed her right hand over her Mom's medallion and asked the MoonCrystal to help her. Jamie watched her mother do this many times.

Multicolored light beams from the gem flickered in all directions of her room. Red beams collected her clothes; golden beams collected photos and other keepsakes; other color rays gathered the rest of Jamie's personal possessions and gently packed them in duffle bags and prefabricated boxes.

Jamie stacked what was left of her drawings and kept Griff's portrait underneath to protect it. She took some family pictures from the mantle over the fireplace and put them in her backpack. Jamie fondly gathered some of her mom's favorite jewelry, including the heart shaped locket that held Kattie's and her baby pictures. She grabbed her dad's whittling knife. *I want a few things to keep Mom and Dad close to me.*

Jamie looked around the house and burst into tears. *I am missing so many of Mom, Dad and Kattie's things. Precious keepsakes. Memories. The dishes we used for family celebrations. Dad's carvings on the bannister.* Then she remembered TimberWood, ran outside, and embraced him, washing him with her tears. Jamie sniveled, "What am I going to do without you? I need your arms around me."

TimberWood's leaves said in a thousand voices. "You're forever in my heart. I will always be close to you and for you. There will be a brighter day. There is hope."

Jamie dozed in his branches. Rowdy noisily loaded up her belongings, jarring her awake.

He roared, "It's time, Jamie."

She kissed her best friend, TimberWood, and ran inside to take one last look. The entire Travelstead stone castle rattled its farewell. Jamie stepped out the front door as all the trees swayed in unison. She rubbed the dragon's cheek. "Hello, Rowdy. Thanks for helping us move to Earth, and for guarding me during the night. You're such a dear dragon."

Grandpa Zack mounted Rowdy with Jamie seated behind him. Light beams strapped her keepsakes behind her. With a strong cord, Grandpa attached larger packages to Rowdy's tail.

Jamie laid her head against Grandpa Zack's back. She prepared herself for a long ride through the wind currents from HallowWinds to Earth. The air swirled around them. They fought against the swift wind currents, hoping to arrive on Earth before mid-morning and settling into her relatives' home.

She could hear someone calling her. The voice sounded muffled and persistent at first. "Grandpa Zack, someone is following us." Jamie strained to hear the words, which sounded raspy like a cat clawing on a door to get its food.

SilverWorm's invitation filled the atmosphere. "Jamie, Kattie needs you to help her get revenge. The three of us can harness the powers of SpiderWood and make her pay for the murders of your family."

Jamie took a deep breath to calm herself and whispered to Grandpa Zack. "SilverWorm wants me to go with her, but she is trying to trick me, right?"

"Lies drizzle from her mouth," Grandpa Zack responded. "SilverWorm is trying to get you to let down your guard."

"Kattie has always been so hateful. Being dead, does not mean she has changed. Now she has chosen darkness; her spirit chose SilverWorm. I feel pulled in many directions. Should I try to help her? After all she is my sister," Jamie said.

"SilverWorm is counting on you feeling awful about your twin sister. She just wants you to join her in overcoming SpiderWood. Then she will get rid of you, Kattie, and anyone else who gets in her way." Grandpa Zack directed Rowdy through easterly winds. "The witches have plotted to take over the universe. It is about power and jealousy. You will quickly learn about your magical powers and intelligence to outsmart evil."

"How are we able to hear SilverWorm talking?" asked Jamie.

Grandpa Zack stroked his well-trimmed beard. "We're traveling along energy currents, which carry images and sounds. We can journey anywhere like Earth, the Light Channel, and HallowWinds."

Jamie had questions. "What about SpiderWood? Will she be able to dominate SilverWorm?"

"At this point, they're about equal in power," Grandpa Zack said.

"Lucky us. Maybe, they'll knock each other off." Jamie grinned.

"I wish, but they each have numerous followers. Their feuds could exterminate many people on both sides."

Jamie hugged Grandpa Zack tighter, but lightened her grip as she stared at the spectacular colors of the universe. Her mouth opened in awe, not terror. They dodged atmospheric debris. Some of it looked like burning coal, which had a beauty of its own. "Look, Grandpa. See that melting boulder. Looks like a zebra with its stripes dripping down into shapes of Clydesdale horses." Jamie pointed, "And that horse is melting into a gazelle streaking toward earth like lightning."

"Well, this is just the beginning. You will see lots of magic, some good and some evil."

With confidence, Jamie declared, "Grandpa, you, I and other good people will overcome evil."

"Yes, our faith in each other will keep us strong. Look at the red sun peeking from around those clouds. Sunrise in its glory. Try to sleep Jamie for a few hours, and then we will be there."

Rowdy gracefully moved one of his wings near Jamie's face to give her shade to sleep. "Sleep tight, Jamie."

****

Grandpa Zack landed his dragon on Dappled Boulevard in Sun Ray Subdivision. This neighborhood had the reputation of always having the gentlest rain showers followed by the most beautiful rainbows. The stars always gave such sparks of light. There was no need for street lamps or outside porch lights.

Jamie dismounted the dragon and skipped around to face Rowdy. "Thanks."

Rowdy swiped his tongue across Jamie's face. She wiped the gook from her cheeks. "Hey there. That tickles."

"He's showing he likes you," Grandpa Zack said, holding his belly in laughter. "I'm going to pop."

Uncle Jonathan and Aunt Esther came running around Rowdy's tail and hugged Jamie. Her uncle held her, and in silence, the pair shared their grief and loss.

Aunt Esther smiled. "We have freshened up Jaden's room with sunny yellow walls and a sky blue border. Go on up and get settled, while your uncle and I get some brunch ready."

Jamie helped Grandpa Zack unload her backpack and toiletry case from the dragon's tail. She touched her medallion and requested light beams to take her other things upstairs. Jamie unpacked smaller items like her hairbrushes, favorite lotions, and shampoos and put them in her bathroom. She hung her clothes in the closet and put sweaters and slacks in dresser drawers. "What is that sound?" Jamie wondered aloud.

A boisterous slurping sound was coming from her bathroom. Jamie ran in and saw Rowdy's head poking through her second story window and his long tongue lapping up what was the water in her toilet bowl. "What are you doing?"

Rowdy looked up with big innocent eyes, "I am drinking water. What does it look like?"

Jamie flushed to refill the bowl. "Okay, my friend, drink up."

Gigantic gulps and a few bowls later, Rowdy burped. "See you later, much later, Jamie. Got to get something to eat and get some sleep."

"Me too." Jamie headed downstairs to the family room. "Yum, that smells so good. I am famished. Where is Judd? Is he in bed?"

Uncle Jonathan set a platter of hotcakes in front of Jamie. "He was playing chess at a friend's house last night and stayed over. You know how he plays late into the night, especially when he's on a winning streak."

"After brunch, I would like to go back up and sleep for a little while. I am enjoying that beautiful border in my room. The sun, moon and stars are dancing all around. Sunbeams kissed me on the cheek. I love it."

"We knew you would like that border," Aunt Esther chuckled.

"And the sunny yellow color," chimed Uncle Jonathan.

As if a dark cloud hovered over her, Jamie changed the conversation, "What about Judd? Are the witches after him?"

"They show no interest in his illusionary tricks or his creativity. He is not magical. Unfortunately, Jaden was," Auntie said sadly.

As if on cue, noisy Judd ran into the house, tripped over the leg of Jamie's chair and landed on the floor with his glasses hanging on his ear.

Jamie laughed and extended her hand to assist Judd. "About time you show up." They embraced.

"He doesn't know. We didn't want to wake him up last night," Uncle Jonathan said. "Sit down, son. We have something to tell you." Jamie's uncle told Judd about the murders.

Judd tenderly gazed at his cousin and squeezed her hand. There were no words to say.

CHAPTER FOUR

Carry Me

━━━━━━━━━━ ✳ ━━━━━━━━━━

T wisting under her covers, Jamie re-experienced the murders of her parents and sister. The witches and other gross monsters took over her dreams and joined Kattie in tormenting her. Kattie spread her fingers apart. Snakes shot out of each fingertip and encircled Jamie. The serpents hissed and bit her. Jamie fought back so hard that she woke up. The top sheet and blanket wrapped tightly around her. She struggled to get them off. Darkness enfolded the sky in all its cruelty. *What time is it? Where am I?*

The border in the room lit up. First, the moon, then the stars and lastly the sun bathed Jamie in light. Recognizing the room, she looked at the clock next to her bed. *Midnight. Have I been asleep since brunch?* She listened, but she heard no sounds in the house. Beams came down over her and caressed her as if to rock her back to sleep.

****

Aunt Esther woke Jamie from a twenty-hour sleep. "Breakfast is ready. As soon as you eat, you can go find a surprise waiting for you in the backyard."

Jamie quickly got dressed, ran downstairs, gulped down some breakfast, hopped out the backdoor and jumped over a rock garden. Grandpa followed her. She stared at the trees in the distance and recognized TimberWood, waving his branches. She hurried to her tree, hugged his large trunk. "TimberWood. Oh my TimberWood."

"Hello Jamie, I've missed you, my friend."

"How did you get here?" Jamie joyfully asked.

"Grandpa used light from his medallion, and the dragons carried us on their backs."

"Us? You mean other trees?"

"Yes, the whole family is here, all twenty of us."

Jamie first pecked Grandpa on one cheek, then the other and lastly square on the mouth in excitement.

Grandpa stepped backwards in jest. "On that affectionate note, I will leave you two to catch up."

Jamie kissed TimberWood. She told him about the move to Earth, her new home with her Aunt and Uncle, and the exquisite border in her new room. "This is great, TimberWood. I can continue to share with my best friend and do my homework in your branches."

TimberWood swooshed his branches around Jamie and embraced her. "I can be with you every day. I insisted on being here today before the funeral. I love you, Jamie."

"You rascal. You did not tell me that you were coming. I thought we had said good-bye." Jamie climbed into TimberWood's branches and rested for what seemed like a long time. *It feels good to be here.*

"Hello up there," a familiar male voice said. "Can I come up?"

Jamie was so excited to see Griff at the base of the tree. "Oh, yes. Come." Griff scaled the tree so quickly and gracefully. He was all dressed in his uniform. "Wow, you look dashing."

"All dressed for my beautiful lady. I am your escort today to Radiance City Center for the service. Many Light Keepers will escort you and your family, and keep you safe. I have to leave in a few hours, but will be back for you around 2:30 p.m."

The two sat together in the tree for several hours. Jamie told Griff the details of the murders. She related how Kattie left with SilverWorm, and her fears of the witches and Kattie. Griff held her hand as he listened attentively.

"Jamie, would you accept a small gift from me? It will make you feel more secure." Griff removed a small velour pouch from his breast pocket, and gingerly removed a tiny diamond shaped brooch. "This is a very special communication device. It is barely visible. You just tap it and speak. I will always be on the other end. See, I have one too." Griff pointed to his small badge on his collar. "Please wear this all the time, day or night. It should always be attached."

"I will wear it twenty-four/seven. Thank you, Griff. I feel special and protected." *He is still my friend, my prince.*

****

Escorted by Light Keepers and trainees, Jamie and her family arrived at Radiance City Center. As Jamie entered, she immediately saw in the foyer two life-size photos of her parents. She leaned into Griff. "They look so alive and beautiful." *Oh how I wish they were real. I want to hug them. And to be held by them. Mom and Dad get me through this.* They walked toward a large photo of Kattie. Jamie tried to choke back the tears, but they ran down her face.

Griff handed Jamie a handkerchief as he whispered into her ear. "I have to join the other guards, but I will try to meet up with you after the service. It depends on when my next assignment begins. So I cannot promise. Just know that I want to be near you." He kissed her cheek.

Jamie, guided by Grandpa, looked at a display of some of her father's best woodcarvings. Touching some of them, memories flooded her mind and heart.

Then across the hall, she saw well-dressed mannequins. "Look, Grandma, these suits and dresses were made from linen Mom spun at her wheel. Wow, look at this, these are the matching linen dresses that she made for Kattie and me. They still look so fresh and cool." She fingered the embroidered daisies on the sleeves and collars.

Next to the mannequins, a table full of dolls revealed Kattie's collection. "Kattie loved these dolls. She spent a lot of time at the boarding school researching different countries on earth, other galaxies and energy fields. She sewed by hand doll clothes that represented each place she researched. Here are all of her meticulous research notes and drawings." Grandma pointed to notebooks full of Kattie's work.

Jamie looked very quizzical. "Where were these dolls? Why didn't I ever see them?"

"We don't know why she did not want to bring them home with her when she left the boarding school."

Jamie took her time to examine each doll and the drawings.

"They are yours to keep if you want. All of these items on display are yours." Grandpa pointed to the next table. "Your grandmother and I want you to have your mother's handwritten notes and research for her book, *Family Connections*. She was very interested in genealogy. Hopefully, someday you will get the actual book back from the witches."

"Gee, I didn't realize my Mom wrote *Family Connections*. No wonder she looked at that book all the time. She was reading it when . . . Oh, I love it. They will teach me all about my family history. Kattie's notes will help me to know my sister better. Thank you so much," Jamie sniffled.

"Let's go into the main hall, Jamie. Everyone has gathered," said Grandpa. He called the assembly together.

Nature's Melodic Pause, her family's favorite piece of music, filled the air. The Light Keepers marched in and formed an honor guard around the family and their friends. When the music stopped, the Guards clicked their heels in unison, withdrew their swords and raised them forming a spire above the group. In the circular opening created by the swords, streams of golden light showered the family. Everyone looked up, as Jamie's parents hovered on the Light beams.

Dad spoke first. "My dearest family, what a wonderful life I had. Fabulous parents and siblings, a loving and beautiful wife, and two intelligent and creative daughters. I thank you all for being a part of my Light Journey. I love you forever, Jamie, and all of you."

In a soft-spoken voice, Mom added, "Light Journeys have endings that are hard for those left behind, but they also are unbelievably peaceful and glorious beginnings for those who walk over. We are at peace. Jamie. You are a young brave warrior who will carry on the family tradition of bringing others into the Light. Your father and I are very proud of you and will always be as close to you as your heart." She gracefully handed down to Jamie a beautiful black urn. "Take care of Kattie. Free her spirit so she can be with us in Paradise."

The beams of light embraced Jamie and then ascended. "I will. I promise."

In unison, the Light Keepers returned their swords to its sheath. They chanted one of the family's favorite hymns, *Your Winds Carry Me on High*. Jamie sang along with renewed strength and grace. The congregation, following Jamie's lead, broke into song.

CHAPTER FIVE

Beginnings

------------------------ ✳ ------------------------

J amie spent that first summer with her aunt and uncle making friends in her new neighborhood. For pleasure, she attended art and violin classes with several of her new friends. Since she missed the final months of the eighth grade, she worked diligently to complete all the requirements.

Jamie sat in TimberWood, practicing her instrument with such grace. All the trees swayed to the melodic sounds that she created. Some pieces were full of grief and others more joy-filled. The birds, butterflies, and squirrels stood in rapt attention, as she soulfully played *Family*, a piece that she had composed. *Tomorrow will bring new beginnings. Family is with me in new ways.*

****

Grandpa Zack, who directed the Advanced Shop Program at WiseMore High, took Jamie to school. As they walked in, the security guard, teachers, and students all cheerfully greeted Mr. Zachary Glosomore.

"Wow, Grandpa, you are such a celebrity around here." Jamie grinned.

Arriving at the main office, Grandpa introduced her to the counselor. "As you can see, Jamie has met all the eighth grade requirements over the summer and did excellent on the high school entrance exam. Here are her academic achievement scores from all of her previous schooling. She is brilliant just like Judd. It runs in the family." He winked and the counselor laughed.

"Your grandfather is quite the character. Jamie, since this is your first time on campus, I will give you a tour. Mr. Glosomore has to get to the Shop Class." The counselor guided Jamie through the school to locate her locker, the gym, and the cafeteria. "This is Maggie, Jamie. She is a student council member and since her schedule is the same as yours, she will take you to all of your classes."

"We met over the summer and have already become good friends," Maggie exclaimed. "You will love this, Jamie. Our first class is art." Maggie guided Jamie to the art and music center.

"Wow, this is awesome. I did not know WiseMore had all of this. This is perfect for my major in art and music." Jamie's heart pumped faster when she saw the complex with rooms for band, music lessons for a variety of instruments, sculpture, pen and ink drawing, painting and more. "There's a gallery, too?"

"And a very large stage for music performances." Maggie was rummaging through her backpack. "I think I left my cell phone in my locker. I wanted to get a photo of you seeing all of this. Do you want to look around the art gallery? I'll be right back."

"You know I can spend all day in this environment." Jamie first studied a charcoal drawing of a girl skipping rope. Gently touching the drawing, the girl became real and jumped around inside the drawing. "Thank you for showing me how to make a little girl skipping rope look real," Jamie told the girl in the drawing. The child smiled and then returned to her motionless pose.

Discovering a clay sculpture of an ice skater, Jamie touched him and it moved. When Jamie touched it again, the terracotta face smiled and then froze in place. *I did not know I could do this.*

Jamie's first class in the art room was magical. Everything she drew looked so realistic. Her figures came to life just long enough for her to sketch them. They danced, jogged, and played soccer. *Thank you for helping me to capture your movements and personalities.*

Caleb, who lived three doors from Jamie, commented on her artwork. "You have really improved since the beginning of summer. Fantastic work."

Jake whispered, "Maybe you should be the teacher." The group at the table laughed.

"Alright, get back to work over there," reminded Mrs. Painter as she walked toward the group. "Jamie, your work is so true-to-life. Have you had art classes before?"

"My friends here and I took one of the Radiance City drawing courses over the summer, but I have always loved to draw."

"You are a natural artist. All of your work from this table is wonderful," Mrs. Painter commended.

****

Maggie was a great tour guide through the rest of the classes. At lunch, Maggie introduced her to some of her other school friends. Jamie felt so accepted.

At the end of the school day, Maggie showed her the bookstore. "Okay, Jamie, I know you have to get books and supplies. It was fun to be your guide today. If you want to meet me here tomorrow, I will help you find all our classes. I know it took me a week to figure out the campus. If you need anything, you know where I live. Call or text me."

"Thank you so much. You were wonderful. See you right here in the morning." Jamie responded.

Maggie sprinted out the door to meet up with her boyfriend, Raz, who was a sophomore.

Jamie bought what she needed for her classes. Walking back into the packed hallway, Jamie thought she saw Griff in the crowd. She raised her hand to get his attention and yelled, "Hey, Griff." He faded among the students.

Jamie leaned up against the wall. *I want to cry. I have not seen him since the funeral. No, I refuse to cry. Not here. Silly me. He does not go to school here anyway. He is at Light Channel Academy. Why do I get so moody and feel suffocated by my emotions?*

Grandpa awakened Jamie from her daze. "You ready to go home?"

"If it is okay, Grandpa, I want to go for a walk in the park by myself."

"Did everything go okay with your classes? What's the matter?"

"School was great. The art and music complex was fantastic. It's just that I'm trying to sort things out."

"You know I am here if you need to talk. Just be careful and be home in time for dinner."

"See you at home."

****

Trying to understand her life, she sat in a park swing and pumped as high as she could to make her toes touch the sky. *I can pretend, can't I?* She daydreamed about the many ways she would punish the witches. *Wish I had the powers to do everything I think and dream.*

Jamie left the swing and sat with her head propped up on the playground gym bars. Her heart filled with rage as time slowly passed. Jamie took out her anger by using a stick and beating up on the equipment. She unchained the swing seat and let it fall in a muddy puddle. *I feel so alone and so angry at the same time. When will I know what to do? When will the anger quit eating at me? Isn't it time I take productive steps to stop evil?*

****

The library was a magical place for Jamie. She went there almost every day after school to study, but also to be close to her grandmother. Grandma reminded Jamie of her mother.

Near Christmas break, Jamie went to the library to do research. She brushed her hair away from her eyes and reached for a stack of books in the middle of the table. She turned the books one at a time in her hands, studying their covers. Her eyes widened with the first one, *Fossils from the American Frontier.* The next one, *Nineteenth Century Native American Artifacts,* got her attention.

Wow, all of these books are on 19ᵗʰ century fossils from western America. I am researching that topic.

Jamie opened a few of the books to photos from archeological digs and began making sketches for her report. The fossils danced and jumped off the pages and posed. One fossil held a bottle and raised it up. *Hey, they found me at an old time saloon.* Another fossil acted like a lassoing cowboy and yet another as an Indian Chief who smoked a peace pipe. The smoke from the pipe formed into pencils bouncing around on their erasers. *Gosh, you are inspiring me,* Jamie thought as she drew the fossils in intricate detail. Her imagination raced like fire burning through a field of dry grass.

The cowboy fossil swirled his rope, rounded up another stack of books, and landed them perfectly in front of Jamie. *I cannot make fossils do that. I do not have that gift. Someone is helping me or is messing with my mind.*

Jamie searched the room for the culprit, and spied her grandmother, the school librarian, rolling a cart of books. Jamie loved her grandmother's soft rounded face framed by combs on either side of her snow-white hair.

Magically, several small birds on the combs flapped their wings and flew off, crowding onto Jamie's fingers. She puckered her lips to kiss the birds, giving them a boost. They took off like planes from a runway and made a perfect landing on Grandma's cart full of books.

Jamie waved. "Grandma, are you or the birds collecting reading materials for me?"

"No, not us," insisted the birds, cozying next to each other.

Grandma chuckled, "Yes, I'm gathering books for you. Hope you don't mind a little help."

"Thanks. Sure is a good thing students are not in here to see the birds and books fly in the air. They wouldn't believe it."

Grandma kept her voice low. "I'm using the odors of mold and dragon manure to drive the students off. Just temporarily, of course, until I get the place cleaned and decluttered. Some badly behaved boys ran around the library, pulled books off the shelves, and tore out pages. I'm glad we're getting a rest."

Jamie sniffed the air. "It smells normal."

"I can make it smell wonderful for us and terrible for them through magic." Grandma Liz snapped her fingers, and the air smelled like roses and lilacs.

"Grandma, why can't others see and smell the wonderful world of magic the way we do?"

"They're too obstinate to believe. If they do not have the gifts, they do not believe that anyone else can have them. Some people get jealous and competitive."

Jamie rubbed her hands over her face, trying hard to focus. "Grandma, I love it that you and Grandpa live right next door and I see you a lot now. I never had a chance before to get to know you. By the way, did I see a miniature dragon, no higher than a German shepherd eating grass from your front lawn yesterday?"

"That's right, Jamie. Only magical people can see my pet Squirmy and other dragons. Therefore, we know that you have the gift."

Just then, two boys entered the library and went to the magazine rack.

Jamie ran her hand through her bangs. She compiled information from the research books on fossils, but she watched the boys to see if they were up to their pranks.

The librarian greeted the boys. "Hello, I am Mrs. Glosomore. Can I help you? I have some great magazines on racing cars and wrestling."

The boys gagged, and held their noses. One boy choked and could barely get his question out. "Did someone die in here?"

Mrs. Glosomore spoke demonstratively. "No, certainly not in my library."

I am going to get those two wise guys. Jamie explained, "Well, I don't know. I just saw a few days ago a boy's head sitting on a library shelf. It was gruesome and blood was everywhere. The principal called the police. Did you miss all the action? It was awful."

The boys stared at each other with bulging eyes, and ran at top speed down the hallway and out the front door, tripping over each other.

"Yippee. We scared them." Jamie raised her arms in victory.

"Oh boy did we!" Grandma Liz clapped.

Jamie thumbed her way through pages on fossils, but her mind kept wandering. She struggled to focus on bones, which she likened to relics of the dead. Even though she appreciated objects left behind by human ancestors, they reminded her too much of her murdered parents. She also wondered if she would see Griff again. He had promised he would see her after the funeral, but he left with the other trainees. *I have had so much loss.* Sadness consumed her.

With a bang, a number of boys came into the library along with a clique of three girls from Jamie's science class. The trio sat down at a nearby table. Marissa bossed her friends. "Sit here and be quiet. I want to ask that strange kid to do something for me." Marissa unloaded her books and walked over to Jamie. "Hey, Jamie, I'll pay you to do my research."

"I've just started my research," Jamie responded. "And I have other projects that I have to be completed before the holiday."

Marissa placed her hands on her hips. "What about your brainy cousin? Get him to do it for me. I will pay you real well if you can talk him into it."

Jamie bristled. *She is the girl who keeps calling Judd and Maggie, pestering them about doing her assignments. She offers to pay well, but Judd and Maggie refuse to cheat. They warned me that she might come after me.* "He's busy. Why don't you spend as much time doing your own assignments as you do trying to get someone else to do your work?"

"I'll never ask you again." Marissa twisted her face, shrugged, and joined her friends.

Well good! I so dislike confrontation. Jamie tried to focus on the task. She propped her head up with her fists. She turned so no one could see her face. Droplets fell from her chin and splashed on her notepaper. The wet marks formed various faces. Her parents' profile lingered the longest.

The library lights turned off and on in sync with her breathing. Jamie walked over to the switches, focused on her breathing and the lights did the same thing. *Hey, I am controlling the lights without touching them.*

Marissa glared at Jamie. "What's with the lights?"

"I'm not sure." Jamie's skin tingled with anticipation. "There's a storm brewing. I guess it's affecting the lights."

Grandma Liz winked at Jamie and telepathically asked Jamie if she could assist her with a scary light show. Jamie nodded. *Let's do it.* The lights danced on and off, changed colors from red to blue to gold, spun in circles and shot light onto the girls' faces.

With a smirk, Marissa wrapped her long blond strands of hair around her beautifully polished fingernails. "You act like you know so much. I bet you think you are a meteorologist, an electrician, or a magician. You will pay for this. No one teases me. My father has a lot of power in this town."

Jamie fidgeted with her pencil. *She is so sarcastic and haughty.* One part of her wanted to smack Marissa—another part wanted to snub her and walk away. *No, I want to be nice. It is so hard.*

Marissa, whispering to her friends, used a marker to draw a teenage girl with the words *Stuck-up* written under it. She slapped the paper down on Jamie's table and strutted back to her seat. The trio giggled.

The sketch twisted out of shape, which made the drawing look utterly ridiculous. Jamie recognized the figure as herself. Her emotions of hurt and anger gushed through her like a waterfall. She searched deep within herself for reasons. *Why make the figure be so ugly? Why is someone using this drawing to get to me? Marissa hasn't the magic to make it move. Who did this?* Jamie stared at the drawing, which became immobile like a corpse in a tomb.

Zap, Rip, Zip. Cracking sounds came from the ceiling above Marissa and her friends. All the girls in the library screamed, "Aaahhh. Aaahhh. The roof is falling. Aaahhh." So did some of the boys.

Mrs. Glosomore spied huge pieces of plaster about to fall on the students. Her eyes turned emerald green and burned with specks of orange. Lights swirled within her pupils and zapped the table size pieces of plaster that hurled downward close to the trio and others. In mid-air, the large hunks broke apart and crumbled showering the floor like sawdust.

Marissa and her friends jumped up, knocked over their chairs, and bumped into each other. She and her friends bolted out. "This place is spooked. I won't be back," Marissa yelled, tripping over her own feet.

Other students grabbed their belongings, and dashed out of the library. They struggled against a whirlwind tossing them in all directions. From the library window, Jamie saw two students landing in the bushes and then scurrying off as fast as their legs could take them.

Jamie grinned. *Marissa is getting what she deserves.* She shook her head. *No, I will not allow myself to think that way.* The only student left in the library, Jamie whimpered, "Grandma, I didn't want to drive the students off. I just wanted to be accepted."

Grandma tried to console her granddaughter. "I know you have a good heart."

"Thanks." Jamie thrilled from the compliment. "I am really glad you made Marissa pay for her rudeness."

"No dear, I didn't. The ceiling did not fall because of me. I am not sure what made the plaster spiral downward. I stepped in to break up the chunks so no one would get injured."

"I thought we were getting even with Marissa for making fun," Jamie said.

Grandma Liz played with one of the birds on her comb. "Using magic to settle a score gives the advantage to the person with power. I will let you in on a trade secret. As a child and young teen, I pretended to put up with others making fun of me. Then I used my mysterious gift to get back at them. Once when I was in my late teens, it really backfired. Instead of the tricks teaching the bullies a lesson, it hurt innocent people. One of those people was someone I knew since nursery school. I learned the hard way, when my best friend abruptly ended our relationship. I have not seen her since age nineteen. From then on, I chose to use my powers to help others in some way. Doing a light show was one thing, hurting others is another."

Jamie bit her lip. "Others make fun of me, big time. However, you are right, Grandma, I need to choose the use of my powers. It'd be so awesome to learn how and when to use magic from you."

"Your mother knew magic."

"Yes, I know that now." Imitating what she had seen her mother do, Jamie raised her hand. She spit out "Commando Fixtusti." Dust particles became hand size chalky pieces. "Gosh, I'm doing it. It worked!" The pieces solidified to become huge chunks. Jamie's magic lifted the chunks so they filled the large gaps in the ceiling, leaving only small visible cracks. The cracks became smaller and smaller until the ceiling looked fixed.

"Except for some dust, it looks like nothing ever happened. But, Grandma, who do you think caused the ceiling to fall?" Jamie reasoned. "Let's see. There was a ceiling falling with unusual noises, but no visible person or persons doing it. That's what level of magic?"

"A person knowing basic verbal commands or has an elementary gem could do it. I like your reasoning. Go on. Tell me. What do you think? Push your analysis further."

Jamie paused for a few minutes. "The tricks or magical abilities seem to be on the same level as what I can do. On the other hand, perhaps it is someone who has had the same training as I. Hmmm … like a twin. Could it be Kattie? SilverWorm could have given her the magical commands or the gem she had promised Kattie."

"Yes, I think you are on to something. Unfortunately, I think it could be Kattie. We know the twin witches are up to no good. SilverWorm could be using Kattie to get to you. The witches will kill anyone who gets in their way to gaining more power. Jamie, they are after you. We have to keep you safe."

Jamie toyed with her pencil, stuffing it through the wire spine of her notebook and nervously tapped her foot against the table leg. "I'm glad you can help me reason this out and learn how to use my gifts."

"Jamie, you are coming into your birthright of magical gifts and power. The wicked witches will not be satisfied until they control you.

Yet you are maturing into a beautiful, strong and gifted young woman. Harness your powers for goodness."

✳✳✳✳✳✳✳✳

Maggie and some other friends walked into the library and sat at the table with Jamie. "Hey, can we study with you for semester exams? You always have such good notes," Maggie asked.

"Sure that would be great." Jamie and her friends pored over their notes, with Jamie often adding insight from her enhanced notes.

"It is amazing how complete your notes are, Jamie. What is your secret?"

Jamie chuckled, "Maggie, I have a secret code – a kind of shorthand. Let me show you." She demonstrated the code to her friends. "When I get home, I read my scribbled notes and use voice recognition on my computer. So I end up with these notes all written out."

"Sure wish you would give us a computer lesson and your whole secret code," one of the girls suggested.

"I would be glad to over break. Let's plan a get together at my house – movies, popcorn and some computer work." *It is so good to have normal friends who are not magical. Wish I could be more like them, but that is not my destiny.*

CHAPTER SIX

Archival Invaders

After the holiday break, Jamie immersed herself in her studies. She became more and more interested in history. *From history, I will find the key to why we keep repeating it in such horrific ways.*

On her way to view special collections, Jamie strolled from the library down a hallway lined with black and white photos of deceased faculty and students. As she passed them, some winked or scowled since they rarely saw anyone going up to the archives. A half dozen of the principals and deans became so excited they fell out of their frames as Jamie walked by. The head dean ran over to Jamie and hugged her. He said in a deep baritone voice, "Welcome to the WiseMore Archives. We haven't seen anyone in here for a long time."

Jamie grinned. "Gee, thanks. What a surprise to have such a welcome." Jamie watched as the school leaders climbed back up the wall and into their frames.

Going up the rickety elevator to the special room to find older manuscripts on fossils and history annals, the hall seemed eerie. *What else will happen?* As Jamie got off the elevator, spider monkeys swung out on grape vines and landed on her head. She grabbed a ruler from her backpack and smacked each one. The monkeys shrieked and scampered back up the vines into the ceiling. *Whew. I was not expecting monkeys. Brrrr it is cold in here.*

As Jamie got closer to the archive door, she shook all over. The air switched from cold to frigid. Fear of the loud whizzing noises churning on the other side of the archives' door also chilled her. *What was that?* Jamie swirled around, startled by the elevator door. "Oh, thank goodness it's you. Watch out, Grandma. Monkeys just attacked me by the elevator." Jamie spoke breathlessly. "And now something inside the Archives wants out."

Grandma reviewed the ceiling for possible monkeys. "No monkeys, but from all the noise, the creatures in the archives must be massive."

The archives' doors rattled, sounding like trucks barreling against them. The massive carved wood doors swung opened. Crash! Bang! Bam!

With nowhere else to go, Jamie pulled her grandmother into the archives. "Quick, hide behind these cabinets."

Flying insects, with bulbous bodies and top-heavy heads, rustled into the archives' main room. Their huge gray eyes with red pupils blinked. The insects made constant clicking noises.

The colossal bugs spiraled and dived like wasps targeting those who disturbed their nests. Jamie ducked under a table, knocking off film canisters. She grabbed two of the canisters, rolled one to Grandma and they both began to swat the insects.

Jamie stared into the face of an insect big enough to ride. Grandma Liz smacked it square on the nape of its neck. The stunned insect fell to the floor, continuing to gawk at Jamie with its bulging angry eyes. With a swollen neck, the bug struggled to hold up its oversized head, which bobbled and then plopped forward to the floor. The canister lay open on the floor with film strewn across the room. The other insects swirled in circles overhead and wailed for their injured comrade.

"Don't you dare mess with my granddaughter or I will slice you up into pieces. You will end up in my roasting pan, and fed to my dragon like I did your great-grandpa."

Jamie cheered. "Yea, Grandma. That bug almost got me."

A deep male voice spoke. "I can get rid of these nasty critters."

"Who are you?" Jamie cried, dodging a bug.

"I'm Texter," said the voice.

Jamie visually searched around her. "Where are you? Show yourself."

Ghost Texter surfaced out of the overturned table. "I'm sorry. Didn't mean to scare you." Neon green letters glowed on his grass-stained football jersey with his name and WiseMore Archive Security Force. He scooped up three research books and handed one to Jamie and Mrs. Glosomore. "I am good with bug combat. Do as I do." Using the book, he knocked an insect to the floor.

They copied Texter. Jamie positioned herself in the open as she held her book up high. "I've got this one." She whacked an insect so hard it sprawled belly-up on a table with its legs kicking in the air. Jamie used her medallion to shrink the bug down to size. She picked up the insect by its back legs, swung it in a circle and threw it against the wall. The insect exploded from the impact, splattering nearby chairs and tables with yellow gook. An obnoxious odor peppered the atmosphere. With each hit, the smelly air worsened.

Mrs. Glosomore's eyes turned a bright emerald green. She stretched out her hand at an insect and recited, "Insecto extinguishotoast." A ball of fire sped from the palm of her hand and zapped the insect, spreading its remains over nearby microfilm scanners. "Jamie, imitate my hand gestures and words. We will get them faster this way."

"All right, Grandma. Let's go." Jamie raised her hand, spread her fingers, and repeated the words, "Insecto extinguishotoast."

Jamie jumped around in celebration. "They're gone. We turned the insects into piles of gook."

"I thought my book smacking was good," Texter interjected. "How did you do that?"

"Just a little magic," Jamie responded with a chuckle.

Grandma quickly added, "By the way, young man, you make a wonderful security guard for our archives."

Jamie extended her hand to Texter. "You're the first ghost I've ever seen." She felt she made contact with a friend.

Texter fluttered around Jamie. "And you are the first human I've ever saved."

"What are you doing in here?" Grandma asked as she chased a black cat out of the archives. Mrs. Glosomore slammed the Archives' doors shut.

Jamie slowed her breathing now that the danger diminished. "Grandma, that cat may have been Kattie. Did she make those insects attack us?"

Grandma Liz placed her hands on her hips with a stern look on her face. "Jamie, I suspect SpiderWood. She rides one of these insects. She caters to the ugly.

"You're funny," Jamie laughed.

"I try to keep things on the light side," Grandma responded. She wiped her face and neck. "SpiderWood runs the GrayStone Castle. She makes these creatures brutally attack and kill people of the Light. If they don't kill us, the witch tortures them and kills their larvae."

"That doesn't seem fair to them."

"SpiderWood teaches their babies cruelty from the beginning." Mrs. Glosomore nodded to Texter. "Make sure to guard the archives doors. We don't want any more visitors."

Grandma Glosomore invited Jamie into the archives' office and closed the door. She pointed to the opposite wall, used as a movie screen. A burst of energy left her fingertip and struck the screen in its center, displaying an underground room with the dimensions of five football fields.

Jamie hid her fright by acting calm. "These visual and audio images are staggering. Are we watching something real or fiction?" Jamie tried to understand as tears rolled down her face.

Grandma had tears welling up into her eyes too. "Oh my child, this is happening now on the GrayStone Castle's campus," Grandma's voice cracked. "The scenes are also predictions of what could occur if we do nothing. Their goal is to exterminate all magical humans first and then the rest of the human race. Only Light Commanders and your grandfather know about what you just saw." Grandma touched the screen and it immediately grew black. Then she escorted Jamie out of the archive office.

Jamie clenched her jaw. "We must do something to save humankind."

"That's a definite yes. Light Channel's staff has a plan that will involve us. Sweetie, you need to finish your research, so we can get out of here and some place more private. I feel like someone is watching us." Grandma scanned the room. "I'll stay up here with you and get this place cleaned up."

Jamie picked out a table spared from the sticky yellow gook of the detonated insects. She skimmed through a stack of research books and studied the photos about diggings in New Mexico. The figures in the illustrations shuffled and shifted when she touched them. *This sure makes reading more interesting.*

Jamie turned toward her grandmother. "Are there other ghosts in here? I feel someone watching too."

"Yes dear, this place has an amazing collection. Some are hundreds of years old. There are soldiers, pirates, and royalty. Others are less notable and ordinary people. Some have personal problems they are trying to solve. It is their unfinished business. Do you think it is a ghost whom you are sensing?"

"Not sure. Maybe. What about Texter? Does he have unfinished business?" Jamie peeked around a partition to see if he was listening.

Grandma Liz whispered, "Just between us girls, Texter played as a football running back and as the leading basketball forward at WiseMore High School. He died last summer from a heat stroke while practicing football. He misses his friends and his neighborhood. He yearns for what he had before he died."

"Aww. Poor Texter. You're good to everyone, Grandma."

"The ghosts, like their living counterparts, have heartbreaking stories. I try to listen to them." Grandma touched Jamie's face, strengthening their bond with each other.

"I want to listen to others like you do. I enjoy talking to Texter. It seems everyone I would like to have as a friend, has a sad story, like Texter and Griff. Do I pick friends who have sad stories because I have a sad story?"

"No, some people gravitate toward people with like stories, but you – I think your choice of friends is varied and healthy – like Maggie, Jake, and Caleb. Sadness has affected my life, too. We have a choice. We can become bitter and angry. On the other hand, we can use our skills to find solutions for others and ourselves. People, who have been hurt, listen better and are more sensitive." Grandma paused for a moment. "You know, when things get too intense, I use magic to get my mind off my troubles. What if I get some cleaning supplies and make them do magic tricks?" Grandma snapped her fingers, making sparks fly, and doubled the amount of cleaning supplies. Mops danced around the room, brooms swept spiders into dustpans, and cleaning cloths washed the windows. Chairs and tables straightened themselves.

"Laughter lightens up any situation. This is fun. This is fun," Jamie chanted as she made dust cloths polish all the tables with the snap of her fingers.

Mrs. Glosomore adjusted her glasses and nodded toward some shelves. "Texter is back. He is taking an interest in you. I think he is the pair of eyes that we felt. He's peeping around the shelves." They both howled.

"I like watching him too. He's fascinating and cute." Jamie winked.

Grandma beamed. "You're like me—we like watching ghosts."

"Is that why you're the librarian—you like the ghosts who hang out in places like this?"

"Yes, I do. I enjoy talking to them. I detect their innermost thoughts." Grandma gave a knowing smile.

"I want to do that too."

"You have the gift. A warm light emanates from your eyes. Light swirls inside your pupils, and a green glow shines on your hands and clothing. The light vanishes after a few moments. You don't see it in yourself, but I assure you, it is happening and people of magic see it."

Jamie placed her hand over her heart. "How d-d-do I?" she stuttered, not really knowing what to ask.

"You have the gift of healing and love. Those words may seem trite, but a time will come when you will not doubt the power of your love."

Jamie briefly felt a deep joy. "I want to believe this with all my heart and hope . . ."

The archives door swung open with a deafening boom, but Jamie did not see anyone. *I need to get a grip. Calm yourself down, Jamie. You can do it. Mom, Dad help me face whatever it is.* Holding her ruler in one hand and swinging her backpack in the other, Jamie yelled, "Ready."

"Follow me," Grandma replied as she grasped her medallion with her right hand. "I'll use my magic."

Texter floated above. "I'll help too."

Jamie arrived at the door first and laughed hysterically when she found Judd collapsed on the floor with books and magazines on top of him.

As Judd crawled to get up, he said breathlessly, "Here I go again, Jamie. It is just me. Real graceful, huh?"

"Elegant enough to be a ballerina." Grandma chuckled.

"Hi, Grandma." Judd laughed sheepishly. "Jamie, I was looking all over for you. You were supposed to meet me at the library door. I was sooo worried. Glad you're with Grandma."

"What's the big deal? I'm only a little late." Jamie pointed at the time on her cell phone.

Boom. Flash. Sizzle. Boom. Boom. Snap. Bang.

"Yikes, it may be too late, but I'm supposed to be a big brother and get you home safely. Mom called and said we are in a winter storm advisory with hail the size of golf balls or larger."

"Texter will see me home," Jamie replied.

"Texter? The only Texter I ever knew died a year ago — a fabulous football player. We need him back on the team. He was a good friend, too. Is there another Texter?"

"No, I am the one and only Texter." A deep voice bounced off the walls.

Judd twisted around to determine the direction of the voice. Texter touched him on his shoulder and gently said "Boo."

Judd leaped into the air and fell flat on his butt again.

Holding out her hand to help Judd, Jamie explained. "Judd, Texter is a security guard here in the archives. Can't you see him?"

"Hey, Texter. There you are." He poked him in the ribs. "You are real." Judd then knuckled Texter. "Good to see you buddy. This is a surprise. I am not so sure you should be wandering off campus and taking Jamie anywhere. You're dead, after all."

Grandma said, "Quit horsing around. Texter, go back to your frame." She pointed to the *In Memory* corridor. "And Judd, get on home before the storm gets any worse. Jamie and I will go together. I promise we will hurry."

Jamie watched the boys obediently leave. She helped Grandma collect their belongings, and then followed her down the hallway into the elevator. *No winking frames, no monkeys on grape vines. It is way too quiet in here.*

CHAPTER SEVEN

Forgotten

When Jamie and Grandma exited the elevator, they wandered into the WiseMore Library foyer.

"Jamie, wait here in the foyer. I will be right back. Just have to get a few things."

The arched doorway vibrated from an ill-tempered wind. Lightning flashed in the circular stained glass window above the door. Jamie looked up at the window and studied it for the first time. *Wow, I did not know this window had my family history told in a variety of patterns and colors.*

Jamie walked closer toward the window and stared. She spoke telepathically. *Magic window, can you tell me more about my family? What is my legacy?*

The glass came alive with multi-color lights highlighting first one section of the window and then another. *Fascinating! Each section is showing different parts of my past.*

Jamie, touched by the tenderness of one scene, used her mother's medallion to transport herself into it. She had been five or six months old. Her mother held her while her father cuddled her sister, Kattie. She looked up at her mother's adoring eyes and felt loved.

Quickly moving to the next scene, nine-month-old Jamie was slowly getting to her feet, using a chair to pull herself up. She fell a few times but she kept trying. Her parents encouraged her to come to them. And she did it. Dad moved further away from her and she got up again and went to him. Kattie was trying also, but gave up and screamed and kicked on the floor. Mom held Kattie while Jamie had walked from chair to chair, giggling.

A branch banged against the window, waking Jamie out of childhood remembrances back into current reality.

The door into the Library Media Center opened to show a dozen ghosts arguing about who would get to check out *Makeup for a Pale Ghost*, and Grandma telling them to settle it by morning. "I'm ready, Jamie. Let's go."

Jamie could not tear herself away from the window. "I've been looking at the stained glass, and reliving my life as a baby." Jamie pointed. "In that scene, Kattie and I are barely two. Look at that. She grabbed some daisies, deliberately tore off the blooms, and threw them at me. Were we ever happy?"

"Look deeper. What is the window showing you?" Grandma said. "Keep looking."

Jamie examined the window. She realized Kattie had loaned her the flower bracelet she had made herself, from daisies. "Wow, she did care."

"That's right. Kattie did have a softer side. There is more. Look in the middle of the window."

Staring at the window, Jamie noticed a familiar car pulling up to a large brick building with the sign reading, *Hermitage of Peace Mental Health*. Her parents got out of the car and instructed her to stay in the back seat. Mom and Dad took Kattie inside along with her suitcase. "Grandma, I thought the Hermitage was a boarding school. Was it a hospital?"

"Your sister had to be hospitalized because of her violent behavior. Your parents did not know how to tell you when you were younger, but early onset bipolar disorder was diagnosed. Her treatment seemed to be successful until recently."

"That explains a lot. I always wondered why she went to a private boarding school, and I did not. I understand now."

A raging wind, full of snow and ice, barreled through the foyer and swung the library doors opened. Jamie and Grandma darted into the library, to get away from the floor to ceiling windows of the foyer and to safety. Or so they thought.

"Guess we are staying here until the weather calms down," Grandma suggested as they huddled under a wooden table. Another gust of cold wind, ice and snow whirled in behind the pair.

With eyes widened, Grandma quizzed, "How is all the snow and ice getting in here? I am going to look. Stay here." She walked tentatively toward the foyer, closed an open door, and tried to lock it. *Boom.* The blizzard blew open the door, as well as the other four foyer entrances, with so much force that Grandma propelled back into the library. The wind howled and whistled, sucking Grandma under the checkout desk like a vacuum cleaner.

Jamie crawled over to her grandmother. "What is happening?"

"I am not sure, but this is not a normal winter storm. Look at the ghosts. They are frenetic and disturbed."

"I can't tell what is snow and what is ghost," Jamie giggled. "It's funny watching them."

"The ghosts are the ones that don't melt," Grandma retorted. They laughed hysterically as they watched the apparitions bounce off each other and slide into the walls.

"They're ice skating. Or maybe that's sledding," Jamie observed. "They can't even stand up."

Another blast of Artic air, scared the flickers and sent them scurrying. As they exited through the walls, the poltergeists noisily knocked keyboards and computers off tables. The cords danced in every direction, pulling table legs and flipping them over. The spooks were badly spooked as they nervously rapped on the walls.

The only ghost left standing was Texter. "Good grief. You would think my friends had never seen snow before. They are acting like a bunch of snowflakes."

Jamie scanned the room as she and Grandma Liz walked toward Texter. "Glad you are in here. I thought you were in your frame upstairs. What's going on?"

"I don't know. The ghosts come in here every day after school to play, but something has spooked them."

"That's funny, Texter, spooked ghosts," Jamie tittered. "I don't think it was just the weather. It is much more than a storm."

"Oh my, watch out!" Texter shouted.

Books soared toward Jamie. She ducked, but a hardback book swiped her forehead. She picked up the book, *The Chase of the Fiends.* The book had a broken spine and rumpled pages. A stench made her sneeze. Jamie cringed. The image on the book cover came to life with a teenage girl running from wide-mouthed and large-teethed wolves. "Gran, why does this girl look like me?"

Grandma walked over to Jamie to look at her head. "Well, the book cover could be a prediction of the future, or someone is trying to scare you. Sit here and let me look at you." Grandma cleaned the blood off Jamie's forehead. "It's a surface cut. We will bandage it when we get home."

Noises like a freight train ripped through the media room. "Watch out," Texter yelled as another book rocketed from the shelves and missed Jamie by an inch. It landed on a table, and emitted horrific groans.

Jamie read the title, *Dungeon of the Forgotten*. The book opened and the pages turned, revealing grotesque photos of gaunt-looking teens shackled in dungeons. Sadly, some photos showed guards beating the teens, and other photos revealed the guards dipping out a spoonful of beans into dirty bowls.

In one picture that filled the entire page, a girl rattled the chains that bound her to a dungeon wall. Magically, she emerged partway from the book, sticking her head and a hand out. The girl grabbed Jamie's wrist. "I'm begging you. Please pull me out."

Jamie clutched the girl's arm. Her gift of Revelation exposed the girl's name as Trish and the abductor's name as SpiderWood.

Trish spilled out her sorrow and pain. "The vicious killings occurred in front of me and my brother. After murdering our parents, SpiderWood kidnapped us in the dark of the night and abducted everyone in this dungeon to silence us."

Jamie gripped Trish's wrist. "I'm pulling as hard as I can. Help me, Grandma." They both tugged until Trish's arms and upper torso became free. "We will get you out," Jamie said. She held on tightly to the girl but stopped pulling for a brief moment to catch her breath.

"You're lucky." Trish said, looking up at Jamie with swollen eyes. "You escaped. Your birthright protected you."

"What do you mean?"

"Everyone here knows you have powers and are destined to be one of the greatest Light Champions of all times. You will save us." Trish let out a blood-curdling scream.

Jamie looked down inside the photo and saw guards violently wrench Trish's legs. She lost her grip on Trish's hands. Jamie wept as the girl's shackled body crashed to the ground, knocking over a water dish and an empty food bowl. The guards beat the girl with whips and broom handles. Powerless to help, Jamie watched Trish cower on the floor in submission. She observed Trish bury her tear-stained face into her folded arms.

Jamie felt like a sword stabbed her heart. She cried out to Trish. "I will come for you and the others. Please keep hope."

"We will not forget you. Stay strong," Grandma compassionately reiterated.

The book went back to its howling, creating a horrific burst of wind, flapping its pages, and blowing loose-leaf papers and magazines everywhere. Jamie slammed the book shut, stinging her hand. *I cannot look anymore. God help me.*

Angry at the injustice she had witnessed, Jamie slung the book across the room. Jamie sobbed, "I'm concerned about the prisoners in the dungeons. Will I have the power and strength to free them? I don't want to fail them."

"I'll assist you in every way I can, I assure you." Grandma Liz put her hand on Jamie's shoulder. "As you know, SpiderWood has a horrific reputation of brutality. Jamie, one day we will participate in the solution to the mysteries surrounding the tortured teens in the photographs. I think the real tempest was in here in the Media Room, not outside. There is that cat again. Suspicious."

"Hmmm. Perhaps the cyclonic winds have stirred up my sense of justice." Jamie stomped over to the book, *Dungeon of the Forgotten,* and snatched it up. "Is this a catalogued book, Grandma?"

"No and neither is *Chase of the Fiends.* Who or whatever created the tumultuous hail and snow storm must have also blown in the books."

"I am keeping both books." Jamie angrily stuffed them into her backpack. "I was literally hit in the head, woken up to my destiny, my calling to help the forgotten ones. I vow to use my birthright and powers to fight for light, justice and freedom."

"Forgotten. You want to take care of them but you have forgotten all about me. Who do you think blew in the storm and threw the books at you?" The black cat sauntered across the table in front of Jamie.

"Kattie?"

The black cat with the ruby collar arched its back and hissed. She skulked sneakily out of the library, took form as a gray mist, and mingled with the wintery night air.

CHAPTER EIGHT

Back Down to Earth

W hat a great beginning – studying two languages and several sciences. *More art classes and music lessons. Back with all of my friends. This is going to be a very good year.* After her summer vacation on HollowWinds, Jamie strolled toward the WiseMore Library at the end of the first day of her sophomore year. She felt the balminess of the air. Sweat beads formed on her brow. *I did not think rain was in the forecast for today.* "Hi Grandma, are you ready?"

Mrs. Glosomore was straightening up the library before leaving to go home with Jaime. "Need a few more minutes."

"Okay, I am going to wait out in the foyer and perhaps sketch some of our family history scenes in the arched window for my genealogy notes. What was that swooshing noise?" Jamie spun around and saw a gray misty shape moving toward her. "Kattie, it's you, isn't it?" Jamie's voice sounded determined. "You have been following me, at HallowWinds and now here. Shouldn't we attempt to talk civilly and have peace between us?"

Housed in her former body, Kattie leapt in front of Jamie. "Oh, Miss Perfect. You would like to talk with me? What? You going to save me? I bet you think you're going to rescue the captives, too."

"What a welcome back to Earth. Yes, I would like to free them, and in my soul, I want to stand up for what matters. I do want to work it out with you. I know about the Hermitage." Jamie looked up at the window, and then reached out to touch her sister.

Kattie slapped Jamie's arm away and spat into the air. "Oh, yeah, you're just trying to make everything all right by being mushy. It may be your birthright to safeguard the world, but not me, sister dear. That ridiculous boarding school could not rehab me. It was no hermitage of peace either. I am dead, and everything goes to the favorite twin. Well, you're in for a surprise."

"You can't blame me for living. Look at you. You are the one who chose to take SilverWorm's side. How could you do that after she murdered our parents?"

"You don't get it. They hated me and I hated them. I did not care that they died. And you don't have any regrets about my death either."

"That is so far from the truth. I wish you were alive, enjoying classes with me and making new friends."

"No way." Kattie zoomed around. "SilverWorm will make me somebody with great power. She wants my help to get rid of her sister. In exchange, I will get her sister's bounty and have wealth of my own. They hate each other, just as I loathe you."

The twins stood face to face, glaring at each other. Jamie clenched her fist, wanting to punch her.

Grandma heard the commotion and rushed into the foyer to see what was transpiring. She positioned herself between the girls. "Listen to me. You're ignoring your chance to settle the past and act human."

"Human? You got to be kidding." Kattie raced toward the doors.

"Do not leave, young lady. Your parents wanted you to get along with your sister," Grandma pleaded with tears in her eyes.

Jamie shook her head as Kattie lumbered away. "I'm so sorry. You tried to bring us together."

"No matter what I feel, protect yourself against the Dark Particles— even if that particle is Kattie," Grandma warned.

"Is there any chance Kattie will change?" Jamie asked.

"I hope so. You know how she was as a child."

"Do I ever." Jamie remembered Kattie's explosive temper with reckless and aggressive behavior. "She could be giddy one minute followed by long bouts of crying the next. If one of us tried to console her, she would get very aggressive. Her mood swings were hard to predict. Grandma, at the hospital, was Kattie given medication or therapy?"

"Yes, she did and those things really helped her, but she didn't always take her medication. Jamie, we are not sure how she will be in death, especially with SilverWorm's evil influence. It's getting late, we need to get home."

Jamie glanced up again at the window. A shrill crackling noise broke out above her. Jamie saw Kattie using a stick to beat on the circular window, shattering it into sharp pieces of glass. Jamie screamed as the glass fell.

Grandma worked her magic. "Uniola celebratio." Blocking the glass from falling, it hung in midair. "We need a permanent display." She used her magic again. "Expecdantae solitate illuminae." The glass pieces recombined to form a new and thicker circular window. Grandma moved toward Kattie. "The renderings in the new window of your family history are for both of you."

"I don't want to share anything with Jamie," Kattie hollered as she raced into a heavy downpour and lightning-filled sky. Sparks flew off her hands and feet as she propelled through the air.

"I don't think Kattie will ever trust me. How can I help her?"

"Be strong." Then Grandma commanded the storm, "Viento tranquilo." They walked outside into the calm.

"I sure am glad you calmed the storm." Jamie swung her purse as she walked along the side of the Student Center with her grandmother. "Ohhh, that chocolate smells so good. Should we get some before we go home, Grandma? The WiseMore Candy store makes the best chocolate rock nuggets. I think chocolate will help me calm down. Kattie sure knows how to churn things up."

"That is for sure, but I think I want their chocolate toffee crunch bar or some of their chocolate mocha bean candies. Yum that will calm me down. Maybe we should get some of each, have some now and save some for later. Even better medicine that way."

They bought the candy and sat on a bench outside the shop to eat it. They looked at a rainbow that arched across the blue sky. Underneath a tree nearby, three squirrels jumped over each other, trying to catch their tails. Jamie giggled at the sight, and then caught herself, remembering the distress she had felt just a half hour ago while her dead sister screamed at her. It did not seem quite real. Yet Jamie knew it was. The sun dribbled through the orange, red and yellow crumpled leaves. *I wish I could have more quiet time. Fall is a reflective season. Life ebbs away in nature with color and beauty before the leaves brown and shrivel. However, spring comes eventually budding growth. Life returns.* "Grandma, didn't you say you wanted to go to the grocery? Why don't you go ahead? I will be okay. I'd like some time alone to think about things."

"Okay, dear. I think that is a great idea. I understand. Quiet time sounds good to me too. It is good medicine." Grandma handed the bag of chocolate to her granddaughter and then headed off to the left.

Lost in her thoughts Jamie wandered aimlessly, and then perched on a tree stump. After a short time, a fog enveloped her as steam rose from the ground. *I wonder if that is Kattie again. If it is my twin, what should I say to invite conversation and healing?* She looked up and noticed 5:07 p.m. on the outdoor clock of the Sports Center. She glanced back toward the mist as the outline of a girl with shoulder length hair appeared.

Jamie jumped up and walked toward Kattie. "Does this mean that you want to talk now?"

With a tree limb in her hand, Kattie raised her arm to strike.

Running up the steps to the Sports Center's door, Jamie yanked as hard as she could, but the door would not open.

"I won't let you escape." Kattie lunged at Jamie again, swearing. The lamplights popped and sizzled at Kattie's command. Live electrical wires dangled from the posts, and some exposed wires fell around Jamie's feet, trapping her. Jamie shrieked as more cables dropped close to her face and torso.

"Go ahead and fuss for all the good it'll do you," Kattie yelled. "No one can hear you."

How do I get out of this one? I do not want to be fried or anyone else hurt. Hmm, something soft. "Transformae en pasteo," commanded Jamie pointing to the wires. She laughed to herself as she watched the cables turn into slender noodles. Jamie doggedly walked through the pasta toward her sister.

Kattie flew off in circles high above Jamie until she was a speck in the sky.

Watching Kattie gain momentum on her descent, Jamie noticed a saber in her sister's hand. It was aimed right at her upturned face.

"Bulls-eye," Kattie thundered.

Charging to the side of the Center for safety, Jamie spied lights in the windows. *Whew, that was close. I am not a dartboard. If I stay close to the building or get in somehow hopefully, I am protected.* Jamie saw students engaged in soccer practice and flailed her arms in front of the windows. She could not get anyone's attention. Bushes under the windows scratched her legs while rope-like roots entangled her feet. She struggled to stand up. *Kattie must be trying to tie me up with these roots. Dad's knife will loosen them.* Jamie used her father's carving knife to rip away the vines. She scampered off. *Maybe I can cross through WiseMore Park to get home.*

As soon as she stepped into the park, the sky darkened and scattered storms hung over Jamie. Water collected in puddles. Jamie splashed through them. The faster she ran—the quicker the cold rain chilled her. She heard what sounded like a pack of running dogs. The growling noises behind Jamie sounded close, so she hid inside a gazebo. The rumbling sounds went past her. *Thank God. They have lost sight of me.*

Jamie stayed in the pentagon shaped structure, with two solid walls and three fenced sides, to conceal herself from the animals chasing her. She squatted down against one of the walls. Two hearts, engraved on the opposite wall, attracted her attention. *G. loves J. I wonder if Griff put that there. Maybe he did.* A faint smile shaped Jamie's face but it quickly dissipated when she heard noises. *They must have turned around. Have the animals discovered me?*

Twisting and peeking around the gazebo's entrance, Jamie spotted shadowy animals, exposing their large white teeth. The animals resembled the black spotted hyenas on the *Chase of the Fiends* book cover.

Jammed against the gazebo's interior wall, Jamie searched in her backpack for *Chase of the Fiends*. She scanned the chapter about diluting wild animal curses. Jamie tossed the book out on the sidewalk to prevent setting the wooden gazebo on fire. She raised her hand and chanted "Curseri inferno." Jamie sent out a flare, encasing the book in flames. The blaze forced the creatures back away a short distance.

Must keep the fire going. Oh, I know. Jamie rummaged in her backpack for the book, *Dungeon of the Forgotten*, which had revealed to her the grotesque images of teens shackled in dungeons. *Maybe I can keep the animals at bay and free the kids.* Jamie thought about Trish and the promise she made, as she set the book on the sidewalk between the gazebo and the fire. She ordered vociferously, "Releasio teenacio." The magic words opened the cages and released the shackles from the ankles of the emaciated teens. *Clang. Bang.* The chains deafeningly fell out of the book. The teens helped each other clamber off the pages.

"Is that everyone?" Jamie asked.

"There are more kids in the dungeons below the other three towers of GrayStone Castle," said Trish. "Can you help them?"

"Are they in this book? I don't remember seeing anything but the south tower."

"You're right. I was just hoping."

"I must torch this book." Jamie threw the book into the flames and ordered, "Curseri inferno." The teens gawked at the bonfire. Jamie explained, "You are free from the witches' traps, their curse on you has ended. Now I have to get you to safety. Gather here in the gazebo, and make a lot of noise to keep the hyenas away. Stay in the group."

Jamie sent a telepathic message to Texter. *I need you immediately to help me get the teens from the dungeon to safety. Bring supplies.* Using her parallelogram brooch, she talked to Griff.

"I will talk to my uncle immediately. Help will be on its way. Please be careful," Griff cautioned.

In a flash, Texter arrived in a 2.5 ton covered army cargo truck with food, water, coats and blankets.

"You are a true friend. That was a speedy response," Jamie said. "You thought of everything."

Texter collected some of the chains. "We can use these as weapons." Two of the stronger 17 year olds loaded them up with Texter.

Jamie quickly helped them climb into the back of the truck lined with benches. Trish hugged Jamie.

"Hurry, Trish. I will catch up with all of you later," Jamie said.

"But what about you? You will be alone. Shouldn't some of us stay behind to help you?" Trish asked.

"I will be okay. Please just hurry." Jamie watched anxiously until the vehicle was out of sight. *Light Keepers watch over these kids. They have suffered enough.*

Then Jamie spotted the fire had extinguished. The pack of oversized hyenas glared at her. *How did that happen?* The animals stood between her and the closest park exit. Their laughter sounded wicked and cruel, like witches' cackling. *I will have to go deeper into the woods and then circle back.*

Kattie rode the pack leader of the hyenas. She belted the animal hard with a whip on its flank. Her eyes narrowed. "Hey Fiend, close in on Jamie. If she gets away, I will beat you to a pulp. Your pack will eat what is left of you."

Jamie leapt over the gazebo railing and darted to the right, going deeper into WiseMore Park. For the moment, she had tricked Kattie and the pack of hyenas, but she knew they were faster than she was. She dashed one way then the other to throw her scent in different directions. *There is a statue of a man on a horse close by.*

Jamie raced toward the large white stone statue that graced the park with its lifeless form. She brushed against its base, causing sparks to radiate from her body into the knight and his charger. They came to life. The animal reared up, spreading its magnificent white wings with green and gold flight feathers. With one mighty launch, the charger cleared the pedestal and turned toward Jamie. He flared his nostrils and displayed his majestic stature, ready for defensive or offensive action.

The knight swept Jamie onto the horse's back. "Hurry. The hyenas are getting closer." Jamie hugged the knight and was surprised she could hear his heartbeat through the armor. Jamie's intuition revealed a secret about the knight.

"You're more than a knight. Your name is Lance. You're serving in the WindSong Cavalry, defending Light Channel."

"I am part of the mounted horse regiment for Light Channel," Lance said, surprised. "You have the gift of revelation."

"Hey, that's what my grandmother says." Jamie held on tight as they raced across the park.

The knight patted his massive charger. "Go, Samson, go." The muscular horse responded.

Jamie looked behind her and witnessed Kattie's cruel treatment of Fiend. She was spurring her heels and striking the hyena's ears.

"I command you to close in," Kattie demanded. Fiend jumped over a large olive bush, causing Kattie to hit an overhanging tree branch. She thudded to the ground. Fiend did not move. Kattie grabbed her whip and beat the hyena. "Take this . . . you'll pay for dumping me. I warned you."

"Stop, Lance. We need to help Fiend." As they circled back, Jamie saw the other hyenas standing to the side for a few moments. The next strongest female positioned herself in front of the pack, and gave the command for the horde to scurry off into the woods with one loud laugh.

Jamie's strong sense of justice compelled her to point her finger at Kattie's whip. "Expungeto." The leather straps went up in smoke.

The injured Fiend hobbled into the dense shrubbery to hide. Kattie ran after the creature and pounded Fiend with her fists. Jamie hopped off the horse and angrily commanded, "Vineis impeditos." Vines near Kattie's feet entangled her and yanked her to the ground. Kattie struck the back of her head on a stone, and laid sprawled out unconscious.

The bloodied Fiend winked at Jamie. "That is the quietest Kattie has ever been." She stood up, shook off debris, and gave a noble bow to Jamie. "I will repay you for your kindness."

"You are most welcome. I heard Kattie call you Fiend. Is that your name?"

With sad eyes, the hyena responded, "No, I don't have a real name."

"Well, you should have an honorable name. From now on you will be known as Victorious."

"I humbly accept such a glorious name. No longer victim, I am Victorious."

"Jamie, catch," Lance said as he tossed a canteen and a small bag to her. "That has some salve that might help Victorious."

Jamie gently poured water over the wounds and smoothed the ointment on them.

Victorious bowed again. "Thanks Jamie and Lance." With broad shoulders straight and ears perked, the injured but proud Victorious slowly marched away.

Swinging back onto the charger, Jamie asked, "Can you help me get away before Kattie regains consciousness?"

"My pleasure, my Lady."

Jamie and her knight rode for a distance, and came to a skidding halt at the park's edge.

Lance dismounted, lowered Jamie to the ground, and calmed his horse. "Jamie, Samson and I possess no life outside the limits of this park. As long as we are in the park, we become alive if a believer in need touches us. If we try to leave, we are cursed to be stone sculptures forever."

"Who would do this to you and Samson?"

"SpiderWood placed a curse on us for five years. Then a command of Light Champions must come to lift the spell. Jamie, I cannot continue with you on your trek home. The neighborhoods are full of dangers. However, our private eyes will be hopping all around you to make sure you get home." Lance picked up a tree frog in a decorated uniform. "Jamie, let me introduce you to someone special. This is Agent Mytee."

Mytee tipped his beret to Jamie. "Glad to meet you, ma'am. I am at your service."

After Lance whispered into the agent's ear, Mytee commanded, "Agent Tynee, send your frog-boys to find out what is lurking near Sun Ray Subdivision tonight."

Just then, tree frogs emerged from trees, rocks, and clumps of weeds. The frog-boys jumped over the park's boundary at Tynee's command.

Agent Mytee explained, "The frog-boys will find out about the witches' activity in the neighborhood. When number one frog gets tired, the word goes to the second frog, and so on until the message reaches its destination. We already know there has been mischief on Weather Avenue."

Jamie said. "I promise. I won't go near Weather Avenue."

Lance hugged Jamie. "I'm glad I could get you safely through the park. The tree frogs will get you home."

Jamie rubbed Samson's neck. "Will you and Samson be safe in the park?"

"Yes," Lance said. "We will stay on our pedestal and freeze frame if necessary until the curse is ended."

"I'll come visit." Jamie waved goodbye to the knight and his charger as they vanished among the trees, heading back into the interior of the park. She shivered and rubbed her arms to keep warm. "Come frog-boys, you're tiny, but mighty." She and the frogs walked across the edge of WiseMore Park. As she passed the Sports Center, the clock read 5:17 p.m. She was amazed. *All that action took place in 10 minutes. That is very strange.*

CHAPTER NINE

Time

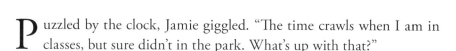

Puzzled by the clock, Jamie giggled. "The time crawls when I am in classes, but sure didn't in the park. What's up with that?"

Agent Mytee responded, "Time is always different in the park and during magical encounters."

The frog-boys sent relay messages throughout the WiseMore campus to keep Jamie safe. They walked by the WiseMore High School Campus, bypassed Weather Avenue, and headed toward home. As they hiked, Jamie showed her medallion to Mytee. "I received this stone from my mother the day she and my father died. I discovered the ability to see any scene I want in the gem. Just now, I saw Kattie still unconscious in the park. Shouldn't I go back to her?"

Before Mytee answered, Jamie sighed in relief. "Oh good, I see my grandfather walking his pet dragon, Rowdy. They are close by."

"Good," said Mytee. "Discuss with him about going back to the park. He is very wise. Commander Glosomore will give practical, safe, and compassionate advice."

"You sound like you know him real well. Have you worked with him on assignments?"

"The frog-boys have performed tasks for him that needed wee soldiers on special missions."

Jamie waved at Grandpa and Rowdy as she took off running toward them. Without taking a breath, Jamie spilled out the things that had happened since she and Grandma split up at the Candy Store.

"We will all go to the park to check on Kattie, but we must be clever. It may be a trick. We will go on Rowdy. Agent Mytee, would you and two of your best frog-boys come with us? Perhaps you can have some of your team keep an eye on the neighborhood, and a few of your relay messengers can go to the park to let Lance and Samson know we are coming," said Grandpa.

"Yes, sir." Mytee gave the necessary orders.

"Grandpa, you already know Mytee, Tynee, and the frog-boys. Do you also know Lance and Samson?"

"Yes, Jamie, we all know each other. Was your grandmother going somewhere after you two left WiseMore Candy Store? She was not home yet. What time did you leave there?"

"We separated at 5:07 p.m. She went to the grocery store after we ate chocolate together."

Pulling out his pocket watch, Grandpa remarked, "It is 5:27 p.m. now. She probably is still shopping. We will go by the store to check on her."

Rowdy, loaded up with his passengers, took off with a roar to the store nine blocks away. Just as they were arriving, Grandma exited the store with a cart of groceries and a smaller package tucked under her arm. Rowdy descended to the street.

"What's going on?" asked Grandma.

"Get on, darling. It's a long story, but we have to go check on Kattie in the park."

"Here, honey, eat a quick protein snack first. You need some protein since we will be eating dinner late." Grandma pulled out of the package some fresh salmon jerky, string cheese and protein bars.

"You had chocolate with Jamie, and I get protein? Did you save any for me?" Grandpa teased as he selected salmon for his snack. "Thanks for getting my kind of chocolate." He gently boosted his wife onto Rowdy and packed the groceries in a container strapped to Rowdy's tail.

"String cheese might balance out the sweet for you," Grandma suggested as she handed some to Jamie.

"A perfect protein snack. Thanks." Jamie yelled, "Oh, no. My medallion is revealing to me that the twin witches are fighting over Kattie who is now leaning up against a tree."

Grandma smiled. "You learned a new skill, Jamie. Can you tell if Kattie is okay? You can make the scene zoom closer by tapping it three times."

Jamie tapped on the gem and saw web-like ropes around Kattie's upper torso, tying her to the tree. "She looks okay but she must have been tied up by SpiderWood. The cords look like webs. I also have a visual on the witches. SilverWorm has reinforcements. There is a gorilla-sized creature with some human and animal parts, and hook-like claws, attacking SpiderWood."

"His name is Gravedigger. He usually stays in the cemetery. This complicates things a little." Grandpa paused. "Rowdy, keep your distance from them, but we need to get as close as possible to Kattie. When we land, I want Jamie and the frog-boys to get Kattie untied. Rowdy, Grandma and I will create a distraction."

Rowdy landed quietly behind some tall bushes and trees. Jamie, Mytee and the frog-boys headed toward Kattie. It was too late. Four feet in front of Kattie, SpiderWood laid writhing on the ground with Gravedigger on top of her, digging his claws deep into her face and chest. SpiderWood squawked and then grew silent.

SilverWorm slashed off the webs around Kattie, picked her up by the nape of her neck, and took flight.

"Oh, my gosh. Gravedigger is rushing up behind us." Jamie bolted back toward Rowdy. Mytee and the frog-boys went in different directions, encircling the gorilla. Gravedigger chased after Jamie with his bones making a horrific clacking sound. With her hair swirling around, Jamie hurdled over bushes, edging stones, and statuary that adorned the park.

Gravedigger struck at Jamie. She jerked on his right hand so hard she ended up with a fist full of phalanges.

"Give me my bones back." Gravedigger grabbed at the boney pieces. In the struggle, the dry bones fell to the ground and began to dissolve. "They're mine," he cried as he knelt to retrieve as many as he could.

"Look, there are replacement bones over here." Mytee and Tynee baited Gravedigger toward a large crater that he himself burrowed earlier looking for bones. Several of the frogs tripped him as he approached and he tumbled into the earth. The frog-boys climbed trees from which they threw a heavy metallic net over the cavern. Grandpa and Lance pounded metal stakes into the ground, stapling the net.

Jamie, using her medallion, chanted, "Commando, cubrir tierra." Dirt filled the gigantic hole. "Well, we buried that bag of bones. Thank you so much, Mytee and Tynee. Please let all the dear frog-boys know my appreciation. Thanks to Grandma and Grandpa, Rowdy, Lance and Samson. We are a great team. You are my heroes."

"We got the catch of the day, Jamie," Grandma exclaimed. Buzzards revolved around their buried prey with disappointment. "Jamie, look behind you."

A stonewall body with one huge eye across its face, and tiller blades for appendages dug up the ground as it tottered. Jamie propelled herself forward, focusing on her strengths. *A day of enemies after me. I can do this. I can.*

Grandpa telepathically communicated to the group. "Lance, create a distraction to get Vaultchaser to go deeper into the park."

Lance rode Samson right up to Vaultchaser, nodded to Jamie and then shouted, "Come on you big block, you wanted to crush Samson and I. Now is your chance. I will even play fair and go very slow like a snail. You can get Jamie later."

Vaultchaser with his heavy body had a difficult time keeping up with Samson and Lance, who would dart off and then come to a complete stop. Lance yelled at Vaultchaser to taunt him.

In her gem, Jamie observed securely from her post with Grandma. Vaultchaser, as he tilled forward, made gaping holes in the sidewalks and grass. The ground ruptured like an earthquake, spewing out gaseous fumes from the pipes below the asphalt. Jamie felt the ground cracking under her. She yelled over the thunderous quaking, "Frog-boys, gather into my pockets. Hurry." She leapt like a bullfrog beyond the ravaged ground to safety.

Grandma climbed onto Rowdy and they took flight.

A streetlight crashed to the ground with the cracking of glass and the screeching of metal. Jamie cleared the utility pole without breaking stride. As more crevices and the landscape changed, Jamie was not sure which direction to go. Nothing looked familiar.

Using her gem, Grandma saw Jamie changing paths. She sent pulsing lights to Jamie as a guide. Jamie's sides ached by the time she found Rowdy and Grandma hovering over a clearing. They landed. Jamie, with her frog friends still in her pockets, breathlessly boarded.

A few minutes later, Lance and Samson arrived. "Vaultchaser just hurtled himself into one of the cracks he had made. I think the fumes got him. It will take him a while to clamber out of that hole. I wanted to watch. Sure it is quite the show."

Grandpa chimed in. "It is. I just saw him, but his tiller legs pulled dirt on top of him. He buried himself. We just checked on SpiderWood. Gravedigger critically injured her. Her spiders wove a web tightly around her, and airlifted her to the north, presumably toward her castle. I am not sure …"

Thunderous roars of SilverWorm's broom caused the group to look up in time to witness SilverWorm torching her sister. A blood-curdling scream, followed by an explosion, pierced the sky. Ashes spewed across the park. A horrible stench of scorched flesh singed the group's nostrils. A medallion fell from the sky at Jamie's feet.

"It's SpiderWood's. Did she mean for me to have it?" Jamie looked into her grandfather's eyes.

"Yes, I think so. SpiderWood met the same demise as your parents," Grandpa reflected. "I suppose this is her way of getting back at SilverWorm for torching her."

"It's such a shock. It's surreal," Jamie added.

"It is justice," Grandma offered as she patted Jamie's hand. "You risked a lot trying to help your sister. We all did. I am so sorry that SilverWorm got to Kattie first. We will put surveillance on her, and rescue Kattie as soon as possible. Gravedigger, Vaultchaser and SpiderWood are gone forever. People of light are joyful. Before we go home, there is something your grandfather and I want you to see in the cemetery."

Lance and Samson gave their good-byes again. Mytee and his scouts went back to work in the neighborhood. Grandma, Grandpa and Jamie took flight on Rowdy over Heat Stroke Drive, a street that experienced blistering heat indices when other streets in the neighborhood did not. Grandma said, "Unpredictable weather has increased with the recent surge of Dark Particles moving into the area from Black Eye Galaxy. You want to avoid Heat Stroke Drive, Jamie, even though it used to be a good short cut from school to your house."

When she went home from school alone, Jamie usually scooted down Heat Stroke, skipped through back yards and jumped over old garden hoses. She sprinted through WiseMore Cemetery's ivy-covered gates. She ran past a row of tall vaults that jutted up into the sky. She felt safe in the cemetery.

Lost in her thoughts, Jamie was unaware that Rowdy had arrived in the cemetery. Jamie studied her surroundings. A drizzling rain ran down Jamie's bangs, onto her face, and into her eyes. She placed her hand on the stone vault in front of her, which triggered a light from the inscription. Tall weeds had grown up around it, but the light allowed Jamie to read the engraved words, which she traced with her fingers:

Lightseekers' Burial Chambers
In Loving Memory of Light Commanders
John and Judith Travelstead,
And their daughter,
Kattie.
May They Rest in Peace

Jamie rocked to her core. *This is my family's burial chambers.* "I didn't know for sure where Mom and Dad were buried. I thought they were at HallowWinds. Are their bodies here?"

Grandma responded, "Yes, dear, your parents' bodies are here so we can keep an eye on their gravesite. Someday soon, we will bring Kattie's urn here too. We are waiting for her spirit to return to her remains, so she can have a body like your parents. There is also a vault for all three of them on HallowWinds to confuse those who would want to desecrate their grave."

"I think the urn should be moved from my bedroom to your fireplace mantel. I wanted her close to me, but don't you think that moving her is more respectful and safer now?" Jamie questioned.

"We want you to be ready to let go. It is a good idea for us to be responsible for her urn. When the time is right, we can have a private ceremony for family closure," Grandpa consoled.

"Whew. I feel better already," Jamie said as she rested her trembling hands on the stone. Sparks of energy came from the stone vault and went into her fingertips. She felt energy strengthen her body. She used her hands to roll the energy into a ball like molding clay in her sculpture class.

Feeling closer to her parents, Jamie reflected on what happened to her recently and came to decisions about how to move forward. She wanted to stay alive and to honor her parents' memories. "They should have daisies on their grave." Within seconds, the blooms shot up and the weeds disappeared. Jamie, with her grandparents and Rowdy, stood in silence. A gentle rain accompanied their mood.

Griff and his uncle approached. "Excuse us. Commanders Glosomore, Ms. Travelstead, we received galactic communication regarding your struggle this evening. You may not have been aware, but with refracted light rays from our ship, we shielded all of you by lifting you over the cracks and gaps," Uncle Belcor enlightened. "We protected you from being swallowed by the earth. Once you left to come here to the cemetery, we made the pathways smooth and the craters filled."

Jamie excitedly responded, "I wondered why we didn't see you, Griff, but I sensed that you were in the park with us. Thank you so much, Uncle Belcor and Griff for safeguarding us."

"It is cool how our galactical equipment allows us to travel in the optical density of light. Jamie, you will learn about the refractive index, how light changes directions and speeds allowing us to manipulate the rays," Griff explained.

"Sounds very interesting."

"Ms. Travelstead, Commanders, a platoon of Light Champions is in the park waiting for you. May we escort you back there," Belcor asked. "Something special is happening."

Sparkling orbs with multifaceted surfaces filtered down through the sky when Griff's uncle, Belcor, touched his medallion. The orbs danced in the rain and exuded light beams that flooded the area with warmth. The Star Particles' cores became brilliant and hot. Their firepower increased, and their impermeable shields transported the group, including Rowdy, back to the center of the park.

When they landed, they entered into a circle of Light Keepers and Champions who stood guard over the statue of Lance atop his magnificent steed, Samson. Belcor along with his nephew, Griff, both released Star Particles from their medallions that surrounded the statue.

"Tonight is the fifth anniversary of the curse placed on this fine young man and his stallion." With a booming voice, Belcor, Commander in Chief of the Luminous Intergalactic Defense, ordered, "Revertio pythonis maldo verbum. Libertatio Senor Lance et caballo."

"What did he say?" Jamie asked.

"He spoke in his version of Spanish, French and Latin. Give freedom to Sir Lance and his horse and reverse the witch's evil words," Grandpa whispered.

Brilliant hues of orange and red embraced the statuary giving off heat. Jamie peered into the light and could see that the statue was moving. As the temperature increased, Lance and Samson glowed white and became more animated. The white heat was so intense that everyone backed away and watched as it changed quickly into incandescent heat. Heat energy turned into light energy, blinding all gathered.

"It's okay. You can open your eyes," Sir Lance said. Before the group, stood a knight arrayed in splendid armor and mounted on his spirited charger. He commanded his steed to gallop to the park's edge.

Belcor displayed a huge screen from his medallion, so all could watch, as the muscular horse sprinted across the park's boundary. Sir Lance threw up a raised arm and clenched fist, a sign of victory. Knight and steed returned to the group and to their boisterous cheers and whistles.

"I am free. I am free," Lance intoned.

The Light Champions escorted Commander-in-Chief Belcor, Commanders Glosomore, Sir Lance, Griff and Jamie along with Samson and Rowdy to the Glosomores' home in Sun Ray Subdivision.

Jamie considered the clock. It was only 6:07 p.m. *In one hour, so much has happened. So much life, liberty, justice, death and emotions. Three of the Dark Particles are expired. I visited my parents' grave. Lance, Samson, Victorious and the dungeon prisoners received the gift of freedom. I do not take my life and freedom for granted. I am thankful for the protectors of the Light. Together, we will help others find the Light.*

Griff spoke softly, "I share your wonder and awe as you stare at the grandfather clock and know you are amazed about the time. When we are defending the Light, we are in a different sphere. Time cannot be measured in human terms."

"It seems like we are participating in something eternal," Jamie responded.

"Okay, earth to Jamie and Griff. You have had your second call and bell ringing. Let's eat," Grandma Liz silenced her dinner bell.

Jamie glanced around the table appreciating each face of family and friend. *It has been a long, but good day. Time is a mystery.*

CHAPTER TEN

Gifts

S unlight danced in Jamie's window as if to a stirring piece of music. The leaves swirled around and spiraled downward on her bedroom wall to the rhythm in her head. *TimberWood and his family are losing their leaves.* She dressed, ran down the stairs, grabbed a banana, headed out the back door and climbed up her favorite tree. "Good morning, friend. It seems like it has been forever since I have seen you. You are changing so fast these days. Look at you in all your oranges, reds and yellows. You smell good too."

TimberWood embraced her with his branches. "Me? You too are changing so fast. Already a junior in high school. It was just yesterday, when your mother rocked you under my branches. Enjoy my color while you can," he said with his deep but comforting voice.

Jamie told him about her violin recital from the previous night and about her art exhibit the first week of December. "I only have six weeks to finish getting the exhibit completed. Good news that I have a week off for Thanksgiving this year. TimberWood, I stayed up until 1:00 a.m. working on a painting of you, but I will have to change it now," she teased.

"No wonder you slept until noon," TimberWood said kindly. "Are you going to show me the painting? I would like to see the magical colors of changing time."

"No, you can't see it yet. But after I completed the painting, I did sleep like a log, pun intended."

"Glad you slept well Jamie."

"Me too," Griff said from below. "May I join you two?" Griff scaled the tree. Immediately Jamie and Griff chatted about the events of the last few months.

"Jamie, it's time to go," Aunt Esther called from the back door.

"Go? Go where?"

"Grandma is taking you to get your nails done."

"Wow. That is awesome. Love you both, my friends. See you later," Jamie said as she slid down the tree.

On the way to the salon, Jamie excitedly told Grandma Liz how she wanted her nails done. "On my right thumb and big toe, I want painted black with sparkling stars. The left I want blue with a bold sun painted on them. Both ring fingers I will have dark blue with a pale yellow moon. All the other fingers and toes will be sunny yellow with orange leaves like TimberWood's."

"That's creative. Help me pick out a design. Your grandfather told me that I needed to get with it, be up with the times since I am working at the high school."

"They can paint little birds for you, Grandma. They can sparkle and look like they are flying."

While they were both getting their pedicures and manicures, Grandma said, "Jamie, I have an idea. Why don't you stay at our house tonight? We can enjoy some of the old ghost movies you always liked."

"That would be fun. Could we fix homemade pizza and get Rowdy to roast some peanuts for us? Oh, he could do marshmallows too."

The two women laughed and had a great afternoon. However, Jamie noticed that Griff and the frog-boys were always close by. *It is comforting but gosh, are they that worried about my family's safety? What do they think will happen? Do they know something that I don't know?*

* * * * * * * *

As her grandmother pulled out some movies, Jamie looked at all the photos of her parents and herself with Kattie, woodcarvings that her father did, and lots of other mementoes that lined the mantle. Jamie enjoyed the flood of happy memories associated with these keepsakes.

"Grandma, let's move Kattie's urn to your mantle. That would make a great birthday present for Kattie and me."

"Okay, we will bring it over from your bedroom tomorrow on the actual day," Grandma responded. "Where is that movie?"

Then Jamie spied more photos and souvenirs on bookshelves across the room. "Grandma, I have never seen these photos before? These are really good pics of the family."

"I found them in a photo box recently and decided to get them framed. Did you notice your first birthday party photo? Your first birthday was celebrated right here in this house."

"Cool." Scratching noises alerted her to a black cat walking along the fireplace's marble shelf. It knocked over a set of wooden carvings. Jamie retraced her steps, picked up the carvings and set them back in their place.

"Kattie, why are you here? Do you want to watch movies with us? Grandma has some old ghost movies like the ones we used to like."

"*Not So Hallowed Ghosts* was one of your favorites and I just found it," Grandma said.

"Tomorrow is our sixteenth birthday," Kattie stated as she took human shape.

"Happy birthday eve, sis."

"Why are you being nice to me? I was getting ready to scratch you with my long fingernails," Kattie said as she clawed the air.

"We share our birthday whether you like it or not. So we might as well be sisters for twenty-four hours," Jamie spoke softly.

"SilverWorm is gone for a few days. She knew about my birthday, but she said dead people do not have them anymore. Besides there is nothing to celebrate."

"Kattie, I am glad you are here. We are making pizza. Why don't you two birthday girls come in the kitchen and select your toppings." Grandma headed to the refrigerator and pulled out all the makings. The girls followed her and remarkably began to knead the dough together. They cried together while chopping onions. Then they placed pepperoni, chopped onions, and green peppers on one pizza, but added pineapple with ham on the other. Both were loaded with lots of cheese on top. The twins remarked how they both liked the same toppings.

The three women shared the pizzas and lots of conversation. *This is wonderful to be with my sister on such a special night. I love to see her smile.*

Grandma, well there are just no words for her sweet spirit and loving heart.
"Where's Grandpa?" Jamie asked.

Grandma responded, "He is next door. Football season, do I need to say more? Poor Aunt Esther with those three guys." The three women laughed together. "The first movie, *Ghost Make-over*, another one of your favorites, is about to start. Are you ready?" Grandma asked.

Jamie plopped into a huge armchair and pretended to lose herself in its comfort. *This is not Kattie from yesterday. Is she being congenial for real or hoping I will let my guard down?* Kattie chose the chair across from Jamie. Grandma sat on the sofa between the two recliners.

As the movie ended with credits displayed on the TV screen, Jamie heard soft noises coming from beneath the carpet. She thought about her friends, the mites, who lived in mite-size motels in the sub floors of her grandmother's home just below where she sat. Her magic gave her access to hearing and understanding the mites who came up through the carpet to give her good advice.

Mites pounded the floor to scare Kattie.

Stop. It is our birthday weekend.

"All of us could bite Kattie, giving her a case of the itch," one of the mites suggested. "Let's vote." The mites tallied their votes to go after Kattie.

No, wait until she does something. Let us give her a chance.

"Too late, we have voted." The mites crawled on Kattie's chair and spring boarded onto her.

"Something is biting on me," hollered Kattie as she bounded to her feet and scratched. They chased her around the living room.

"Stop," Jamie yelled. "I want to get along."

"I'm not doing anything. Something is really biting me." She got away by exiting through an outside wall.

Jamie was going to try to stop her, but she was gone. She fussed at the mites. "Next time wait till you get my signal please. You just ruined our birthday eve together."

The mites returned to the sub floor, waving goodbye to Jamie. "Sorry, Jamie, let us know when you need us to bite Kattie again."

"Grandma, I wanted Kattie to stay as long as she could."

"Hang on to the moments you shared, sweetie." Grandma picked up the dishes and carried them into the kitchen.

"Do you want me to help?"

"No, enjoy the fireplace and relax."

Jamie stuffed her socks into her shoes, piled them in front of the fireplace, and stoked the fire. She sat alone in the living room, captivated by the flickering cinders.

The black cat with the ruby collar purred next to her. Jamie said, "I'm sorry, Kattie. I didn't want the mites to attack you."

"Happy birthday, Jamie." The cat dissolved through the wall above the fireplace.

Jamie slept well another night. She dreamt that her parents were giving both she and Kattie a surprise birthday party. All of their childhood friends on HallowWinds were there.

****

Jamie woke to Rowdy's face in the bedroom window. "Go away, Rowdy, I want to sleep a little longer."

Rowdy kept bumping it with his forehead until Jamie had to get up to see what he wanted. She opened the window and got a gentle, but slurpy lick on her cheek. "Happy Birthday, Jamie. I am taking you for a ride, but there is someone who wants to see you," Rowdy said as he motioned down.

Jamie leaned out her window and saw Griff holding a large box wrapped in bright yellow paper and a twelve-inch wide red bow. He sat the box down, and then belted out the Light Champion's version of *Happy Birthday* with words about Light, Love and Joy being the best gifts of all. Jamie giggled as she watched all the animation and motion put with his off-key singing. "Not so great a singer, but I loved it, Griff."

"Jamie, I am coming up. I want to be the first to give you a gift." Griff climbed on Rowdy's tail and made his ascent upward with the box. Jamie quickly threw on an oversized flannel shirt over her pajamas and brushed her hands through her hair.

Griff managed to get the box through the window. As Jamie took the box from him, she remarked, "It weighs less than air. What is it?"

"Well, open it, Jamie." Griff swung his legs into the window and sat on the window seat.

Jamie carried the box over to her bed and carefully unwrapped it. "Oh, you. It's a box inside a box." She was not as careful unwrapping the second container. She tore into the third and the fourth, throwing the paper everywhere. Finally, the fifth was the size of a tiny box. Jamie took her time opening it. *Jewelry from my prince. No, it cannot be. A friendship ring?*

Griff walked over to her and held out his hand motioning for the ring. He gently slipped it onto her finger. "Jamie, I promise my friendship forever." Griff stood tall with straight shoulders, as he placed his hand over his heart. "And I pledge my protection, support and respect."

Jamie stood there speechless while Griff swung his legs back out the window and climbed onto Rowdy's shoulders.

"Where are you going, young man?" Grandpa Zack asked standing in Jamie's doorway. "You are invited to stay for breakfast."

"Whew, for a minute I thought I was in trouble for being in Jamie's room."

"You are trained to be honorable at all times. We trust you, Griff. But it might be best in you came in the door," Grandpa chuckled. He went over to kiss his beautiful granddaughter on the cheek, picked up her hand and nodded his approval. "Birthday breakfast in twenty minutes."

Jamie got dressed in a bright red and yellow checked blouse, a pair of black jeans and black riding boots. Rowdy promised to take her somewhere.

A friendship ring with promises. Distracted by the ring, Jamie gently slapped her cheeks. *This is not a dream.* Jamie skipped downstairs. She was not sure if her feet touched each step or not.

Griff stood at the bottom of the stairwell and escorted her out the back door with his right arm interlocked in her left.

"Where are we going? Breakfast is ready in the kitchen."

"Yes, it's ready, but not in the kitchen," Griff said. He led her into her aunt and uncle's backyard next door.

Jamie squealed with delight. Filled with multicolored streamers and balloons, TimberWood's branches provided the perfect canopy for the birthday breakfast picnic. *So this is why I was taken to the nail parlor and stayed overnight at Grandma's house. Sneaky.*

Blankets and cushions spread out under the trees. Hot breakfast casserole, stacks of French toast, and jars of maple syrup sat on a table with a red-check tablecloth.

Under TimberWood's branches, a Queen Anne chair had Jamie's name on it. Griff showed Jamie to her seat. TimberWood lowered his branches toward Jamie and wished his dear friend, "Have a wonder-filled birthday."

Grandma placed a crown of her head, as Aunt Esther laid a large napkin on Jamie's lap. Uncle Jonathan sat a TV table in front of her. Clumsy Judd carried her a plate of food and placed it in front of her without incident. Each one kissed her on the cheek and whispered some greeting.

After breakfast, Jamie watched Griff and Judd pull on ropes to lower a large dark blue cloth draping the house's back wall. It became the backdrop for the Star Particles' light show.

The Star Particles parted to each side and showered the center of the backcloth with floodlight. As if from nowhere, the frog-boys dressed in kilts danced an Irish jig in front of the screen. Agents Mytee and Tynee played frog size bagpipes. After their dance, they each threw a handful of beads up in the air. The beads magically came together and made a beautiful necklace.

While Jamie looked up to watch the magical beads, she saw the black cat with the ruby jewelry sitting on a second story windowsill.

The beads swirled and danced to the bagpipes and slid over Jamie's head. *Such love. What a great birthday. It does not get any better than this.*

Rowdy and two other dragons roared in unison. Everyone laughed to see such bulky creatures in tuxedos. "It's time for my birthday gift for you," Rowdy exclaimed. Jamie's grandparents got on one dragon; her aunt, uncle and cousin boarded another; Griff and Jamie sat on Rowdy. "Off to HallowWinds," bellowed Rowdy.

"Surprise," yelled a big group of teens and adults as Jamie entered her former Middle School. She was delighted to see so many of her old school friends. To her horror, Jamie learned some friends were killed, others captured by the witches.

Kattie followed us here. Guess it is not safe for her to show herself to everyone. Happy birthday, my sister. The black cat glided across the hall.

From HallowWinds, the family rode off. "I thought we were headed home. Where are we going?" Jamie quizzed.

"Your grandmother and I have another gift for you," Grandpa hollered across the winds from his dragon.

Just then, Jamie saw the beautiful planet that looked like pure gold. "Wow. We are going to Light Channel."

The dragons parked in front of a mansion with enormous white columns and *Light Channel Academy* painted in gold letters lined in black across the front façade. Grandpa handed Jamie parchment paper rolled up and tied with a gold ribbon.

Jamie gently untied it and rolled it out. She cried.

Griff, standing behind Jamie, read from the scroll, "Jamie Travelstead, after observation and evaluation, you have been unconditionally accepted as a Light Keeper apprentice to begin in January."

"Congratulations," boomed a stately white-haired man in uniform. "I am Head Master Scott Powers. Welcome. I believe you know Commander-in Chief Belcor Williams."

"Uncle Belcor, so glad to see you again."

He bent over and gave Jamie a kiss. "Congratulations and happy birthday." He then walked toward two other young women with some family members. "Maria de los Angeles Perez and Patricia Robinson, after observation and evaluation, you have been unconditionally accepted as a Light Keeper apprentice to begin in January," he announced.

Jamie strolled over to congratulate them. When she got close, she recognized the young women as Trish and Maria from the *Dungeon of the Forgotten*. The three of them excitedly hugged and introduced their families to one another.

"Wow! What a reunion. You both look so good. I heard that you are at optimal health now. You have done well in school, too, and are athletic stars."

"Guess you having been keeping us with us. We are proud of you. I think I speak for Maria, too, that we want to hear you play the violin, especially some of your own compositions," Trish suggested.

"That would be fun, if you play the cello, Trish and Maria plays her sax."

"You know about that, too. A girl cannot have secrets. Let's make a date for the jamboree," Maria giggled.

"Yes, I know the three of you are fantastic musicians. However, back to business, this is an important day on Light Channel. I officially want to say these young women have shown remarkable courage and strength amid great adversity. They have unmatched powers and keen sense of justice. Proof is obvious that they are already protectors of the Light, and deserve this high honor given to them today. We do not normally accept new apprentices mid academic year. That we making an exception is a testimony of your advanced skill, knowledge and love for the Light. Congratulations, ladies of Light," Commander-in-Chief pronounced as he warmly shook their hands.

Everyone clapped.

"Now I have a surprise for these young ladies. Griff has a special request for Jamie's birthday. Shall we get started?" Belcor asked and then slipped away.

Griff moved closer. "Yeah, you bet." He touched his medallion, sending out flashes of red, pink, and white. The beams formed four Tapping Beetles that were only one inch tall and dressed in black tuxedos with red bow ties. Pink carnations brightened their lapels. Griff blew on the Tapping Beetles and they turned into life size figures, singing and tap dancing to *Come with Us, Jamie, Come,* a song that Griff made up for the occasion.

As the Beetles played on, Griff held out his hand in an invitation to dance. Jamie ecstatically danced with Griff. He gracefully swirled Jamie like an autumn leaf in the fall breeze. Everyone else grabbed a partner and danced too.

"I expected lots of fun," Jamie whispered in Griff's ear, "but this is beyond what I ever dreamed."

Griff gave Jamie a quick kiss on her cheek. Her face grew warm, and she let out a nervous chuckle. He picked up small stones and burned a letter into each of them with his hands. Then he tossed the stones upward and they sparkled like fireworks spelling out "Friends forever."

Jamie swirled around and threw a pebble at Griff. "Here. Catch this."

Griff retrieved it, squeezing it tight. The small nugget tickled. He opened his hand, revealing a white heart trimmed with red. With a big smile, he threw it back to Jamie. She jumped up, caught it, and held it close to her heart. "Awesome." Her heart beat faster. "I want this moment to never end."

Griff rubbed on his gem. "Oh, it's not ending yet," Griff pointed. *You are invited to come to the Light Channel Command Center* in red, white, and pink flashed on the wall.

"Really? Great. I would love to see and experience it." She stared at Griff's medallion. It flashed and hummed a tune. "Is this my next surprise?"

"Uncle Belcor is calling from the Light Channel Command Center."

"I didn't realize he wasn't still here," Jamie said as she spun around to see the group.

"Belcor is saying something." Griff touched his LightStone to hear the sender. Instead, noises surrounded them. "That's odd."

"What is it? Is something wrong?" Jamie quizzed.

"I can't understand him." Griff detached his LightStone from its chain and tossed it into the air. "We'll use a different type of transmission as our backup." The suspended medallion transformed into a large viewing screen, which showed Belcor in a master control chair, handling transmissions and collecting information from multiple computer screens and rows of instrument panels. The white-haired commander stroked his beard and rustled around in his green satin robe. Wide bands of gold trimmed his garment down the front and around his long sleeves.

"Hello birthday girl, Maria, Trish and your families" Belcor said.

Jamie reminded herself to close her mouth. "I like your robe with the moving scenes filling in the borders. It is magnificent." The magically interactive pictures from nature mesmerized her.

"You can reach through the screen and into the band on my robe and touch whatever you like, Jamie," Belcor responded.

Jamie loved the deer, raccoon, and squirrels. She reached into the panoramic screen and picked up a rabbit from the gold band. She gently patted it, and placed it in the band by a stream of water. Her heart swelled with delight. "Your robe is awesome."

A wide smile played across Belcor's face, as he pointed to a little creature perched on Griff's shoulder. "Thank you Jamie. I have heard from the cute chuckwalla, Scrunch, that you wanted to tour our command center. How would you, Trish and Maria like to have that tour as part of your surprise?"

"Oh yes, *YES*." Jamie danced around. "What a fantastic gift."

Belcor put out his hand and Jamie entered through the greatly enlarged screen. Griff, Scrunch and the whole group followed Jamie into the Light Channel's Control Center.

Belcor cautioned everyone. "We can only view certain areas of the castle."

"Oh, that's disappointing. Are some areas restricted?" Trish asked.

"Yes, some parts of the center contain security sensitive equipment and maps." Belcor explained. He took them to an arched doorway and tapped the brick border in a precise diamond pattern. The door opened into a domed room. Multiple computer monitors around the room displayed the castle's chambers, towers, and dungeons.

Jamie touched the screen for a dungeon. The viewfinder became red. A large X marked the screen as not accessible. "I guess that's one of the restricted areas."

Belcor nodded.

Scrunch, perched on Jamie's shoulder, leaned toward a kitchen scene and tapped it. He and the others landed in a massive food preparation room. Jamie laughed. "I should have known what you'd choose"

"Sorry," Scrunch said. "They're running specials on the menu, like pop-eyed flies and worm-delights. I couldn't resist." Scrunch tested a worm, holding the specimen between the tips of two fingers. Everyone chuckled.

Jamie muttered under her breath, "Gross."

"I heard that," Scrunch replied.

Griff and Jamie, with Scrunch back on her shoulder, and the whole group toured the rest of the kitchen, which bustled with activities. Chefs prepared thousands of roasted chickens, baked breads, and cauldrons of thick vegetable soup for the Light Keepers, Champions and officers. Of course, everyone enjoyed tasting the many delectable and mouthwatering dishes of food.

Taking turns, the three girls picked out one scene after another to tour. Jamie loved the game room with its dart competition and archery. Her last and favorite place to visit was the outside of the castle with its seven ascending stairways lit with lamps. At the end of each landing, a tower with telescopes let her view the stars. The telescopes were so powerful she felt as if she were up in the stars themselves. They were so breathtaking. The lamps were as bright as the stars.

"Light Keepers watch over these lamps to keep them lit. If they go out, the Light Channel's power will weaken. The lamps are a source of our strength and our pride," Belcor described.

"Can your enemies kill you by putting out the lamps?" Maria asked.

"It's a possibility. As the lamps weaken, we lose strength as well." Griff explained.

"We have ourselves covered. If the Light Champions falter, the Star Particles take over. They light the sky from dawn through dusk." Belcor gestured toward the arched, glass ceiling above him. "This area is formed by the bodies of incubating Star Particles. They're becoming beautiful lights that will one day adorn the firmament." Belcor's smile glowed so brightly that his face radiated.

Jamie put her hands together, and rocked them in approval. "I like the castle's lamps, but I love the Star Particles. They're cute huddled together."

"I knew you would be fascinated by them." Belcor touched the scene depicting the Light Channel's Command Center. "Let's go back."

The group landed near the MASTER, the control center. Belcor sat down and adjusted knobs on a panel in the master's chair, zooming in and showing details on the star particles. "We have the finest command center in the universe."

Jamie studied the details in the wooden archways, furniture, and inlaid floors. "Griff told me that you've spent a lifetime building up the Light Channel. We are grateful, sir. I'm sure you see all that happens and you're not afraid to take action."

Belcor nodded. "The Light Keepers and Champions work hard to maintain the Light Channel's reputation." He clutched the medallion that hung around his neck. "The Genesis is responsible for much of my success. Its gem is the mother stone of all the genuine light stones."

Jamie cherished Belcor for his fatherly and detailed tour. She gratefully said, "Thanks for the spectacular surprise." She reached up to hug him around the neck. Trish, Maria and all in the group nodded with gratitude and respect for Belcor's leadership.

"Jamie, I am delighted to be a part of your birthday surprise. Maria, Trish and Jamie, you each have grown into strong, beautiful and intelligent young women." Belcor touched the scene showing the steps of Light Channel Academy. Jamie, Griff, and the others stepped out of the screen for Light Channel Command Center. "Happy Birthday, Jamie," Belcor said and faded away.

Jamie could feel the glow on her face. She looked at her hands. They too were aglow.

The black cat with the ruby collar sauntered across the Academy's porch. *Kattie is here? How can that be on Light Channel?*

CHAPTER ELEVEN

Soulful

J amie boarded onto Rowdy's back with her grandparents to begin the journey from Light Channel to Earth. Griff and the rest of her family were on dragons nearby.

Grandpa gently shook her. "We're home," he said. "Do I need to carry you in?"

"Huh? Oh my, I fell asleep. No, I can walk. It has been a glorious day. It is still my birthday, isn't it?" Jamie asked.

"We are not done celebrating your birthday. There are more gifts and another birthday cake," Aunt Esther announced. "Are you joining us, Griff?

"No, I have security detail this evening. But thank you for including me in the party." Griff kissed Jamie on the cheek.

"Jamie has a boyfriend. Jamie has a boyfriend," Judd chanted.

Griff playfully drew his sword and pointed it at Judd. "Good night, everyone," he said as he slowly walked away from the group.

"Grandma, is this a good time to take Kattie's urn to your house?"

"Hmmm, I was thinking the same thing, Jamie. With both of us thinking about it simultaneously, that means this is the right time. Go on up to your room and get the urn, we will meet you here at Aunt Esther's front door."

Jamie ran off to her room and spotted immediately the black cat, sitting next to the urn. "Another surprise! Hi Kattie. You have traveled a lot today, but I am so glad you are here for the transfer of the urn."

"That's why I am here. I like it, Jamie, and really appreciate your thoughtfulness. It is a great birthday gift from you to me."

"You are a birthday gift to me, Kattie. I love it when we can be true sisters to one another."

Jamie, with the cat strolling next to her, carried the urn with both hands elevated to her shoulders. The front door, of Aunt Esther and Uncle Jonathan's home, magically opened to a choir singing *Your Winds Carry Me on High*. The family, Griff, and numerous Light Keepers and Champions in full uniform made up the choral group and the escorts to Gran's house. Light Keepers led the way, with each one carrying a golden lantern. The Champions raised their swords pointed to the sky, under which the family promenaded with Jamie and Kattie in the middle. Each family member also carried a golden lamp. When the parade reached Gran's home, the door opened to reveal an extremely well lit house and Commanders John and Judith Travelstead standing in rapt attention.

Grandma had the center of the mantel cleared and ready to receive the urn. Jamie majestically displayed the vessel, and stepped to the side. Her parents gracefully positioned eternally lit candles to each side of the final receptacle.

Grandpa invited family and friends to a moment of silence. In the quiet, everyone heard the cat purring. Kattie soared onto the mantel and rubbed against the ornamental vase in approval. As she did, the color changed from black to a brilliant gold.

Awestruck, the group continued to stand in silence until Kattie leapt from the marble shelf and disappeared.

"Well," Grandpa awkwardly suggested. "I am ready for your cake, Esther. Shall we go back to your house?"

"Sounds good. Everything is ready. There is enough cake and ice cream for everyone to have as much as you can eat."

They all sat around the tables, both inside and out, and enjoyed red velvet cake with cream cheese icing.

After the group departed and only the family remained, Jamie's aunt and uncle gave her a dark blue backpack to replace her old one with the broken zipper. Luminous stars and brilliant planets covered its surface. Pleased with the gift, Jamie kissed her aunt and uncle on their foreheads and gave Judd a high-five. She took the new backpack to the shelves at the rear door and laid it near her old one. To her amazement, her things in the old bag packed themselves into her new one. Several stickers came from nowhere and decorated the bag with images of her favorite rock group, the *Jagged Crevices.*

A side pocket on the new bag moved. Jamie reached in and found sparkly confetti that shot out of her hand and floated in the air, spelling out *happy birthday.* Jamie thrilled at the surprise. In small letters, she saw the words*, color design by Griff.*

"I have a gift for you too. Mummy movies. Let's watch one," Judd said. Jamie and Judd headed to the family room and plopped on the couch.

In the movie, the mummy wrapped in layers of filthy cloth ripped away the walls of a tomb to escape his prison of stone. He stalked and attacked a young girl who dodged plants and tomb decorations tossed by the winds.

Kattie stared in the window at Jamie and Judd for a brief moment. Then she swooshed through the exterior wall, stood behind the couch and stared at the movie.

Jamie felt Kattie's chilly presence and pulled the lap cover over her legs. "Do you want to join us for the movie?"

Judd added, "Yeah, you can sit next to me."

For a moment, Kattie looked like she might give in. Instead, she swished back outside. With Kattie gone, Jamie felt warmer.

Fine dust particles surrounding the mummy filled the TV screen and filtered into the family room. The air became denser. Judd sneezed. "This is insane. How can dust come out of a movie? It's all over our furniture and us."

Jamie grabbed a pillow and covered her nose, coughing into the cushion. "I can't breathe, and my skin is itching." She frowned. *Kattie is getting back at me for the mites.*

Judd ran his hand along the lamp stand and pinched the dirt between his fingers. "This stuff is sticky. I am freaking out. Go ahead. Work your magic. I'd like to see it."

Jamie raised her hand. "Stutio storma no breatho," Jamie commanded as she laughed her head off. The dust settled down and dissolved.

A groaning sound came from the TV. The mummy meandered along, trailed by a swarm of flies. The insects escaped from the TV screen and chased Jamie and Judd, causing them to stumble over a rug.

The teens' screams filtered throughout the house. Aunt Esther demanded, "Jamie, Judd, quit hollering. If you keep it up, you won't watch any more scary movies."

"OK, we'll tone it down," Judd said.

Jamie acted quickly. "Grabado estendica." Newspapers on the coffee table rolled up and swatted the flies. The bodies of the bugs disintegrated. Another dozen flew up the chimney.

"Look at that," Judd said, scratching his head. "You're great with magic."

Booming noises outside intensified. Aunt Esther stood in the doorway, "Stay clear of the windows. The lightening is fierce. You might want to turn the television off."

"Sure Aunt Esther," Jamie said, hoping none of the glass would break and hit them.

Aunt Esther stared at the room. "What happen in here? How did it get so dusty? A broken lamp and newspapers everywhere. I should ground you both. I have a bridge party tomorrow evening. Clean up this mess."

"We're sorry," Judd said. "Jamie and I will get your lamp fixed." When Aunt Esther left the room, Jamie used her magic.

Jamie attempted to stay calm, but all the noises in the backyard alarmed her. She darted toward the family room windows and ducked below the windowsills. Judd followed her, staying low. Jamie got the courage to peek at the lightning strikes stabbing the darkness and lighting up the backyard, which revealed odd shadows.

The TV's volume went up by several decibels. The girl in the movie screamed as she tried to get free of the mummy. Jamie ran back into the living room and grabbed the remote control. "What's wrong with this TV?" Jamie pushed the off button several times.

The mummy turned, and gawked directly at Jamie from inside the movie screen. Jamie stood within inches of the TV. The mummy thrashed its arms with its binding tape coming off. It tried to pull her inside the screen. *Kattie stop please. Watch the movies with us.*

Judd yanked the TV cord out of the wall. Jamie watched the screen go dark.

Scratching noises took them both back to the window. They stared at the billowing clouds dropping low in the sky. Muted laughing noises accompanied the growing darkness. *The hyenas are back. As a people of Light, we are gathering our forces and making our plans. Are we ready for another attack?*

The hyenas snarled at the home's rear windows and backdoor. They scratched the glass panes, making the window frames rattle.

"Sounds like the storm is throwing things at the windows. Best move away from them," Uncle Jonathan suggested from the kitchen.

"What are those things?" Judd asked, as he peered out the window.

"The hyenas that I told you about. We should be safe with Griff and his team out there, but I am surprised the hyenas are in the backyard."

Jamie and Judd went into the kitchen to check the back door and window. Aunt Esther held out her hand to collect her winnings from Uncle Jonathan. He winked at Jamie "I had to let her win. It keeps her in a good mood. Speaking of moods, this storm is affecting mine. The wind sounds like cats crying. In addition, I keep hearing voices. Do you think Griff and the others are okay out there?"

Before Jamie could answer, there was a scuffle at the back door and noise like cats screeching. Jamie separated a slat apart on the blind, and saw TimberWood and all the other trees swinging their branches in a furious frenzy. She could see Star Particles darting back and forth, sending out bolts. In the light, she could see Griff and other guards with drawn swords. Jamie heard the hyenas yelp, leaves whistling and voices shouting. Then deafening silence. Jamie strained to see any movement. *Nothing.*

A tapping sound at the window where Jamie stood frightened her. She quickly closed the slat and backed away. *Human laughter?* "That better be you, Griff, and you better be okay."

"Come to the door. A friend of yours is out here," Griff said.

Cautiously going to the door, Jamie opened it and saw Griff with Victorious. Jamie ran down the steps and hugged her. "Oh, it is so good to see you. Are you okay?"

"All healed. I am now on your team to help fight the dark particles. Regaining my position as leader of the remaining hyenas," Victorious said, "you will have nothing to fear from them. They are convinced to follow the Light."

"Remaining hyenas?" Jamie quizzed.

"The others are destroyed. Ma'am, we will remove the carcasses tonight," Victorious said looking at Aunt Esther. "Sorry about the disturbance. We will be guarding your home the rest of the night as quietly as possible."

"Thank you, Griff, Victorious and you too TimberWood," Jamie said, as she blew a kiss to her dear old friend. He and the other trees waved their branches gently.

"Griff, was Kattie here?" whispered Jamie.

"She and SilverWorm were both here but managed to get away. We have your perimeters secured. Sleep well."

"Good night. Thank you everyone for a great birthday." Jamie closed the door. The four family members went upstairs to bed.

With her ear up against Judd's door, she heard him wedge a chair under the doorknob. "Judd, are you okay?"

"Yes, but my teeth are rattling."

"Get under your covers and get some shuteye." Unknown to Judd, Jamie sat on the floor outside his door. After a short time, Judd's room was as quiet as a coffin. The soft snoring from her aunt and uncle's room convinced Jamie they were asleep. She headed downstairs to recheck the family room doors. Halfway down the stairs, Jamie leaned over the handrail, searching the shadows. "Kattie, where are you?" Suddenly, she flipped over the banister. Jamie landed in a standing position.

Kattie tossed a framed photo, which hit the floor and broke. Jamie picked up the pieces. "This photo is priceless. It shows Mom and Dad. It even shows you and me. Why are you being so mean? I thought we were on better terms. It is past time for you to come to your senses."

"See what SilverWorm gave me for my sixteenth birthday. However, my own sister did not give me anything except moving my urn out of her bedroom. Didn't want me close anymore? Bothered you to have my ashes nearby?" Kattie played with the ruby around her neck.

"You know better. The feelings I expressed earlier were sincere. You have swung again to the other side. SilverWorm decided she believes in birthdays after all?"

"Yeah, even witches can have a change of heart," Kattie responded sarcastically.

"That would be great if the witches changed their hearts."

Kattie stuck out her tongue. "You don't know what I'm going to do. You haven't seen anything."

"You're bluffing," Jamie said. "I don't want you here. You made your choice. Everyone else is asleep."

Kattie hissed. "You'll have your wish." She evaporated through the front door.

Jamie sneaked out past her security and trailed after Kattie. She came to the five avenues, which converged to a garden called Fountain Circle. The garden contained black metal benches and potted mums placed along a paved, circular walkway around a huge fountain. Jamie plucked a mum, yellow with rust colored stains. *Oh, these flowers—they look like they have blood on them.* Jamie ducked behind evergreen bushes. *Kattie is not satisfied. She and SilverWorm want my powers of revelation and transformation— everything I have.*

Jamie stared at the fountain's sculpture. It looked different with the night shadows. The six stone figures seemed frozen with their bodies twisted in different contortions.

StoneCrasher, another one of SilverWorm's cohorts, arrived with thirty of his followers called StoneThrowers. Several of the throwers were dragging some slimy weed-like creature into the center of the circle. SilverWorm and Kattie were also in the group.

"Throw RootRot in the fountain for letting Griff and the others escape in backyard battle," commanded StoneCrasher.

Jamie watched as SilverWorm stirred the fountain's water, which began to bubble like a cauldron. She lugged the slimy weed, RootRot, to the fountain where she held his torso over the boiling liquid.

Out of the waters came Dark Particles that lived below. They pulled RootRot closer. He screamed when the steam burned his face. The six sculptured figures pushed and shoved his legs and torso until RootRot immersed in the fountain. The dark particles below and above rejoiced over his demise.

"StoneCrasher, you messed up on this one. Choosing RootRot was an obvious mistake. Perhaps you should be next in the fountain," Kattie hinted.

SilverWorm, without missing a beat, demanded, "Yes, absolutely. This is not his first screw-up. This would not have happened if he had consulted us. You StoneThrowers are now under my command. Lock StoneCrasher up in solitary confinement in GrayStone's north tower. He can just stew until we decide his fate."

"We have another agenda item," StoneCrasher said. "We need a soul snatcher, whose task will be to suck out Jamie's soul and prepare her body for Kattie to possess."

The sculptures and the dark particles in the fountain, along with all in the circle, chanted *"Snatchio soultis."* Their words became louder, bolder, and full of evil.

"I have been trained as a Soul Snatcher. I will do it," StoneCrasher offered. "Give me a chance to make up for my mistake."

"Okay, one last chance. If you mess this up, you will be history. Follow me," SilverWorm commanded.

The group walked in the middle of the street and headed for the Travelstead home, which sat in a row of other two-story brick buildings.

Jamie stayed at a distance while following the Dark Particles. She watched as they ripped off unlocked doors and tossed them around like mangled kites. They twisted gutters and from them produced sculptured, metal dragons that roared in pain. They tore off shutters and sailed them through the air like white sailboats on a brutal sea. After they passed by, Jamie used her powers to return everything in place. The residents came out to thank her and others followed her.

An older couple invited Jamie to ride with them. "You're Jamie Travelstead, the Glosomore's granddaughter. Get in. You'll be safe with us," the woman said.

The couple slowly made their way up Dappled Boulevard with their headlights off. Jamie asked the couple for their names. "Willow," the woman replied, "Marie and Bill Willow."

"Thanks. I'll let my grandparents know how kind you are." Jamie used her medallion to send a message to the Glosomores about the Willows, and about the entourage headed toward their home and hers.

"Griff. Trouble is brewing. They want my soul."

"Where are you? Judd came out and told us that you were not in the house. He found a framed photo broken and glass on the floor."

"Kattie was there and I followed her. StoneCrasher, about thirty StoneThrowers, SilverWorm and Kattie headed that way. Very close now.

I am behind them with the Willows and a bunch of neighbors. Where is Judd?"

"Judd, Esther and Jonathan are safe at home. Your grandparents are with me. Jamie, please head north with the Willows so the dark particles don't see you," Griff advised. "Blast it. Static. Jamie, are you still there? Jamie …"

Jamie had disconnected. "I'm getting out of your car here. Please, you and the others need to stay out of this. Head north."

"We'll be okay. We are magical and so are your neighbors." Mr. Willow spoke for the first time. "Put this on," he stated with authority as he handed Jamie and his wife a mask. He popped open the car's hood. Hundreds of smooth black pebbles shot out from the engine in all directions, hitting the dark paraders.

Griff and his Star Particles, wearing masks, rushed from the Travelsteads' house to the scene. They blinded the evil marchers' eyes with their bright lights, forcing them back toward the flying gravel.

The light from the Star Particles shone on the pebbles and activated them, motorizing their electrical currents. Each pebble emitted a green gas that surrounded the dark particles, reducing them in size, and then sucking them inside the stones. The StoneThrowers struggled to escape from the pebbles on the street.

Only SilverWorm, StoneCrasher and Kattie remained. "Oh no, those captured inside the stones will exist as prisoners forever," StoneCrasher said. "It is just us. We need reinforcements."

Jamie laughed as she watched SilverWorm and Kattie squirm. "You are outnumbered. Neighbors and friends behind you, the Luminous Intergalactic Defense in front of you. The circle around the Travelstead home is secure. I will not let you take my soul or my body," she adamantly declared.

The clock on a nearby church rang out the *St. Michael's Chimes* twelve times. A flurry of flying debris and the influx of more Dark Particles in spirit form surrounded the area. Jamie sensed their presence. *No one else seems to notice.*

"Blasted, it's too late," SilverWorm said. "We will be back." SilverWorm and Kattie boarded their brooms and flew off. StoneCrasher scampered off to the cemetery. *That is odd. Why are they leaving when the other dark particles show up to help them?*

The frog-boys and Light personnel went back to their posts. The Willows, neighbors, grandparents, and Griff stayed with Jamie. "Do you sense other dark particles here?" Jamie asked.

"Feels eerie. I am calling Uncle Belcor for more assistance," Griff responded. "And I plan to sleep on your floor tonight."

"My husband and I are staying with your grandparents. We are here to help," Mrs. Willow said. "Your neighbors will either be in your house or the Glosomore's."

"Good, maybe I can sleep better," Jamie said. "Guess we should all get some slumber. Good night and sweet dreams."

"Hopefully," Grandpa Zack responded.

Jamie laid on her bed, closed her eyes and took a deep breath. One of her eyes opened. Something cold touched Jamie's hand. She shot up. "Who did that?"

Griff jumped up with drawn sword.

"It's Kattie," Jamie said pointing to the black cat with the ruby collar.

Sculpting into human form, Kattie declared, "Soon, your soul will be sucked out and I will be in control of your body."

Jamie kept a straight face. "According to legend, it's past the hour to extract a soul. You lost your chance at midnight."

Kattie stared at her sister's hands. "Best not to believe in legends. You're trembling—you're afraid."

"No, I'm shaking because the room is cold whenever you are here. Why do you let the Dark Particles control you?" Jamie pulled the blanket up over her nose. "It is freezing in here."

Kattie squirmed, "The Dark Particles are all I have. After the death of our birthparents, SilverWorm offered me a magical medallion—so I went with her. I thought the medallion's power would help me feel alive."

"You had family with you just a few hours ago, but you chose to turn against us. It is a cruel misuse of power," Jamie advised. "You don't have to do evil to feel alive. There are many ghosts and spirits moving freely throughout the earth who are kind and good."

"Sorry, but it may be too late," Kattie said as she glanced out Jamie's bedroom window.

Jamie walked over to the window and spied StoneCrasher and SilverWorm on the front lawn, looking toward her window. Before she could tell Griff, they disappeared.

Kattie morphed into the cat and pounced on Jamie. He ran to help, and in the struggle between the three of them Griff fell through the window, breaking it into pieces. Jamie screamed, "Griff. You pushed him. Why did you do that?"

"I don't like your boyfriend," Kattie announced. "He needed to be out of the way of progress."

StoneCrasher appeared from thin air and stood in between Jamie and the window. He pulled out his gnarled hands from under his cloak. "SilverWorm will take care of Griff, your sleeping family, and busybody neighbors. We will torture them to death while you watch. You have an option if you do not want them tortured and killed. Cooperate with us. Soul snatching is quick and painless unless you fight." He stomped toward Jamie.

Kattie used her medallion to propel a jewelry box straight at StoneCrasher, breaking his nose. "Stay away from her," she yelled.

"Whose side are you on?" he queried. "You won't have a body unless I do this." He reached for Jamie, gripped her face, and forced her to stare into his red eyes. Inside his pupils, Jamie glimpsed captives struggling to free themselves from their metal cages. Dark Particles poked at the captives with sizzling iron rods.

Jamie caught sight of herself in shackles in GrayStone Castle, which formally belonged to SpiderWood, the witch who murdered her parents. *Guess SilverWorm, her twin sister, inherited GrayStone. My head feels so weird. What is wrong ...* She felt her soul pulled up through her chest and toward her head. Jamie collapsed to the floor.

StoneCrasher knelt over her with his foul breath close to Jamie's face. *Ugh, that would wake the dead.*

Kattie stood over him pounding him with her fists.

Is she on my side again? Jamie choked and swallowed hard, desperately trying to speak. *Those eyes are robbing my soul.* "Nooo. This will not be my future. I will not let you imprison my body or my soul. Never." She fumbled for her medallion around her neck, and flashed it in StoneCrasher's eyes.

Swirls of green emanated from her eyes and moved with rhythm across the floor.

StoneCrasher glanced around the room. "Where is that light coming from?"

"You will see. Commando verde caliente," Jamie commanded her eyes to emit scorching emerald green light toward StoneCrasher.

He backed away. "No. Stop. I'm burning up from the inside out," he screamed. "I feel like I am in a microwave oven." Whimpering, StoneCrasher soared out the broken window.

Jamie's eyes cooled and turned back to normal. Kattie helped Jamie to the window and stared.

SilverWorm plucked him off the ground and tossed him about. "You're a stupid fool. You have let a little girl outsmart you. You could not finish sucking out her soul. That was your job. Guess I will have to take care of it myself."

The witch ripped her broom through the window as fast as lightning and knocked the twins down. "Find me something to tie her up," the witch ordered Kattie.

"You tried to protect me a little while ago, Sis," Jamie pleaded, still foggy headed.

"You did what? What an ungrateful brat. You will do as I say now or I will terminate you," the sorceress decreed.

"Jamie is lying. Of course, I will help you." Kattie got some of Jamie's belts out of the closet, and winked at her sister.

"Commando cincio," Jamie hollered. The belts flew from Kattie's hands and tied the witch's arms and legs. One strap made a noose around the witch's neck and tightened. Jamie jerked the witch's medallion from around her neck. The noose wrenched SilverWorm up and tossed her, broom-less, out the window. The girls laughed in relief.

Griff banged through the bedroom door. "Jamie, I'm here." He brandished his sword.

"A little late," Jamie chuckled. "Oh my, what happened to you?" Griff was covered with blood.

"Fortunately, Rowdy broke my fall out the window, but SilverWorm pummeled us with glass shards."

"Is Rowdy okay?" Jamie asked, as she wiped the blood from deep scratches on Griff's face and arms. Jamie snickered at the sounds from her bathroom. Rowdy stopped his slurping long enough to let them know he was okay.

"Looks like you took care of StoneCrasher and SilverWorm finished him off. You got SilverWorm with a few of your belts. She is under a very tight guard now." Griff gently touched Jamie's arm. "Good work."

Jamie boasted, "Kattie helped by retrieving the belts." Looking at her twin, Jamie added, "Thanks, Sis."

"I don't like to admit I am wrong. I do not need your body or soul to be happy. And it's not crucial for me to live with SilverWorm." The twins hugged for the first time since their parents were murdered.

* * * * * * * *

Jamie finally was able to drift off to sleep with Kattie next to her, and Griff on the floor. She dreamt about tunnels from her house to HallowWinds, Light Channel and other kingdoms.

Kattie jumped from the pile of blankets and floated near the ceiling.

Griff was upright watching, ready to draw his sword.

Jamie demanded, "What are you doing up there? We haven't had enough sleep. I was dreaming and you interrupted. I dreamt about secret tunnels accessed in closets in a few houses on Dappled Boulevard. They connected with those on other levels like HallowWinds and Light Channel. A person of magic can travel between parallel universes by way of these closets. Magnetic fields control travel along currents. What am I saying? I need to go back to sleep."

"Did you just steal my dream?"

"What? Did you dream it too?" Jamie ran to the wardrobe with its double-doors. "I have to see this. I love mysteries."

"For your information, I'm traveling between these closets to discover other worlds. I don't know when I'll be back." Kattie elbowed past Jamie, opened a secret door in the back of the closet and disappeared.

Jamie shook her head in disbelief. *What a show off. What is she up to? Ok, breathe deep. Stay calm.*

Bumping noises came from the secret compartment. Jamie pushed aside her clothes, opened the door where Kattie disappeared and strained her eyes. "It looks like some sort of tube, like an elevator. I cannot see a way to get into the tube. Are there secret passages, Griff?"

"Could be. I might be able to figure it out if I wasn't sleep deprived." Griff rubbed his eyes and peered inside the tube. Brown eyes stared back. Griff jumped back and fell over boots, trying to get out of the closet.

"Brave man, it is just your favorite chuckwalla." Scrunch crawled out.

CHAPTER TWELVE

The Move

"Well, dear friend, here I go. Wish you could go to Light Channel with me," Jamie spoke softly to TimberWood. "Sorry, I haven't spent much time with you lately." She climbed into the stately oak, brushed snow off one of his branches and snuggled up to his trunk.

"I have missed you, but I understand. How did your exhibit and recital go?"

"A master violinist from Russia was there. He wanted to give me a scholarship to study in Russia. In addition, I got first prize in several categories – pastels, charcoals, acrylics and pottery. Am I making a mistake in not pursuing a career in these fields in which I do so well?"

"No, I think you are following your heart and your passion by going to Light Channel Academy."

"Tomorrow is the day that I leave. The winter holidays are over," Jamie said with tears filling her eyes.

TimberWood wrapped his branches around her. "We will spend spring break together and the summers. All will be well, my dear young friend."

"I wrote another violin piece for you. I'll be right back." Jamie hopped down the tree and ran to the house to retrieve her violin. As she played, Jamie and TimberWood watched a gentle snowfall, with flakes spiraling around and downward. She turned her face upwards and felt the soft moisture dance on her face and tickle her nose. The music suggested chilly air, but also the warmth of family and friends. Jamie and TimberWood swayed to the music, as if doing a slow and graceful dance.

When she finished, her grandparents, Judd, Aunt Esther, Uncle Jonathan, the Willows and other neighbors gave her a thunderous round of applause.

"I didn't know you all were listening," Jamie said.

"So beautiful, Jamie. I think you call it *Friendship in Winter*," TimberWood guessed.

"You know me so well. I will write you another for the spring." Jamie reached over and patted her tree. "See you in the morning before I leave, okay?"

****

Inside the warmth of the house that had become her home in her darkest hour, Jamie sat in the living room with her family and friends. There were gifts galore, good food and lots of laughter. *My life is dramatically changing once again. Mom and Dad be with me.*

Kattie, in her cat form, brushed against Jamie's legs and then jumped in her lap. *I will be with you on Light Channel, too.*

That is amazing we have never talked this way with each other before. My sister is in my thoughts. How cool.

I am learning that I can speak heart to heart, mind to mind. Learning some good magic, Kattie responded to her sister.

Kattie, are you being sincere? Have you really changed?

I am changing. I want to change. Conflicts still surface within me. Confusion and temptation still haunt me. Did you know that SilverWorm escaped this morning? She has already visited me. She is still promising me your body and soul.

What did you tell her? Jamie asked.

No, we are sisters. Besides, I do not need a body anymore. She said she would think of something else to get me back into her friendship.

Kattie, please, try real hard. Jamie watched as Kattie jumped down and tiptoed away.

"Where did you go, Jamie? Are you daydreaming?" Her grandmother sat down next to Jamie and handed her a gift.

****

To her amazement, Jamie arrived at Light Channel Academy without incidence. *This is much harder than regular high school. Second day, I am already inundated with homework. Oh no, it is time for martial arts session.*

Jamie grabbed her sword and ran to the martial arts building. Japanese sword training was so interesting. Jamie especially loved the deeper aspects of the art. She combined her spiritual and personal qualities with physical skill.

"Master Liu," Jamie gave a deep bow. "My apologies for being late."

He waved his hand at her as if dismissing her apology. "We will begin with a wooden sword, called the bokken. You will not use your own sword. Do not bring it to session again."

"Yes, sir."

"This is a life long journey, one in which great humility is required. No one of us is ever a master. Because of this, you will not call me master, but Sensei. I am your guide and teacher. I am only as good as my students," Sensei Liu explained.

"Yes, Sensei." For the next three hours, Jamie's Sensei went over basic Japanese fencing skills, beginning with ritual and etiquette. She gracefully transferred the sword from the left hand to the right, and smoothly placed the sword in its belt. They practiced over and over four basic cuts.

As Jamie was packing to leave, she picked up her own sword and the bokken.

"No, Jamie, do not take the bokken."

"I would like to practice, Sensei, between sessions."

"Practice only occurs here with my supervision. Right technique is very important. Practice on one's own boosts the ego into thinking that they are excelling, only to find that the Sensei will have to force unlearning. Humility is key." They both bowed.

✳✳✳✳✳✳✳

Trish, Maria, and Jamie shared an apartment with five suites. They each had their own bedroom, bath and study area; but shared a kitchen and large open living area. The threesome were cooking dinner together, when a knock and female voices sounded.

Jamie ran to the door.

"Hi, Jamie. Are the other young ladies here?" asked their dorm mother, Mrs. Johnson. "I want to introduce all of you to your new suitemates." Mrs. Johnson and two more girls entered. "Oh good, everyone is home. Look at you girls being so domestic. What are you cooking? It smells scrumptious."

"There is enough here for everyone and it's ready. Are you hungry? Hi, I'm Trish."

"And I'm Maria. Grab a plate." She reached for three more plates from the cabinet.

"This is BirdSong Leigh and Lois Chan," Mrs. Johnson said. "Thank you for inviting all of us for dinner. However, I must leave you to enjoy getting to know each other. I'll let myself out."

The five young women immediately and comfortably chatted about everything – from school to boys, dreams and disappointments.

"We haven't done the usual questions. Where is everyone from? Ages?" Trish noticed.

"That's right. So where is everyone from?" Jamie echoed.

"I'll start," Trish began. "I am originally from Kenya on Earth. My parents and brothers were killed, and I was imprisoned in a dungeon in the United States from age eight until fourteen. Jamie was instrumental in my release. That is how we met. We have been through a lot together the last two years. My grandparents have been like parents to me these last two years and are so very supportive of my being here."

The group then learned that Maria was Mexican American and was in the dungeon with Trish. Her family lived in Arizona. She and two of her brothers were kidnapped on their way home from school. Her murdered father left Maria's mother with just their baby sister. "Jamie rescued all three of us. We all owe a debt of gratitude to her."

Adopted at age five, Lois was from mainland China. Her parents lived on Light Channel. "Several years ago, my parents realized I have magical abilities. So here I am."

Jamie offered her story. "My parents and twin sister were murdered in our home on HallowWinds. Since their deaths almost four years ago, I have been living with my aunt and uncle in Radiance City, Kentucky on Earth. My grandparents, Commanders Zachary and Elizabeth Glosomore, live right next door. I have a long history of family members in the Defense. I believe it is my destiny to be here."

Birdsong described herself as part Native American and English. "My father was a Canadian photo journalist. My mother was a Mohawk. Our people call themselves Kanienkehaka, which means 'people of the flint' because the ancestors were strong and courageous. I am the middle child, with an older and younger brother. I like to say that we are rock solid and therefore, we have a good foundation." Everyone laughed at Birdie's humor. "I want to take some to send to my family on Earth. Is that okay?" BirdSong inquired. "It is so cool that we all have different skin tones and ethnicities. We will make a beautiful photo together." BirdSong beamed.

The girls giggled as they posed in various configurations.

"This is a lot of fun." Jamie enjoyed taking turns with her suitemates in the roles of model or photographer.

CHAPTER THIRTEEN

Body Search

The last evening of break, Jamie invited Griff and his new suitemates over to their apartment for dinner and board games. They had just arrived earlier that day from other high schools.

Griff began to introduce his friends, "This is Udo who is Nigerian. His name means peace."

"There he goes. I told you Griff would have to explain everyone's names. He is obsessed," Jamie giggled.

"Well, I love knowing the meaning of names also. My name means sea in Chinese, but two in Vietnamese. I was the second child, and I love the sea," Hai interjected.

"Roberto is from Columbia. We met twenty years ago?"

"No, seventeen." Roberto answered with his mouth full. "This pizza is great."

"His name means bright fame, but he jokes that he is both bright and famous. We are not too sure how he is illustrious, except that he is notorious for eating before anyone else. And this is my dear friend, Keme, whose name means secret. He is from the island of Tierra del Fuego in Chile. The island's name means 'Land of the Fire" where the Ona Tribe settled." Griff concluded.

"We better get started eating before Roberto consumes it all." Maria teased.

Just as everyone relaxed with their pizza and soda, bizarre sounds came from somewhere near the front door. The group stared, expecting it to open. It remained closed.

"Boo," said a booming male voice. Everyone jumped. "Hi Jamie and Griff. Ladies and gentlemen."

"Who are you?" Jamie asked, looking at the front door. "Where are you? How did you get in?"

"I am from your past," the young man said from the foyer coat closet.

Griff started to laugh. "I recognize you now, Jaden."

Kattie burst out of the closet and into the room. "I found him. He was wandering around our old house on HallowWinds. He is a ghost just like me. I told him he had to come here to see you. He showed me how tunnels connect from earth to HallowWinds and here."

"Well, cousin Jaden, come on out, so we can enjoy your company," Jamie said enthusiastically. "Hey everybody, this is my twin sister, Kattie."

"I can't exactly come out like Kattie, even though we are both ghosts. My spirit can, but I do not have the power to come back physically. A curse, placed on me the day I was murdered, prevents it forever."

The chuckwalla's eyes bulged as she floated out from the tube about six feet in the air. "This is my friend, Squeezey," explained Jaden. "She likes to ride on my shoulder, and thinks she is just a small lizard."

"Your varying shades of yellow and gray bands are beautiful. And what are you, eighteen inches long? And how did you get that name?" Jamie asked.

"I am twenty inches long and when you squeeze me, I giggle," she said with a childlike laugh that was contagious for everyone in the room.

"Okay guys, keep eating. Guess the game we are playing tonight … let's see, we can call it *Jaden's Corpus*. On a more serious note, Jaden, there must be a way. By whom and how can the curse be reversed?" Jamie inquired.

"Didn't want to scare you by my invisible presence in Kentucky. The night that you and Griff stared into the closet tunnel and you saw Scrunch? Well that was Squeezey and I saying good-bye to her brother, Scrunch. I have been in your room on Earth many times trying to find my childhood medallion so I can unblock my magical powers. I hope that my childhood abilities will be strong enough to release me. By any chance, have you seen it? The gem was jade."

"Did you have it on the day you were killed?" Griff asked.

"No, it was stored in a forest green box lined in sage green satin," Jaden described.

"Uh oh, I have seen the box but nothing was in it," Jamie responded. "I couldn't get the bottom dresser drawer open one day without a fight. I pulled out the drawer above it and there was the small chest. I love that box so much. I keep jewelry in it here." Jamie went to her bedroom and brought it back into the living area.

"All right, Jamie. I am excited you have the box here with you. Very convenient," Jaden clapped as he jumped.

Icy air brushed across Jamie's arm. "I am right next to you and I am taking the box from your hand," Jaden explained. "The box has a secret compartment." Jamie watched as her jewelry floated to the coffee table. The interior bottom peeled off to reveal an oval black pillow. A loosely seamed pocket on the pillow opened and bulged. The medallion slid out, drifted upward and settled at Jamie's eye level.

"It is beautiful, Jaden. It needs a little polishing though." Jamie grabbed a soft cloth from the kitchen and buffed it.

To everyone's amazement, Jaden momentarily took shape and then vanished.

"We can put our childhood medallions together," Kattie suggested. "But I'm not sure where mine is stored. Do you know, Jamie?"

"My childhood trunk is in that corner over there," Jamie pointed. "Maybe Aunt Esther packed some of your things too. I'll call them."

"Oh, don't call Mom and Dad or Judd up here just yet. They are not magical and this would confuse them," Jaden said.

"I will become my cat self and go sneaking around. Promise I will not let anyone see me. Nobody is awake anyway. It is 2:00 a.m. there. Be back in a jiffy," Kattie exclaimed.

Griff introduced Jaden to everyone in the room. Jamie heard the guys talking about their childhood gems. She overheard Griff explain that he had his boyhood stone inset into a ring, which he wears all the time.

Jamie knelt in front of her ornate cedar chest, positioned near the bay window, and spoke softly. "I know a secret code protects your contents but these items belong to me. I just want to look at them. Only my parents knew the code. Mom, help me."

Her mother's medallion pulsated with light and eight numbers flashed into Jamie's mind. *Cool. 86421357. Thanks, Mom.*

Unlocking the trunk, Jamie shielded her eyes from the neon light that squeezed out. She reached into the chest and touched a baby blanket, which brought a flood of childhood memories. *I remember this blanket. I carried it with me all through preschool.* Jamie lovingly went through things collected by her parents since her birth. Grandpa Zack and Rowdy brought the trunk to Light Channel shortly after she moved.

Jamie rummaged through the chest and found a decorative container holding her childhood medallion. The gem saved her at age three by hiding her from the wicked SpiderWood. Jamie picked up the medallion and rubbed its surface, gave it a shiny look and sparked its magic. It responded to the owner's commands.

Kattie ran into the room. "I found it."

"I have mine too. Let's try it."

The twin sisters, Griff and Jaden huddled together with their stones touching. "Commando ionicas transformae," Jamie started. The others chanted the words three times with her.

Jaden appeared long enough for everyone to see him smile. Kattie reached over to hug him, but he passed quickly from sight. "I'm sorry, Kattie. It did not have anything to do with you. It was a power failure," he hooted.

"Power? More energy? Wait. Who actually murdered you? And who made the curse?" Jamie quizzed.

"SpiderWood. Why do you ask?"

"I have her medallion," Jamie responded. "The day SilverWood killed her, the gem literally landed at my feet. We could try to use its power to reverse the spell."

"It would have to be purified before it could be used," Griff said. "There is a decontamination process, but I don't know the details."

"Okay, I'm calling for help." Jamie grabbed her phone "Hello," she said, cocking her head to hear the speaker. "Texter, could you bring the book, *Undoing a Witch* from the WiseMore library. Look in the health section under detox." Jamie paused to listen. "You know about the tunnel? Okay, good. Use it. See you soon."

No sooner than she hung up, Texter was there with the book.

"Wow, Texter, you are magic in more ways than one. Thanks a bunch." Jamie flipped pages.

Griff made Texter acquainted with the group and offered him pizza. "Sorry, the pizza is cold, but so is the soda." Griff pulled a drink out of the refrigerator. "Make yourself at home."

"That's my kind of pizza. Ghosts like the cold."

"Here it is in the chapter on releasing toxins from a witch's gem. I will summarize. We have to take SpiderWood's gemstone to St. Michael's back home. He is the archangel who cast Lucifer into hell and defends against all evil. Hang the medallion on Michael's sword. The angel will drop it in the fountain to purify it. When the muddy color of the stone begins turning red, four magical people with the angel will stir the water until the stone becomes opaque. We need four of us to go do this now."

"What about me? I have dark particles in me. But I do want to help," Kattie cried. "I am afraid that my presence or touch will ruin it. SilverWorm still controls me more than I want. She might follow us. Guess I will have to bow out."

"I can do it. Your grandma helped me volumes with my magical powers," Texter suggested with confidence.

Trish announced, "We are all going with you just in case there is any trouble. We are all magical. Team work, right?"

"Down the tube I go. It is best that I don't know any more plans." Kattie disappeared.

"Thanks, Kattie. I appreciate your contribution to Jaden's release from the curse. I will see you soon, Sis."

"Wow, she is changing in front of our eyes. I know a lot of that is your influence, Jamie." Griff kissed her on the cheek.

✳✳✳✳✳✳✳✳

When the group of twelve, plus Squeezey, arrived at the church, they stared up at the elegant nine-foot alabaster sculpture of the archangel with its gleaming sword pointed to heaven. As part of the stone art, Michael stood on the neck of Lucifer the devil.

Griff volunteered to climb up the sculpture, but Squeezey took the medallion and flew up to the sword's point. The gem pendant draped from the saber.

St. Michael gracefully moved his sword into the fountain at the sculpture's base and churned the medallion around in the water. The brown medallion changed drastically. Jamie, Griff, Jaden and Texter swirled their gems in the pool with Michael, allowing Jaden to take physical form.

"He's baaack." Jamie squealed with delight. The group hugged and celebrated by using their medallions to create a light display. Angelic song broke out and multi-colored wings fluttered around them. The spectrum of colors swirled in harmony with the joyful sounds. "Oh, how breathtaking this is. I love it."

Griff's medallion signaled him to return to Light Channel. He said his good-byes and headed off alone. Watching Griff march through the trees, Jamie spied a dark robed sinister looking creature following Griff. She motioned to the others to follow as she paged him on that small diamond shaped brooch.

Jamie's skin felt clammy. Her throat became dry. She waited anxiously to hear from Griff. Worried about him, Jamie could not delay any longer. She used her medallion to relocate herself and the others beyond the path taken by Griff. She thought she saw him behind a stack of old cars in Ruben's Junk Yard on the other side of the alley.

"Griff is in here somewhere. Let us split up into teams. I will take Udo and Trish with me as lead group. Hai, since you are 'second', you, Lois and Texter are the second team; and, Roberto, Birdsong and Keme, third team. That leaves Maria and Jaden along with Squeezey for the fourth," Jamie directed.

With each group responsible for a quadrant of the junk yard, they maneuvered between discarded vehicles and corroded parts. Clanking of metal and rushing sounds startled Jamie and her team. She felt something near her face. It felt very familiar. It was Kattie.

Kattie tilted her head and put her hands on her hips. "Humph, I watched you ogle Griff. Then, you scouted his trail through the woods. Now you are trying to sniff him out like a hunting dog."

Jamie's heart rate seemed to double. "What do you mean?"

Kattie huffed, "Well you are wasting your time. Your four teams are in danger for naught. Griff will not live long because Lucifer plans to kill him. Then, his delight will be your death. And the other eleven lives will be his sadistic recreation before he slays them."

"Who is Lucifer? The devil is under Michael's feet? That does not make sense. Michael is the most powerful of all the angels. He is with us on our missions. Lucifer will be defeated in his attempts to kill any of us. You need to stay away from evil, too." Jamie stood in determined conviction. "Why does Lucifer want to kill Griff and me?"

"I decided I want Griff for myself."

"You sound jealous," Jamie frowned. "Griff won't be interested in a ghost, especially one attracted to the ways of witches. Get real."

"When Griff gets killed, he and I will be ghost-friends, or you meet your demise and I will be in your body. Griff won't know the difference since we are identical."

"Believe me; he knows the difference between bad and good. Before, you wanted my body so you could have power. Do you want my boyfriend now? That is so immature. You swing back and forth too much. I thought we were okay with each other."

Kattie pushed Jamie into a bumper on a rusty car. "We'll see who comes out on top. Lucifer will succeed."

"Peace between you," Udo said as he blocked Kattie from striking her sister.

Jamie demanded, "I thought we were bridging the gap between us. You bowed out from our team, so we would not have this craziness, and here you are acting as if you are on Lucifer's side. Why are you cheering for him? You have enough trouble on your hands with SilverWorm. Why didn't you tell me about Lucifer back at my apartment? Our plan could have been more strategically prepared."

"You don't understand. I am advising you now that he is worse than the devil. Listen to me. He can make hell freeze over. Watch out." Kattie morphed into a cat and slinked away.

From the rear of Ruben's Junk Yard, a garage door light revealed the dark creature hovering over a motionless figure on the ground.

Lucifer called, "Jamie, do you want to know what I am doing to Griff? Let me demonstrate on that owl in the tree above you."

Jamie looked up. The bird stared with wide-open eyes. It moved around on its branch and spread its wings with a whizzing noise. The owl screeched and shivered. Icicles formed on its feathers, beak, and feet. The bird solidified as a block of ice. Shiny silver daggers hung from its body.

"No. I do not want to know what you are doing. Go away," Jamie shouted.

Kattie gave me a clue – Lucifer can freeze hell. Jamie recalled her recent science lesson on hypothermia. She wondered if Griff's heart, lungs, and other organs had chilled over, and his blood had frozen in the chambers of his heart. *Griff is like the bird. However, it will take longer to freeze Griff to death. There is still time.*

"Ha, ha, you make me laugh, Jamie. I am not going to miss today's fun. Don't think for a moment that I'm going away," Lucifer responded.

Planning what to do, she crawled with Udo and Trish between rows of old, rusty cars and curled underneath a Chevy. From where she lay, she could see Griff sprawled on the concrete behind chunks of wreckage. He was clutching his chest. *Perhaps his hand is near his medallion.*

Jamie used her MoonStone to send a message to Jaden and Texter. In an instant, they were there. All the others were to make a circle around Griff's location. Maria was instructed to team up with Hai's group. Jamie pulled her bangs to the side. *Griff, I wish I could communicate with you without alerting Lucifer.* She fiddled with her medallion. *Griff, I can hear your thoughts and your heart. Our medallions have the power to keep Lucifer from hearing us.*

Knowing you are near warms my blood. I can move my thumbs and fingers, but nothing else, Griff replied.

Jamie clutched her medallion close to her heart. *Keep going. We cannot give in to Lucifer.*

He just left to get something to eat. Hurry. Come now, please.

We are almost there, Griff. Stay strong.

"Hey look. A full gasoline can," Texter whispered as he held up the container. "I used to work on cars. We can gas up several vehicles close to the garage to create warmth."

"Since I am a ghost, I can let go of my new body long enough to get in the garage and flip on all the lights. That will create more heat, also," suggested Jaden.

"Lucifer will not pay attention to lizards. I can go in the garage where my brother, Scrunch, is. He can help me to revive Griff with our hot breath." Squeezey flew to the garage. Over their medallions, Jamie heard her make lizard sounds to attract her brother. "Scrunch blow on his head and upper torso, and I'll start with his feet."

Jamie bit her lip. "I hear odd noises. Sounds like angel wings fluttering."

Scrunch said, "You are right. They are creating warm yellow light."

"That kind of help comes from our protector, St. Michael."

The cars started, all the lights clicked on, angel wings flapped, and the chuckwallas blew as hard as they could. Big chunks of ice fell from Griff's arms and legs. Griff twitched.

Ghosts Texter and Jaden, with help from the angels, lifted Griff's ice-laden torso out of the garage and gently put him behind some old trucks.

"Who was in here?" demanded Lucifer. The bright lights blinded him. "Where is my victim? I won't let you have him."

Kattie, in her cat form, purred. "I turned on the lights to try to see where Griff was. I don't know who took him." She spoke into her childhood gem so Jamie would hear everything.

Griff, stay where you are. He cannot see you behind those trucks. We will create a diversion. Udo and Trish ran noisily toward some garages on the other side of the alley away from Griff, as Jamie ran to her prince.

Lucifer yelled, "I know that's you, Jamie. Now you will die first." He sprung from one garage rooftop to another, looking inside cars and trucks to find his prey. His taunting bone-chilling words seemed to ooze from the mortar between the concrete blocks that made up the garages. "You just think you tricked me. Your friends think they are clever. I am behind you, Jamie. I am in front of you. I'm everywhere."

With Jamie's help, Griff touched the powerful LightStone hanging around his neck. His LightStone sent out piercing bursts of light. "Jamie, we have to locate Lucifer. Let's touch our stones and tell them to work together."

Jamie did as directed. The arcing rays from the gems combined. Then they split apart, chased after each other, and jabbed at dark crevices. Sending sparks everywhere, the light rays did not detect Lucifer.

"Is he the devil?" Jamie inquired, as the group searched the junk yard for Lucifer.

"No. He thinks he is, but he is just a shifty-eyed, scheming beast that looks like an overgrown weasel," Griff replied.

Texter added, "We studied weasels in science class. They have long slender bodies with short legs and a grossly small head. It is believed they have the ability to shape-shift."

"That's interesting, Texter. I wonder what shape he's in now." Jamie vocalized.

The beast laughed. "I've changed forms every few seconds," Lucifer announced with a condescending laugh. "I went from a possum to a rock to an old milk carton to a puddle of water. You will never guess who or what I am now."

"Help me to stand," Griff requested. Jamie and Texter helped him to his feet. "Lucifer, I loathe your arrogance—we haven't found you, but we will." Griff stepped out into an open space. Jamie and the others stood courageously with him.

"You think you're powerful," Lucifer yelled. He lunged at Griff scratching his face.

"Where is he? All I saw were monstrous claws," Jaden stated. The group flashed their medallion lights again but could not expose the beast.

"Back away from me everyone before . . ." Griff collapsed and convulsed violently on the ground.

Smelling gaseous fumes around Griff, Jamie backed away and quickly recited, "Commando purifient l'air e respirar." The air cleared.

Jamie looked down at Griff and noticed one of the chuckwallas was trying to draw out the toxic gas. The lizard's low voice beseeched him to continue to fight. The tremors stopped but Griff did not rouse. "I'm not strong enough to help," the creature cried.

"Let me try," Jamie offered. She knelt beside him and pressed her mouth against Griff's to give him the kiss of life. "Lucifer is nearby. I can smell him. He still controls the air." Jamie kept trying to resuscitate Griff.

Griff choked on the vapors exhaled from his lungs and throat. The chuckwalla took Griff's right hand and placed it on the medallion. "Do it, Griff. You must try." He stroked the gem. It glowed red-hot beams of light, which revealed Lucifer in human weasel form. The fiery beams scorched him inside out as if he were on a rotisserie rod. The entire group of twelve, Jamie included, combined their powers against Lucifer. The projection of energy worked, and the polluted air changed into purified air for healthy breathing. Howling and staggering from the pain, Lucifer finally disappeared in the atmosphere.

Griff lowered his head and fainted.

The angels fanned their wings, blowing cool air across Griff's face and lessening the vaporous hold on him. His friends all knelt around him waving whatever they could find to fan him too.

Griff opened his eyes and took in a deep breath.

"Are you ok?" Jamie asked. "You lost consciousness."

"I am fine now. Is Lucifer gone? What about you? Were you hurt?"

"I was scared. My heart sounded like the pounding of a basswood drum." She patted Griff's shoulder. "You defeated Lucifer this time. Do you think he'll come back?"

"More than likely, he and the Dark Particles will regroup." He held his head. "I feel like my brain has turned into mush, but at least, we survived Lucifer this time."

"Thank you Squeezey and Scrunch," Jamie said, giving the lizards a high-five.

"This little guy almost lost his life trying to save yours," Jamie smiled and placed Scrunch in Griff's hands.

Jamie patted Scrunch as he basked in Griff's hands. "What beautiful colors, black, rust, gold, and cream."

"What about my cute face, and stowaway wings on my back?" Scrunch asked, twisting himself to show his best side and flapping his wings.

Jamie ran her fingers along Scrunch's back.

Scrunch turned over for a belly rub. He wrinkled his nose and wiggled his toes. "Ooh, that feels so good."

"What about me? Do I get a rub?" Squeezey chanted. "Why does Scrunch get all the attention?"

"You are absolutely gorgeous," Jamie said as she lifted Squeezey to her lips and kissed her on the head.

CHAPTER FOURTEEN

Healing Balm

———————————✴———————————

Jamie walked with Griff along the poorly paved alleyway and its potholes with the rest of the group following. She stumbled on the uneven surface. Scrunch slipped to the ground. "Hey, take it easy."

Jamie giggled as Scrunch climbed up Jamie's body and regained his footing.

"Hey, you aren't making fun of me, are you?" Scrunch asked.

"Of course not." Jamie scooped him up in her hands and petted him on the head with one finger. "You're so darn cute."

"Aww shucks," Scrunch's cheeks turned a rosy color.

"Who lives in that ugly house?" Jamie pointed to the back of a house. Parts of the building had collapsed. The gray paint on the doors, windows, and shutters had peeled off. The bricks were as black as charcoal. A dim light in an upstairs window revealed a black cat huddled on the windowsill. A dark human-like shadow moved in a first floor window.

"That is SilverWorm's house," Griff answered. "Even though she spends most of her time now at GrayStone Castle, SpiderWood's former home. Looks like she has left her place in shambles."

"I guess this is where Kattie lives too." Jamie added sadly, as she eyed the black cat. "I thought she had changed. I am so disappointed. Do you think she told me about Lucifer's freezing technique to warn me?"

Griff smiled at Jamie and moved near to her. "Possibly. Kattie is in the process of changing. It is a long journey. Jaden will be assigned to help her make right choices." Griff and Jaden exchanged glances.

"Yes. Your sister's conversion will happen. I am proud of you, Jamie. The Dark Particles could not defeat you. You have special gifts and a magical birthright. Our grandparents were known for their magic in other worlds, as were your parents. You have quite a legacy to carry on to our next generation," Jaden encouraged.

Jamie cocked her head. "Yes, I do have gifts. I'm learning what they are, and I want to use them wisely."

"For sure, you are going about this in the right way. It isn't easy, but you are already working your way through several murders, like I am," Griff said. "We're doing the best we can. I am convinced that in time we will be among the best of our magical society. The day will come when all the people of Light share freely their gifts. Peace is the goal for all the galaxies of the universe."

The group of ten live humans, two ghosts, and two chuckwallas crept down the alley for a short distance where they could still see inside the open window. Out of exhaustion, they sat on recycling containers filled with old newspapers and magazines.

Several people came out of the houses along the alley, entered their garages, and backed out their cars. Jamie perked up, listening to the rumble of the motors. She wondered if the drivers were leaving for the graveyard shift.

Scrunch jumped up. A swirling orange color filled the LightStone, giving off a hissing noise.

Jamie drew closer to Griff, and tightly closed her eyes to shield them against the brilliant orange light. "What's happening?"

"We are receiving a warning." Griff touched the LightStone to determine the problem. "Message is about a female driver who is wearing a nurse's white uniform."

"She's harmless, isn't she?" asked Jamie.

"LightStone is saying she has the persona of a human, but she is an Illusion." Griff barely got the words out of his mouth, when they saw the illusory woman raise her hand as if to wave. Instead, she threw a black ball with dozens of sharp pointed spikes protruding from its surface.

"It's a bomb. Get back everybody, it may explode." Griff jumped in front. He moved with such agility that the bomb did not explode when he caught it, but the spikes pierced his palm and made his hands bleed.

Griff threw the ball back at its source, blasting the Illusion full of holes. The deceptive woman ripped apart. A large explosion lit the sky, and it hastened to return to blackness.

Another Illusion, dressed in a business suit, propelled an explosive. Jamie sprinted into the middle of the alley, caught the bomb, and then halted.

"Hurry—get rid of the bomb," Griff yelled.

Jamie aimed and threw the bomb at the figment in the business suit. The sky lit up like a fireball from the impact. A few bomb fragments sailed through the air.

The group caught most of them, threw them back, and blew up the Illusions in rapid-fire succession. The mirages gave off ungodly screams and then whimpered on the hot pavement as they died amid blazing flames.

Griff placed his hand on Jamie's shoulder. "That was Lucifer and your twin trying to kill us."

"You mean you saw Kattie? Why didn't you throw a bomb at her?"

Griff fumbled for words. "Well … I didn't think you wanted me to torch her. She is your sister. She looks like you. It would be like destroying you."

"I don't want her destroyed. I still have hope." She wondered if Griff liked Kattie. Her face took on a puzzled look. "Do you hear my thoughts?"

Griff's forehead furrowed. "You think I'm attracted to her, don't you?" How can you think something so ridiculous? And at a time like this?"

Jamie felt her face warm. "Well, she's bold and spirited."

"That's true, but she has murder in her heart," Griff said. "Zero attraction, but I couldn't forgive myself if we struck her down and later regretted it. You could begin to hate me."

"I could never hate you," Jamie said. "We have a common destiny to deliver others from the evil of the Dark Particles."

Griff turned and stared straight into Jamie's eyes. "Yes, I feel a bond between us." He spoke in a soft, deliberate voice. "Your sister has aligned herself with the Dark Particles. This may cause more confrontations with her. I could never get along with someone who is filled with jealousy and revenge. We all hope she will change. Jaden and Texter, as good friendly ghosts, are here to help us with Kattie for your sake, Jamie."

Jamie brushed her bangs away from her face. "Thanks, guys. What's next?" She hoped that things would ease up for the rest of the week.

Squeezey yanked on the hem of Jamie's slacks. "Can you believe this? The explosions left only a few scorch marks and dents on garbage cans and cars. The earlier winds did much more damage. How is that possible?"

Griff picked Squeezey up, held her in his hands. "Our Light Channel and the Earth have only certain surfaces and objects in common. Magical people see the Illusions and their bombs, while non-magic folks see only residual marks and wonder what caused them."

Scrunch, still sitting on Jamie's shoulders, whipped his wings. "That's confusing."

"It's baffling to me, too." Jamie stated.

"Well, Illusions can't act on their own. They are not independent," Griff said. "They're empty on the inside. Magical persons, good or evil, can make and control Illusions with their powerful medallions."

"Did Kattie control the Illusions that we encountered?" Jamie asked.

"Lucifer did it for Kattie." Griff gently swung Jamie around and took her hands into his own. "Ok, now it's time to take care of you. Look at your hands. They're cut and swollen."

"Yeah, now show me yours." Jamie inspected Griff's palms. Blood and tissue mixed with the fibers of his torn black gloves.

Griff removed them. The leather stuck to his hands. He placed his fingertips on the LightStone. "Jamie, touch your MoonStone. Everyone else do the same."

Each teen rubbed their stones, which exuded therapeutic gel onto their skin. The gel turned colors as it seeped into their bodies. All of their wounds began to heal.

Jamie held up her hands and swirled around, marveling at the healed puncture wounds. "My skin looks unblemished. That is exciting. I love magic."

Griff studied his mended hands. "Now I need a new pair of gloves."

"That's a gift I can give you. Consider it done." Jamie felt her face blush. She noticed Griff's strong jaw line and magnificent emerald green eyes. *Griff's eyes look brighter tonight.*

CHAPTER FIFTEEN

Fire

Aharsh laugh pierced the night. As Lucifer peered around the trash receptacle, a dim light revealed a dark red hooded robe to the group. His face was weasel-like with horns embedded in his forehead. Lucifer showed up whenever he wanted, even when people thought he was gone.

"Did you like my Illusions that I created just to get what I desire, your deaths?" Lucifer licked his lips. "With your kind gone, I will have sole control. I am irate that you are still alive. I will become Rage to make you pay. I will show you what ripping apart feels like."

Lucifer mounted a dumpster, balanced himself, straightened out his cloak and yelled. "Watch this drama."

Out jumped Rage from the same spot, clothed in a black robe covered with embers of fire and wearing a perpetual flame necklace. Rage moved his wand over a jungle embroidered on the trim of his robe. He dictated, "Lions, come to life and tear Jamie and Griff apart."

Two mountain lions' images roared, shaking the ground like an aftershock. The lions jumped off the robe and became full-size.

Jamie and Griff rubbed their medallions. Light rays landed on the lions and turned them into black and white rabbits. Scrunch shooed the rabbits to safety.

Rage waved his wand over two jaguars painted on his robe and brought them to life. The jaguars chased the teens and swiped at them with their claws.

"Hurry, the jaguars are way too close," Maria reacted.

Hai raised his eyebrows and fingered his medallion. Rays shot out and wrapped the jaguars in light. "They'll be ok in a wild life refuge." Away they went.

Rage sent flames from his claws, set several bushes on fire, and disappeared.

As Jamie headed northwest up the alley with Griff and the others, she tried to recognize forms within the thickening fog.

A gravelly voice broke the silence and became louder. "Beware. Only fools dare to stay out on a night like this."

Griff hollered. "Does that mean you and I are both fools, since we're both out?"

"No-o-o, I own the night." The vaporous creature spewed out vomit. "Let me introduce myself. I'm Strangler." He picked up the disgorged matter with his claws and threw it at the teens. The stench was disgusting.

Jamie yelled at Strangler. "So, you think that a stench will humiliate us. You don't scare these teens."

"I have more in mind than degradation," Strangler howled as he heaved more gook. "Your team and you two will become intimidated very soon."

Griff scolded the creature. "Your odor is enough to cause a victim to barf and choke on it. Is that why you are called Strangler?"

"Yes, you're right," Strangler grumbled. "My odor is permeating your body and will soon deaden your senses."

Lois and Birdsong bent over with cramping pain, swayed and tried to keep their balance. Some of the other teens developed queasiness that made them lethargic.

Hearing a sucking noise, Jamie saw Griff collapsed with Scrunch on top of him. Jamie whispered. "Scrunch, is Griff alive?"

Scrunch nudged Griff. "Barely. Do something." The lizard continued to suck in the stench, showing no concern for his own safety. Jamie did not know how much Scrunch could absorb.

Jamie massaged her stone. "Aqua surgento." Crystal blue water gushed from her gem, creating a stream that ran the length of the alley. It coursed around Griff, reviving him. The water carried away all the toxins and smell. Griff sat up in the water, holding Scrunch.

Standing up with Keme and Udo's assistance, Griff rocked back and forth, rubbing his nose. He gasped, "That smell was worse than a firebomb."

Everyone breathed fresher air. "Whew, we survived again. Thank goodness. He has a thing about our breathing," Roberto triumphantly shouted.

"Yeah, he wants us to stop breathing," Jamie's mouth opened wide.

Not too far from her, Strangler shifted skin, clothing, size and shape. He rearranged his particles, changing back into Rage.

"Go away, you freak." Trish squealed loudly.

Rage boomed, "Who are you to tell the most powerful creature in the universe what to do?" He bounded toward them.

Griff crawled closer to Jamie. He did not want to let on that he feared Rage's control over them. He encouraged Jamie. "Let's stay calm. We'll think of something." Griff looked around. "Where's Texter and Jaden? Scrunch, where is your sister?"

A gigantic fireball rolled up Tornado Alley, like a colossal bowling ball. It barreled straight for Rage. The luminous ball showered an intense blinding light so pure that Rage shrieked in pain. "Holy spitball, what is this light?"

No one answered.

Rage ran from the brilliant light, which chased him until he turned into a tiny speck in the distance. The light left no memory of itself.

Jamie remarked, "I wonder who sent that fireball to save us. It worked. Thank you Light."

⁕⁕⁕⁕⁕⁕⁕

Scrunch unfolded his wings and groaned. His voice rose in pitch. "I feel like something has possessed me. What's wrong with me?" The dizzy lizard bumped into things and babbled, "I'm scared. This is too weird."

Grabbing Scrunch, Griff rubbed his belly area and heard the gases gurgling in his interior. His chest seemed to bubble like a cauldron of boiling water. "Scrunch, you are acting crazed. I think parts of Rage are inside you."

An evil-sounding Scrunch hissed. "If Rage remains in me, it's my business. So, stay out of this!"

Griff confronted Scrunch. "You're talking, but it doesn't sound like you. You look like you're going to self-destruct."

The voice coming from Scrunch sounded like Rage. Scrunch spun out of Griff's hand with such force that smoke followed him. Rage yanked him here and there like a yo-yo on a string.

Griff grabbed Scrunch, hurled him skyward, and yelled, "Hurry, turn around and come back to me."

Scrunch arched with such power that he slung the evil glob out of his mouth and far into the dark sky. He raced back. Griff caught Scrunch, giving him to Jamie. She cradled him while he slowly returned to looking like himself.

Scrunch patted his belly. "I'm as cute as ever, aren't I?"

"Now, you sound like yourself, Scrunch," Jamie commended.

"Hey, where is my sister?" Scrunch's eyes darted furtively.

Jamie and Griff shrugged their shoulders.

"Squeezey, where are you? Squeezey." Scrunch kept yelling her name.

"Hello. Hello, can anyone hear me?" asked a muffled voice.

"Who said that?" Trish said as everyone twirled around to see who spoke.

"Jaden, your friendly ghost. We're over here and can't get out."

"Keep talking so we can locate you," Scrunch said. "Is Texter and my sister with you?"

"Texter is, but we haven't seen Squeezey. Sorry, Scrunch."

"Their voices are coming from over here," Maria pointed. Roberto and Lois pulled away an enormous pile of leaves, unearthing a large bubble.

"Well, this is a sight. How did you get in that thing?" Jamie laughed.

"I had this bright idea that if we encapsulated ourselves we would be protected from that awful smell," Texter explained. "But I don't know how to reverse my own magic. Mrs. Glosomore didn't teach me that."

"We can just poke a hole and let the air out," Keme said laughing and waving a branch. "Maybe it will deflate a few ghosts too."

"That's not funny," Jaden complained. "Do something. We can hardly breathe in this thing."

Jamie called on her MoonStone, "Bursteo caseo. Bursteo insalato. Burst the darn bubble. I don't know the magic phrase for this scenario." All the teens hooted.

"I know what to do." Scrunch was on top pouncing on the clear membrane until it squeaked. The bubble puffed-up and then expelled all its air, sending Texter, Jaden and Scrunch into the trees.

Jaden took ghostly form and served as parachute for the chuckwalla's descent. Texter, in typical ghost fashion, perched in a tree with his jersey caught in its branches.

"Please, we have to find my sister. Now," Scrunch demanded.

Griff hoisted Scrunch onto his shoulder. "Let's go find her." The group headed down the weed covered alley. Suddenly, the luminous fireball emerged in front of them.

With the flutter of magnificent and mammoth wings, Michael emerged from the ball and sat Squeezey on the ground next to her brother. The glorious angel proclaimed, "Your brave little friend came to get me. Lucifer is gone forever."

The light beams from the teens' medallions merged in a beautiful light show, celebrating victory. The angels sung *Triumph of Goodness* as they glided away.

CHAPTER SIXTEEN

Dragons

Jamie called Aunt Esther. "I came to Earth for a special assignment, but it is now finished. If it is okay with you, I would like to spend tonight and tomorrow with you and Uncle Jonathan before I have to be back at the Academy."

"Sure, it is more than okay with us. Is anything wrong?"

"Just very tired and hungry, Auntie."

"We just finished dinner, but there are plenty of leftovers. We had one of your favorite meals, ginger chicken over fried rice, and I have a red velvet cake in the oven now," Aunt Esther responded enthusiastically. "Judd, Uncle Jonathan and your grandparents are all here. We cannot wait to see you. Are you alone?"

"Griff is here with me. A bunch of our friends were with us, but are all headed to their homes. They want to meet you tomorrow. Can you stand a bunch of teens in your house?"

"Oh, absolutely. I would love to have all of you. I love teenagers, as you know. This is exciting. I will cook a big meal, too. How many should I prepare for?"

"Well, there will be ten teens, two or maybe three ghosts, and two chuckwallas," Jamie said. "Is that too many?"

"Sounds like a great party. Grandpa and Grandma have a very special gift that they have been waiting to give you. TimberWood will be excited to see you too."

"Fantastic. Griff and I are almost there. See you shortly, Auntie. Love you very much."

"We all love you more than you know, Jamie."

"Three ghosts?" Griff quizzed.

"Yes, if Kattie comes," Jamie answered.

"Seriously? You think she will come after all that just happened."

Jamie stomped her foot, "Remember, I told you she warned me about Lucifer. I will not stop believing in her."

"I like the sound of that, believing in me. Good thing. I am following you. Do you really still trust me?" The black cat with the ruby collar appeared in front of them. "I wouldn't blame you if you didn't."

"Kattie is trying," Jaden interjected. He and Texter appeared next to the black cat. "She told Texter and me at the junkyard that if Lucifer got the upper hand, Michael would intervene. She had talked to Michael and his army."

"Then show yourself in human form," Jamie demanded.

"I am so sorry. I wanted to make sure that we were okay first," Kattie said as she took human form with her arms intertwined with Texter and Jaden. "These two kind men are showing me just how much fun it is to be a good ghost. I was invisibly with you throughout the evening, helping as best as I could without letting old Lucifer know. My magic is not very strong, but I am learning from these good guys."

"Oh, Kattie. Thank you. I do believe you and trust you," Jamie responded tearfully. *Miracles do happen. Just keep believing.*

The twin sisters hugged as Griff, Jaden and Texter looked on.

****

The door opened to the tantalizing aroma of ginger chicken fried rice and red velvet cake. An overwhelming feeling of homesickness surged through Jamie's soul. She wept as she fell into her aunt's embrace. "Oh, the sweet smells of home and such beautiful faces. I missed you, all of you so much."

Everyone hugged and shared the events of the last three months while Griff and Jamie ate their dinner. It was a wonderful evening with family and Griff. Jamie drank it in with an insatiable thirst. *This will have to sustain me for another three months.*

"It is a warm spring night. Can we eat dessert outside?" Jamie asked.

"I thought you might want to do that. You and Griff go on out to visit your best friend. I already have chairs set out. We will bring cake and ice cream in a few minutes," Grandma directed.

Griff and Jamie headed directly to TimberWood, who embraced them into his loving arms.

"You two have drawn very close to each other. More than friends," wise TimberWood said. "That's really good."

"Yes, I love Jamie. We are best friends. I feel closer to her than to anyone else in the universe," Griff verified.

"Like soulmates," Jamie added.

"Hmmm, I see that truth in your tired faces, but I also see sadness. It is close to your parents' anniversary, Jamie. How are you doing?"

"In many ways, I feel them closer to me than when they were alive. It is like they are here inside of me," Jamie tapped her heart. "Yet in other ways they seem so far away."

"You have your father's fortitude and your mother's wisdom," TimberWood affirmed. "I see both of them in you."

Jamie's grandparents came out carrying an ice cooler with boxes of ice cream in it. They sat the chest under TimberWood. "We have moose tracks, butter pecan, creamy vanilla, chocolate walnut, banana cream and several other flavors of ice cream. After dessert, we challenge you two to a word or number game. Or maybe a game of dominoes," Grandma Liz said.

"I have the most fun grandparents in the galaxy," Jamie said as she and Griff jumped down from the tree.

"Actually, all the adults in your family are cool, Jamie," Griff praised.

"Could you go get the folding tables, please, Griff? They are right inside the back door," Grandma asked.

"Yes ma'am. I'd be delighted."

After Griff ran in, she added, "Come with us, Jamie, to the side of the house to see your gift from us."

Grandpa reached for Grandma and Jamie's hands.

"Hey Rowdy. I am happy to see you. Who do you have with you?" Jamie patted Rowdy on his neck.

"This is my wife, Rowena, and our baby girl, Winnie."

Winnie immediately licked Jamie's face. "Hi, I'm your new dragon. Hop on and I'll show you what I can do."

Jamie looked at her grandparents with surprise all over her face. "Wow. My very own dragon. Wow-weee."

Rowdy and Rowena gave their permission to Jamie and Winnie to ride around. "It's okay. Rowdy and I are so proud of our sweet and smart daughter. She is more than ready to serve you and serve you well, Jamie."

Winnie whisked Jamie around the neighborhood so fast, that she felt a bit dizzy by the time they landed. "I am strong, fast, and magical. I can do all kinds of tricks. Like this." Winnie magically lifted Jamie up about three feet off the ground and spun her around three times before she gently sat her back down.

"You are wonderful, Winnie. If I wasn't dizzy before, I sure am now," Jamie joked.

The rest of the family and Griff delighted in seeing Jamie so happy. They spent hours outside eating cake and sharing more stories until midnight.

****

Everyone gathered at the Travelsteads' backyard. Uncle Jonathan and Grandpa Glosomore, the grill chefs for the day, barbequed chicken, ribs, and corn on the cob. Grandma, Aunt Esther, Jamie and Kattie readied potato and three bean salads.

"I'm so glad you came early, Kattie." Jamie and her sister arranged red-checkered cloths on the two long tables.

"Me, too. You have such great friends and they all accept me as a friend too. I just love my ghost buddies, Jaden and Texter. Did you know that Texter and I are sort of dating?"

"That is wonderful, Kattie. Congratulations. Speaking of Texter, there he is with Jaden and Griff."

"Are you spying on me, Texter? What have you three been up to?" Kattie quizzed.

"Well, yes, I am spying. I love watching my two favorite girls working together like sisters. When do we eat?"

Jamie chuckled. "You sure have an enormous appetite for a ghost. I think everything is almost ready. Look, here comes the rest of the crew."

All the teens arrived, Griff's uncle, the chuckwallas, Scrunch and Squeezey, along with the Willows and other neighbors. Jamie watched the group with pleasure and love. *What a great afternoon with all those I love in one spot. Griff and I, Texter and Kattie are in love. I know you must be smiling, Mom and Dad, to see your daughters like this.*

****

On the way back to Light Channel on dragons, a particle with enormous wings soared low on the horizon, switched directions, and headed toward the group. The fire-breathing she-monster had two heads, one of a lion and one of wild boar. It had a goat's body and a serpent's tail.

Scrunch pumped his greenish-gold wings and shot back and forth in front of Jamie. "What's that huge thing?"

Jamie put her hands to her mouth. "I don't know."

Griff kept his cool. "It's SnakeDragon and its venom is as poisonous as a rattler. SilverWorm controls him." Griff circled to face the dark particle. "Get lost, you evil thing."

SnakeDragon roared, "Lucifer has sent me to destroy all of you." It slashed out with its tail, causing a bloody abrasion on Rowena' side. Griff, riding on her back, used his medallion to put salve on her wound and then circled back toward the monster.

"Mom, are you okay? Can you take Jamie?" Winnie inquired.

"I am fine, Winnie, but what are you going to do?"

Winnie lifted Jamie from her back and sat her on Rowena's back with Griff. "I am going to show you some real magic, Jamie." She flew straight up at lightning speed and spiraled tail first into SnakeDragon's side, exposing his ribs. Fire spewed from Winnie's mouth, scorching the monster in one of its faces. The monster shrieked in pain, but continued to slash with its tail.

"Scrunch, if we fly closer, will you drill holes into its wings? Disabled appendages will throw him off balance." Jamie steered Rowena to the monster's injured side. Scrunch climbed onto SnakeDragon and bored holes as fast as he could.

The monster flipped Scrunch into the air. She screamed, "Get off of me."

Jamie swung around, squarely facing the creature and stroked her medallions. Light rays gyrated in the air, fashioning armor for Griff and Jamie. Griff's LightStone produced two steel swords, each with glistening sapphires at its hilt. The other teens encircled the monster with drawn swords. Jamie lifted her bokken and used the movements she had learned in martial arts. She lowered it signaling to the group to attack.

SnakeDragon shook his injured heads and blasted the teens with fire. Several dragons with their passengers turned just in time to avoid a direct fireball strike. Rowena and Winnie rapidly fired back multiple times.

"Circle close to the monster again and set up for a group attack after we poked out its eyes," Scrunch directed. As they drew near, Scrunch and Squeezey jumped onto SnakeDragon's one good head. Together they aggressively attacked the boar's eyes and then climbed back onto Winnie as she circled close again.

With the monster blinded, the teens formed an impenetrable wall of dragons and humans, quickly moving toward the monster. The teens propelled their swords into SnakeDragon's heads and torso.

SnakeDragon screamed and thrashed about. With pierced wings, gouged eyes, and multiple stab wounds, the monster shook its rattler and spewed one last ball of fire as it tumbled out of the atmosphere back to Earth.

"I will send one stronger than SnakeDragon. Kattie, come here now," SilverWorm demanded.

"No, I will not. Leave me alone." The ruby that hung from a chain around her neck singed her. "You can have the ruby," Kattie screeched as she ripped it from her neck and hurled it at the witch. "And this useless stone." Kattie tossed the medallion given to her by the sorceress. SilverWorm swooped down and caught the jewelry.

"No defenses now you little brat. You are history," the witch cackled and shouted obscenities as she zipped away on her besom.

CHAPTER SEVENTEEN

Love Conquers

Jamie and the other teens were exhausted when they arrived back at Light Channel. Griff invited Jaden and Texter to stay with him for the night. Kattie stayed with Jamie. The two dorm buildings situated right next door to each other, looked like a grand duplex. Across the street was a large structure for housing the students' pets. With their dragons and chuckwallas settled and fed, the teens and ghosts drifted off into a sound sleep in the comfort of their own rooms. Jamie turned her light off and glanced over at her digital clock. The lighted time read 11:11 p.m. With a soul-lifting smile, she whispered, "Eleven-eleven, a hug from heaven."

"I remember Mom used to say that when it was eleven-eleven. We always teased her about it only happening twice a day. Guess she is thinking about us. Good night, Sis." Kattie rolled over, pulling the cover over her right ear.

"Yeah, I believe she is. Sweet dreams." Jamie yawned.

At 11:11 p.m., Jamie and Kattie both sat straight up in bed and looked at each other quizzically.

"The clock hasn't changed, but I feel like we slept for eight hours or more." Jamie picked up her cellphone and noted it had the same time. "Weird. Really strange."

"It is strange. I feel rested as if I slept, too. However, I did not want to wake up yet. I was dreaming about Mom and Dad," Kattie said. "It seemed so real, like they were here talking to both of us."

"Really? My dream too. Must be highly classified messages to stop time. Let us write down what they told us in our dreams and interpret their meaning. What happened in your dream?"

"Mom told me I am talented in drawing maps and diagrams in great detail just like Dad. Commander-in-Chief Belcor Williams had an important briefing with them that involved both of us. Mom said it is imperative that we work together. I am supposed to allow myself to be captured by SilverWorm. Once there, I am to sketch the interior of the castle, especially the three dungeons that remain full of captured teens and children. They showed me images of other buildings on the witch's compound. Dark Particles, who inhabit those buildings, are under SilverWorm's supreme spell and control. Their plan is for me to present a complete architectural drawing of each designated building to Light Channel Command. Dad told me that when I awoke, I should tell you everything. He proudly dubbed us his 'Team Twins', with that wise twinkle in his eye. Dad said your dream would provide all the other necessary details. Jamie, he laughed so hard when he hailed 'Watch out universe. Here comes double trouble like you have never seen.' Mom was laughing too. I feel his presence right now. Do you see them both in our room?"

"Not yet, but wow, what a dream, Kattie. Your dream is different from mine but very similar. Our dreams linked cleverly together by our magical parents." Jamie winked, jumped up, grabbed her backpack, and retrieved their father's medallion, CastorStone. "Dad told me in my dream that his stone is named for the second brightest star in the constellation Gemini. It is one of the clearest stars in the night sky. This was Daddy's zodiac sign. People under Gemini are very independent. More than anything, they desire freedom. They will not let others dictate to them. He said you have the same spirit. Dad wants you to know how proud he is to present his stone to you today through me. He also told me that he wanted me to hold up this gem and for us to repeat together the words of our family pledge. Do you remember it, Kattie?"

"With your help, I can say it."

"We promise to always protect the Light within our own beings, in each …," Jamie started and Kattie joined her sister. "… family member, and all seekers of the Light. We pledge that we will humbly and stoically use our magical powers and medallions only for goodness, justice, and peace."

"What does stoic mean, Jamie? I have never understood that."

"I asked Mom the same question a few months before she died. She told me that it comes from an old school of philosophy that holds wise people should make decisions free from passion and emotion. All judgments should be based on unconditional love and a strong sense of justice."

Tears freely rolled down Kattie's face. "I had forgotten to live by this."

"We can all start over again, Sis."

"I am so ashamed of myself for turning away from this pledge and for living in the darkness. My journey was horror and terrorism. I clearly know if it were not for forgiveness and the renewed belief in the Light, then I would not be here with you today. I am ready to make my mark in this world and all others for the truth of Light. Thank you for not giving up on me."

"I see the Light and its mighty power at work in you, Kattie. I am very proud of you. You described the way of Light very well. Dad wants you to have his stone to protect you and enhance your magical Light powers." Jamie placed the chain around Kattie's neck. "This is yours now. Our parents knew this is the right time."

"I will cherish it always and protect it with my life." Kattie held the jewel in her hand and stared at its beauty. "The gratitude and love I feel in my heart is overwhelming. I am scared of messing it all up. I want to use it wisely. Please mentor me so that I will use my medallion for the greater good. Show me how to use it well."

"In my dream, I was told that twelve months of rigorous courses begin tomorrow here at the Academy. Invitations, to advance in your knowledge and use of medallions, have been sent to you, Texter and some other ghost friends of the Light. The other classes will hone your Light skills. Orientation is tomorrow morning at 10:00 a.m. in the Academy's auditorium with a luncheon afterwards. Per dream instructions, I am supposed to accompany you for the event. What do you think, Kattie?"

"Sounds great. Awesome details, huh? What happens after my learning phase? Does your dream continue?"

"You will be asked by SilverWorm to lure Griff, some of our other friends and myself to the GrayStone Castle as a way for you to prove your loyalty to the witch. I am to allow myself to be taken to the castle. All this will take place when you and I have completed our coursework. This mission will be your field placement and final exam. By that time, you will be ready. A plan, developed by Light Channel commanders and officers, needs our undercover work at the castle. Mom was adamant when she said, 'you two daughters of mine must trust each other with your life and spirits'. I am ready to commit if you are."

Both teary eyed, the two girls hugged. "I am ready, too," Kattie responded as she surrendered into a bear hug with her sister.

As she hugged her sister, Jamie looked at the clock. "It is still eleven-eleven, a hug from heaven. We know Mom and Dad are on a high beam of Light right now to see us be this way with one another. I feel them here, wrapping their love around us."

"They are here, participating in a life-giving group hug," Kattie agreed.

CHAPTER EIGHTEEN

Rites of Passage

The combined high school graduation and the enrollment as a Light Keeper apprentice took place on the first day of June. They also honored many ghosts, who met their early death before they completed school, with a diploma. Enrollment as Light Keepers Special Manifestation Forces was given to deceased graduates. Kattie and Texter joined Jaden, who had been in this special unit for two years. It was a proud day for all.

After the ceremony and the banquet, Commander-in-Chief Belcor Williams of the Luminous Intergalactic Defense had his personal guards escort Griff, Jamie, Kattie, Texter, Jaden, Trish, Maria, BirdSong, Lois, Udo, Roberto, Keme, and Hai to a special gathering at his home.

When they arrived, they each received a hood to put over their head and face for security purposes. The group was gently guided through an intricate pattern of lefts and rights, down stairs and up and down again. Lastly, their guide led them to a seat at a huge oak table.

"You may now remove your hoods. The Commander will be with you shortly," one of the guards announced. "You each have a folder in front of you that contains your military orders. In absolute silence, we ask you to read your assignment details." The guard clicked his heels and perfected his posture with sword in hand across his chest. He stood on guard at the only entrance into the room.

Jamie eagerly read the contents of her folder about her first official mission. When she finished reading, she closed her folder and looked around the room. There had been only two sounds in the room – the turning of papers and breathing. She watched in silence as everyone read their assignments and closed their folders.

Kattie was the last to finish. She closed her folder and looked right at Jamie. *She has been crying.*

Yes, Sis, I am sorry for how ugly I have been. Now I will make it up to you. I love you.

And I love you more and more ...

"Please stand," commanded the guard. Everyone stood up and attentively turned toward the door. A gentle breeze from above their heads made them instinctively turn back to the table. The Commander-in-Chief and many of his officers were present.

"Please be seated," Belcor started. "As you can tell, we are inviting you to participate in a top secret mission. If you have any reservations about our Light Command orders, then you are to leave now. No dishonor. You will be held in highest regard for your achievements thus far. Of course, this mission may cost you your life, so you must choose courageously with that fact in mind."

Jamie stood, "I am with you, sir." She saluted and remained standing. Griff quickly made his declaration to follow the orders of this mission. Each one of the other teens did the same.

Only Kattie stayed seated. "May I ask a question, sir?"

Belcor nodded. "Everyone be seated, please."

"If I should fail ..."

"The mission depends on you, Kattie. You cannot fail. If you do, your sister and others may die. And you will cease to exist in any of your forms."

"I am frightened. I don't want to fail for their sake – all of these good people are friends of mine," Kattie responded as she moved her right hand in a circular pattern. "I also don't want to fail those who are held captive. They have the right to be free."

"There is only one powerful silencer of fear and that is the more powerful gift of love, my dear daughter, Kattie," her father spoke gently yet very strongly. Mom and Dad had come in with Belcor but had remained in spirit form until this moment. "I promise to be as close to you as your CastorStone. You and Jamie can do this."

Kattie stood to face her father. "I am sorry …"

"Shhh, my baby. We know your heart," Dad uttered.

"We forgive you and love you," Mom said motioning to Jamie to come.

The four Travelsteads embraced and in that moment, Kattie showed the effect of Light. Her being took on an iridescent and redeemed form, a new self.

"You are beautiful." Jamie remarked in awe and with tears in her eyes.

"And I will be brave. Okay, Commander Belcor, I am ready to go full speed ahead into this mission."

CHAPTER NINETEEN

Capture

─────────── ✶ ───────────

J amie, with Griff at her side, watched anxiously in her medallion as Kattie travelled alone on a borrowed dragon to Travelstead Castle on HallowWinds. Kattie arrived without incident and entered into their old home. "I'm here." Kattie used the CastorStone to communicate with Jamie.

"I have you in visual and the troops are ready as needed."

Kattie left the front door open and rummaged through closets and riffled through drawers. She deliberately tossed stuff everywhere. A gust of wind stirred the papers and photos into a tornado shape that stood in front of Kattie.

"What are you looking for? Where have you been?" SilverWorm demanded.

"I … I have been in hiding," Kattie acted scared.

"Afraid of me, are you?" The tornadic witch moved closer. "You didn't tell me what you are looking for."

"I need protection. I thought I could find my father's medallion here."

"You had protection, you silly child and you threw it away."

"I am sorry. I had to do it or Jamie would put a curse on me. She threatened to freeze me in place."

"You didn't think I would rescue you? Protect you?"

"I thought you would be mad at me for hanging around my sister and helping her out. I was torn, but I am not now. I cannot stand her. She lies and is not to be trusted. She has gained a lot of power. It has gone to her head. I need protection from her. I will stay loyal to you, I promise."

"Are you asking for my help?" SilverWorm inquired as she formed into her witch shape.

That is too easy. Be careful, Kattie. Jamie told her sister telepathically.

"Answer me, child," the witch demanded.

"Yes, I need your help desperately."

The witch flew around Kattie several times, using her medallion to search her. "You have some sort of stone on you."

I just deactivated it, Kattie. We still have you on visual and audio. Will reactivate when safe.

"Yes, I just told you I came looking for my father's gem. And I found it, but it doesn't even light up."

SilverWorm snatched the stone. "You don't know how to use a powerful stone like this. I'll show you." The witch commanded, rubbed, and cursed the stone, but could not make it work. She held her stone up against it, but nothing happened. "Stupid thing does not work. It has lost its power. This won't help you." SilverWorm flung it across the room.

"But it was my father's. Jamie got everything else. I want to keep it." Kattie ran across the room to retrieve it.

It is reactivated now.

Kattie hung it around her neck and stuffed the gem under her blouse, and buttoned her jacket. "Can I go home with you, please? I will serve you."

"Get on. Do not forget for a minute, little wishy-washy girl, I will be watching you very closely. One false move and you will be history." They sailed off on SilverWorm's sweeper to Earth with an entourage of followers behind, beneath and all around them.

✳✳✳✳✳✳✳

When they arrived at SilverWorm's castle, the witch had Kattie handcuffed, blindfolded and thrown into a dark room alone in one of the dungeons. "Shackle her," the witch commanded.

We still have images and sound, Kattie. Texter slipped in with you.

Okay, Jamie. Good to know. After all the steps down, I was not sure if I could be seen.

"Tonight you will stay here. I am leaving you with this thought. If you lure Jamie and Griff here for me, I will give you back your ruby and a supremely powerful stone. You will have life in ways you have never experienced it. I will make you my witch apprentice and share my power. For tonight, you, the rats and the cockroaches will be together. Hope all of you get along. Elevate her. Teach her a few lessons about what happens when I am disobeyed."

Chains attached to the shackles lifted her five feet off the ground, dangling by her arms. Several ape-like creatures batted her back and forth, wrenching her arms and making her wrists bleed. They then placed shackles on her feet and anchored them with chains to the floor. Pain shot through Kattie's ghost form every time she moved even slightly.

"You will do anything I want by morning, I assure you. Tighten the chains and lock the door." The creatures did as she commanded. The door slammed. Kattie listened to their footsteps and counted.

Thirty-three steps, I think, and two landings before another door. These chains are tight.

Texter, can you loosen Kattie's chains? Are you hurt, Sis?

Not really, just in pain. I am good, Jamie.

I am untightening them for you, but we should wait a little while before I let you down, Texter consoled. He flew up to her face and tenderly gave her a kiss on each cheek.

Texter, you always make me smile, no matter what is going on around me. You are so sweet. Jamie, there is a small window over to the right about eight feet above me, Kattie described.

Good cat eyes. Noting your environment is good strategy. It is located by the ceiling and has a grate over it. A lot of underbrush on the other side. I am going out to explore. Texter whispered as he floated through the long and narrow grill. *Jamie, Kattie's room is on the north side of the castle. A moat surrounds the fortification. A drawbridge leads to the front entrance. It is about fifty feet to the window's left. First window is Kattie's. There are another nine windows to our right. Shall I go peek?*

Sounds good, Texter. This is Griff. I have you on my gem screen to allow Jamie to focus on Kattie and the interior rooms.

Okay, little kids asleep on the floors behind each window. Maybe fifty in each of these nine rooms. Holy baloney, after the second door, there are nine more windows and another large door. Sending you images now. I have a visual on teens in … in each of the second group of nine windows. Looks like thirty in each room in this section. Oh no, there are a group of overgrown weasel like creatures, snorting and sniffing around. They may be on to my scent. Guess I have a scent. I am going back.

You have a strong scent. You are dead after all, Griff teased.

You do not really smell, but it is a good idea to go back to Kattie's room before they sense your existence, Jamie advised.

Sounds on the stairwell, Texter, hurry, Kattie pleaded.

The door opened just as Texter tightened the chains back up. One of the ape creatures flashed a powerful light into Kattie's face. She moaned and groaned for effect. Then the creature scanned the light around the room.

He just does not know how much he helped. We got a clear image of the whole room, Kattie. I think the next cell check is in two hours.

The room darkened as the creature grumbled and stomped out of the room. He clanged the thick door shut and secured the lock. Texter and Kattie counted the steps and heard another door slam.

✳✳✳✳✳✳✳✳

For the next couple of hours during the night, Kattie and Texter, in their ghost forms, toured the north side of the castle. Griff kept an eye on Kattie's cell in case someone came back to do a prisoner check before the scheduled time. Jamie recorded images on her medallion as the ghost team walked through several corridors and rooms.

As you know, Jamie, all castles have secret rooms and hiding places. Four walls are very cold, like freezers perhaps behind them. Those walls are impenetrable. Texter and I have covered most of this spooky place, but now we are ready to communicate our mission to the captives.

Griff and Jamie granted permission to proceed. The other teams received their alerts regarding captive preparation.

Kattie gently awakened the oldest teens in each cell. "Shhh … don't be afraid. Be very quiet. My name is Kattie. This is my friend, Texter. We are ghosts, but we will briefly appear to you." Kattie and Texter showed themselves in bodily form. "We are protectors of the Light and are planning to rescue you real soon. There is a team of us are here in the castle. Hang in here but stay alert for our cues. Texter and I promise we will be back for all of you." The duo waved and then disappeared.

The two ghosts discovered the walls and doors leading out of the north side were impermeable. *We cannot access the other parts of the castle from here. Hard to believe a ghost cannot get through places. That is really funny.*

The sun will be up in about thirty minutes. You should head back to the chains, Kattie.

Ugh, the chains are awful, Jamie. Want to trade places with me? Just kidding, Sis. Kattie and Texter zoomed back to the cell in a nanosecond. *Yikes, I hear their footsteps.* Kattie quickly slipped back into the chains as Texter tightened the exact links.

You are an excellent illusionist and actress, Kattie. You can do this. Jamie encouraged. *I know this is scary. Believe in your strength and courage. You are doing a great job.*

Kattie immediately feigned agony by moaning and coughing. She was barely audible as she spoke. "Please let me down. I will do anything you want. My wrists and ankles are bloody. My shoulders feel dislocated."

"I don't want to hear about your pain. I want to know how you are going to get Jamie and Griff here unarmed – no medallions, no weapons. That is what I want and that is what you will do. Let her down." The witch looked at Kattie's bloodied arms and legs, and felt of her shoulders. "Give her some water, bread and a chair. Bring in one of the first aid kits. She can tend to her own wounds. One more thing, bring me a chair. Snap to it." SilverWorm rapidly spewed out her orders. "So begin explaining your grand plan. Prove your obedience and loyalty to me."

"Jamie has her mind set on releasing the imprisoned teens. Let me go tell her how she and Griff can get inside of the castle. That is the perfect way to get them here. I cogitated this all night. I finally figured out all the angles for me to bring them to your castle unarmed."

"I will decide if it is a perfect plan or not. Go on. I still have not heard your complete plan. You are stalling."

"You have metal and stone detectors, right?"

"Yes. Go on."

"I will show them the detectors and request they leave their gear outside behind a bush, stonewall or wherever you wish. You should tell me the best place. When I take them into the dungeon's corridors, your crew can capture them without difficulty because they will be unarmed."

"Sounds good so far. Anything else in this juvenile plan of yours?"

"I will need to see the entrance, the corridor to take once inside and the dungeon, right?" Kattie put on one of her best innocent, naïve looks.

"Hmmm, I guess I can trust you. Follow me. Guards come with me too, just in case she is up to something." *The strategy is working. The old woman is giving me a visual of the castle entrance and the path to the dungeons, Jamie.*

After the tour and more discussion, SilverWorm showed her delight in Kattie's scheme. She ordered lunch that included two large pizzas, drinks, cookies and ice cream. Then the pair enthusiastically worked out more details, as Jamie and Griff listened to the whole conversation.

SilverWorm led Kattie to her old suite of rooms. Texter followed undetected. Kattie and Texter carefully counted the steps from the dungeon to the suite and made detailed mental notes of the corridors to use.

Kattie's suite was spacious and ornately decorated. It had a comfortable queen size bed, a pillowy sofa with two matching recliners, and a daybed by the computer nook. Texter spied a dorm refrigerator, a microwave, and a coffeepot with everything they might need. *I am hungry. Glad this stuff is so accessible.*

"I had it freshly cleaned for you this morning. The refrigerator and pantry are both well stocked with your favorites."

"Thank you so much, SilverWorm. I won't let you down."

"I will have one of my attendants come by to get you by 9:00 a.m. tomorrow for breakfast with me, so we can work out final particulars. And oh, just in case you are lying to me, guards are on duty and have orders to destroy you immediately should you try anything."

****

Fantastic work, Sis. SilverWorm fell for it completely. Or did she? Jamie asked.

Thanks. I think she bought it. Hope so.

Kattie, do you think there is a way to find out what is behind those cold walls you and Texter found. Belcor thinks SilverWorm may have scientists trying cryonics, freezing bodies of magical teens and bringing them back later.

Wow, I will see what I can find out.

I do not think SilverWorm's threats were idle. Please be careful, Kattie.

I will be okay. Sleep well, Jamie.

Thanks. Sending you a hug your way.

I feel it, Sis. Jamie watched Kattie place her hand over her heart. *One back to you, too.*

Kattie was unaware that Jamie and Griff were taking turns watching her all night. Jamie had first shift.

Kattie and Texter waited about an hour. Then taking their ghost forms, they slipped past their sleeping guards. They retraced their steps to the dungeon and cold walls. They measured the space and calculated that there were three refrigerated rooms.

"Texter, I don't remember the exact commands we learned in our classes, but let's see if we can get in." Rubbing her CastorStone, Kattie commanded, "Permitir la entrada." She and Texter floated through the walls of the three rooms, taking many images.

"Cool, it worked," Texter responded.

"It's not cool. It is brrry cold in here. I'll send these to Jamie in the morning."

"Maybe you should do it now. Jamie will need some time to check with a scientist or doctor as to how best to thaw or move these frozen bodies. They appear to be in different stages in the freezing process, and they may need to be handled differently," Texter suggested.

"Good point, I'll get in touch with her now."

Kattie, I have been observing, watching out for you. Impressive use of commands, Kattie. Good work. I have the images and will begin research now. The guards are awake in your hallway. I have created an electronic lightshow as a diversion down the hallway from your room. Quickly return while I keep them guessing where the light is coming from.

Kattie and Texter returned to the room. Once inside they laughed hysterically at the comedy outside the suite's door.

Whew, that was close. Thanks, Jamie. Glad we were still on visual. The guards went crazy with the lights.

We have to take care of each other.

Good night again.

****

Early the next morning, Kattie awakened to a knock at her door. "SilverWorm wants me to bring you to her breakfast nook in one half hour. I will come back to get you. Please be ready. She doesn't like tardiness."

"Okay, I'll be ready." Kattie waited until she heard the footsteps move away from her door. She dressed quickly and then woke up Texter, who was asleep on the daybed by the computer nook.

SilverWorm kept Kattie close all day. In spite of her, it was a fairly pleasant day. Kattie had plenty of time to think about the rescue mission, as she became more familiar with the castle.

"What are those buildings used for?" Kattie asked as she pointed out a castle window on the west side.

"Guests stay there. I do not let too many people get into my personal space. A woman has to have her secrets."

"Oh, do you have horses in those barns over there to the left? I love to ride," Kattie hinted.

"No, army supplies are kept in those and lots of food in those silos," SilverWorm shared freely. "They are all heavily guarded, so don't get any ideas."

"I can't believe you are still suspicious of me. We have been together all day."

"You gave me good reason not to trust you fully, you little twerp," SilverWorm quipped. "You best not betray me again or you will be antiquity."

★★★★★★★★

At the same time as Kattie's breakfast with SilverWorm, Jamie, Griff and their group met with Belcor. He commissioned Griff as team leader with Jamie as second in command.

"Uncle Belcor, we have more to share with you about the dungeons." Griff began. "Jamie, fill him in about last night."

"Kattie and Texter were able to get into the freezer areas, and some older teens have been frozen. Approximately thirty are in coolers packed on dry ice and others are in nitrogen tanks. Griff and I plan to visit when we are finished here with the lead cryopreservationist at Light Channel Medical Center. We wanted to see what the process looked like in person. As you know, Light Channel has cryonics capability as well as the nanotechnology to repair the suspended bodies of whatever illnesses or injuries they may have had," Jamie reported.

"Not so sure about this process. I have not had a need to know. What actually happens?" Belcor quizzed.

"The doctor told us on the phone this morning that his team of scientists have found a way to pump the chemical substance, called cryoprotectant, into human bodies. They place the bodies of the suspended humans on dry ice until they reach-202 degrees Fahrenheit, and deposit in large tanks of nitrogen to keep their temperatures stabilized. With the nanotechnology, Light Channel medical staff may be able to mend damage caused by the freezing process. However, if SilverWorm's team erred in technical stabilization or suspension, then it may not work."

"So, does that mean we have to verify if the right amounts of cryoprotectant have been infused? And if the right temperatures of those packed with dry ice as well as those in nitrogen tanks have been achieved before they are thawed?" asked Belcor.

Griff responded quickly, "Since we probably do not have time for that during the rescue, the doctor suggested that a satellite medical station be readied. It can hover near the castle. The teens can be moved from the castle in the coolers or tanks, and then onto the satellite which would transport them to the Medical Center. There they can more safely make the calculations and wake the suspended teens."

"Wow, very enlightening but that does complicate everything. Sounds like we will need more team members to help transport the tanks to the satellite, medical staff in the dungeons to assist with the transfer as well as the hovering staffed medical unit. Okay, I'll call Dr. Stein and get the medical part set up, and will assign a larger company for the rescue," Belcor decided. "Make your team selections and I'll be in touch about the details. I think it is an excellent idea for you to visit Dr. Stein's setup. Well done."

****

The pair selected their team of three young men and three women, who would travel to HallowWinds.

The team included Trish and Maria, former prisoners in the south dungeon at SilverWorm's castle. Their experience with dungeon life, schedules and security staff provided key information for strategic activity.

As bait for SilverWorm, they would allow themselves to be captured with Jamie, Griff and Lois.

With her name meaning beautiful warrior, Lois used her physical and spiritual beauty to enhance her position with the enemy. She could trick the devil into complete trust, which made her combat skills surprising and unsurpassable.

Keme, with his penchant for camouflage, possessed the uncanny ability to move about unnoticed. He was able to change his identity, clothing, hair, body size and physique, as well as facial appearances at a moment's notice. As part of his disguise, Keme convincingly changed his speech patterns to that of a male or female, young or old in almost any language of the universe.

Jaden, with his extensive research on sorcery, understood their divination techniques, curses, and communications with animals. As a master ghost, Jaden was undetectable whenever he deemed it necessary.

Hai, whose name means two, duplicated himself. He possessed the talent of being in multiple places at the same time. He rounded out the highly skilled team.

Jamie led the group in a detailed review of the strategy and several contingencies. She and Griff packed their gear on Winnie and readied for their journey to HallowWinds.

"Time for us to send out our alerts," Griff suggested to the team.

"Kattie, Texter. Commence," Jamie proclaimed.

Keme sent out a communication in the top ten languages of Earth, including Mandarin, Hindustani, Bengali, and Malay-Indonesian. He also sent messages to Black Eye Galaxy, the birthplace of many evil sorcerers. He disguised the message source so it looked like it was coming from Tyranny, the code name for the person believed to be the commander-in-chief of Black Eye. His real identity was not yet known. Keme hoped that SilverWorm would respond. "Tyranny's fake message worked. SilverWorm is on her way to HallowWinds with Kattie."

"Great." Griff sent a relay message to Lance, the Glosomores, Agents Mytee and Tynee, and Victorious. They passed the message on to all the friends of the Light on Earth and elsewhere in the Milky Way Galaxy.

"Uncle Belcor, all is ready. Up in ten," Griff declared through his medallion.

"Roger that. This is Commander-in-Chief Belcor Williams. Southern Pinwheel Galaxy activate. Ten, nine, eight …" As the countdown completed, the enormous whirlpool galaxy that makes up Light Channel glowed in vibrant pulsating pinks and purples. Supernova exploded creating immense UV energy. Light Channel looked like an effervescent flower springing into life.

As the group circled near Black Eye, Jamie noted, "M64 is redder than usual. Think I studied that red means more stars are being formed, right? I hope that doesn't mean more Dark Particles will show up."

"Right, Jamie. Monitoring the formations now," Uncle Belcor responded.

"I am always struck by Black Eye's odd beauty with its stars and hydrogen gases rotating in one direction, while the immense cloud of dust rotates in the other. It looks sinister," Griff remarked.

"Evil keeps things stirred up and causes its victims to feel pulled in different directions," Jamie added. "We are approaching Sombrero Galaxy, Uncle Belcor."

"Roger that."

"Landing on the bulge now. I have always loved the hat's center, where the night sky reveals the star clusters all around the brim. HallowWinds, the cosmic giant head of the galaxy, will always be home for me."

"Roger that, Jamie. It is home for you, but you must put that thought aside today."

"Done. Griff, Trish, Maria, Lois and I are entering."

"Have you on visual." Belcor kept vigil as the five teens were cruelly assaulted when they entered the Travelstead castle. Kattie and eleven other necromancers took them prisoners, as SilverWorm supervised.

CHAPTER TWENTY

Freedom

With her hands manacled to granite wall, Jamie woke up. Her badly bruised face and her throbbing head made it impossible for Jamie to see through her swollen eyes. "Griff. Trish. Maria or Lois are you here?"

"The three female members are here on the opposite wall from you. Are you okay?" Maria answered.

"I think I'm okay. I see you. I am a little beat up. Not sure how bad the injuries are. Who else is over there by you? Where is Griff?"

"There's other teenagers over here," Trish answered. "Heika is sitting next to me, and on the other side of her is Rosita. They told me that a man came in to bring everyone rice and beans earlier, but said he would come back when we were awake. Heika told me that the male prisoners are usually housed in a room across the hall. Presumably Griff is there."

Jamie leaned her head over touching her left shoulder and spoke softly into the diamond shaped communication device. "Griff, can you hear me? Griff? Are you okay?"

She heard moaning but could not tell if it was Griff. He made a sound again. "Is that you, Griff?" Another grunt. "Did you just say yes?" Same kind of utterance. "Are you gagged?" Uh-huh. "Are you handcuffed or chained?" Another yes. "You are … Got to go. Door is opening."

A tall, gaunt looking man came in with a tray. "Food and water for the sleepy heads. I only came back since this is your first day. From now on, if you want to eat, you best be awake when we come in." He leaned over and sloppily placed two bowls in front of Jamie, one with water and one with a few beans over rice. He walked over to the opposite side and did the same for Lois, Trish and Maria. "Right or left handed?" he barked at them, and unshackled the opposite hand from their answer. He roughly asked Jamie, "Left or right handed?"

"Left," Jamie said even though she was right handed.

The man unlocked the shackle on the left, but did not remove it. "Holler when I kick you," he whispered and then pretended to kick Jamie in her left side.

"Aghh," Jamie yelled.

He pretended another kick, at which she moaned again. "Brat," he screamed. "You thought you could trick me? I should take these bowls away," he fussed loudly. He leaned over, unshackled her right hand, dropped a tiny intricately folded piece of paper in her lap, and exited the section.

Something metal. Feels like a small key. Jamie quietly removed the shackle from her left hand. Gently unfolding the paper, she found four small duplicate keys taped to it and a message, which read: "Duplicate keys for shackles. Release team first. Then u 4 undo all. One hand left loosely in shackles. Same act across hall by male team. Hai is one of three SW guards for men. Security check and bowl pick-up in thirty. Me, with two guards for u. Far left toilet tank for weapons. Ninety-four to be freed. Keme."

Jamie acted swiftly. The four female team members unchained the fifty-one emaciated teenage girls. All were ready with swords or knives by their sides and out of sight.

****

The heavy metal doors on both sides of the hallway opened almost simultaneously. As Keme collected her bowls, one of SilverWorm's guards approached Jamie to restrain her. In accord with one another, they tackled the guard knocking him off his feet. Jamie held him down as Keme, took on his bodily appearance, gagged and constrained the guard. Trish and Maria worked together to padlock the other sentry in the now empty shackles.

"Ladies free your hands. If someone needs help getting up, will you kindly assist one another or let me know who needs help. We need to act fast. Stay together. My team members will lead you out," Kattie said as she entered the room. "The men are ready to go."

Wow. What a sight. Everyone helping each other. This is Light. This is hope. This is the way it is supposed to be. Jamie carried a young girl about ten who could not walk. Her tiny legs had atrophied.

"I will carry her. You may need your hands free as a warrior." Texter gently received the girl from Jamie into his arms.

Griff and Jaden dragged several more guards from the hall into the dungeon rooms and fastened them to chains. Kattie bolted the dungeon doors with the guards inside.

"Okay, everyone waits here. No one goes out of the castle until I give the signal." Griff and his ghost buddies slowly opened the door to allow in a team of medical personnel and their assistants.

"This way. Follow me." Kattie led the group to the freezer sections. "Permitir la entrada." Kattie entered through the wall, opened the door of the first freezer vault from the inside, and quickly ran to the next room. She repeated the process two more times. The medical team hastily checked all the instruments and stages of cryonic process for each person. They promptly removed all the coolers and tanks.

Twenty-one coolers and twelve nitrogen tanks were carried out first. Light Champions surrounded the medical staff, moved at a brisk pace down the hall, out the backdoor of the north dungeon, and toward the moat. Other team members assisted the medics get onto the cloaked satellite. They quietly lifted off and headed toward Light Channel.

After the removal of the frozen prisoners from the castle and safe in the medical satellite, Kattie led the ambulatory teens out the castle door. "Victorious and her pack of hyenas have secured the yard. Temporary bridges are in place across the moat. Oh no. Team alert! They are on to us," Kattie yelled. "Move quickly."

The group of ninety-four freed children and teens as well as the entire Light team moved rapidly toward the moat.

Jamie noted that the unkempt stone path had weeds sprouting through the crevices. "Stay off the walk," Jamie suggested. "The weeds will entangle …"

Suddenly, the weeds wrapped and twisted around the legs of several teens, entrapping them. Jamie and the other team members slashed the weeds to free them.

Three young people began screaming. They were struggling and flailing in quicksand. Jamie ran over to them. "Please listen to me. Do not move around. The more your arms and legs wave or kick, the further down you will sink. Be calm." Jamie kept talking to them. "Help is on the way. Light Champions are bringing me a large limb or a plank from one of the bridges. When they come, I will get the wood as close to you as possible. One by one, I want you to roll onto it laying on your back. Once you are on it, you can paddle a little closer to the edge of the firmer ground, and we will lift you out. Okay, thanks for bringing us some wood. Place the planks here," Jamie pointed. "What is your name?"

"Tommy."

"Well, Tommy, there is a piece of wood behind you. I want you to put your hands on the plank … okay … now roll onto the lumber, but try to stay on your back … good job. Can you pretend you are on a float in a pool? Move just your arms and paddle closer to me."

Two Light Champions reached Tommy and pulled him to safety. Jamie moved the wood closer to the next two children. "One by one, I want you to do like Tommy," Jamie encouraged.

"Sure, glad you knew what to do, Jamie. Good work," Griff commended.

Mechanical flies flitted around in a thickening mist. The creatures were about five inches long and had large bulging yellow eyes. The flies snapped at the young people. The teens slapped at their arms and faces to no avail. A few of the teens tumbled to the ground and became very ill. Jamie rubbed her medallion, "Commando insecto inhabilitar." The light behind their eyes fizzled and the flies dropped to the ground.

"Those flies were webcams. SilverWorm knows we have broken free. We need to carry the ill. Hurry," Kattie encouraged. "Go straight ahead. Cross the planks about ten feet ahead."

Temporary wooden bridges stretched out across the moat. Muscular Light Champions secured the timber on both sides of the fosse. Light Keepers aided those bitten by the flies and scratched by the weeds. Once all who needed assistance safely transferred across the contaminated water, the ambulatory teens raced over the deep trench.

"Next hurdle is the fence," Kattie pointed ahead. "Grandpa has a team of dragons on the other side yanking it down."

The twelve feet tall black iron fence, with barbed wire wrapped around each vertical railing and foot long spears at the top of each rail, looked deadly. Jamie observed Rowdy, Rowena and Winnie, along with many of their dragon friends, tugging on the barrier.

The clamorous cries of the witch echoed from an upstairs window. "Kattie, not again. Nooo. Nooo." The discordant sounds continued until she reached the moat with thousands of rodents thronging at her feet. Their pointed snouts and elongated bodies jumped in the water and quickly approached the escapees. "Commando. Infectados con la peste bubonica," SilverWorm shouted. The rats raced toward the kids. One bite and Black Death would consume them.

The special mission team, with Griff and Jamie in front, stood between the rodents and the rescued youth. With one voice and medallions linked together, Jamie and Griff led the chant, "Commando morte a rodentas."

All the Light Keepers and Light Champions, the Glosomores, the Willows and other Light neighbors, Victorious and the hyenas, Lance and other knights on their horses, all the dragons, and agents Mytee and Tynee with the frogboys chanted with thunderous raucous, "Commando morte a rodentas." Each rat trundled to its back with all fours up in the air. Haggard, SilverWorm darted back into the castle and bolted the doors.

The stench of death permeated the air.

Jamie commanded. "Rodentas incendio." The rats engulfed in flames.

"The death vapors and smoke are a horrible mix. I think I am going to pass out." Scrunch sniffed at the air as he emerged from Griff's pocket. The chuckwalla jumped to the ground, keeled over and sprawled out with eyes closed.

Jamie leaned over and picked him up. "Are you okay?" She stroked his belly. He did not answer.

Squeezey crawled out of Jamie's pocket and down her sleeve toward her brother. She held her face close to his. "Hmmm, just what I thought." She tickled his left foot. Her brother's eyes popped open and he squealed with laughter.

"You scared us." With a scowl on her face and hands on her hips, Squeezey added, "Bad joke. Very bad joke."

A loud explosion behind them made everyone turn and jump. The flattened fence propelled debris, chunks of dirt, rocks and water everywhere.

One resounding cheer sailed through the sky.

One loud scream.

One very long wail echoed throughout the galaxies.

Jamie leapt over the downed barrier toward the wail and knelt beside her sobbing grandfather holding his bloodied wife. A spear from the fence pierced her grandmother's chest, stabbing her heart. Her breath slowed.

"Liz stay with me. Stay with me," Grandpa begged.

CHAPTER TWENTY-ONE

Light Channel

Before a blink of the eye, Commander-in-Chief Belcor Williams ordered intergalactic sonic transport of Commander Elizabeth Glosomore to Light Channel along with her husband, children and grandchildren.

Light Healer Assistants ushered the family into a glassed balcony that overlooked a spacious six hundred square feet surgical theater. It was stunning with its pure iridescent white walls and ceiling. An enormous multifaceted and multicolored glass orb, about twelve feet in diameter, hung suspended in the middle of the room.

Jamie and her family observed as the robotic technology provided the Light Healer team of physicians and nurses with images of the penetrating spearhead, the heart and surrounding tissues. The long, flexible arm moved at many angles around Jamie's grandmother. It revealed a traumatic puncture of the muscular chest wall and a blood-filled pericardium. On a huge screen, the surgeons and family visualized the injury in the minutest detail.

Maneuvering robotic arms from their individual computer stations, one of the surgeons located a small laceration of her upper left lobe of her lung and pulmonary artery. It was actively bleeding and leaking pulmonary fluid. He performed endotracheal intubation immediately.

Two other surgeons explored the wound of the left ventricle, which hemorrhaged significantly. They opened the pericardium, removed the spearhead, evacuated the blood from the chambers, synthetically patched the left ventricle wound and sealed it with biological glue.

Commander Elizabeth Glosomore's respiratory and heart rates stabilized. To increase her mortality chances, the medical technicians transferred her from the surgical table into a cylindrical tube, called Light Passage.

The group watched as robotic arms strapped the patient in and covered her with spun gold cloth. The surgical bay lights dimmed. Mesmerized, Jamie and her whole family watched the Light Healing process. The tube filled with pulsating rainbow colors, alternating with brilliant sunset colors and back to pastels. The cylinder rotated clockwise, counterclockwise, horizontally, and vertically in repetitive patterns. During each cycle, the colors of lights intensified. At each significant step, the technicians gently ejected Commander Glosomore from the tube and examined her. Respiratory and heart rates had rallied. The surgeons repeated this process multiple times.

After her grandmother's eighth transport through the Light Passage and discharge, Jamie watched the assistants lower the suspended sphere, roll Grandma's gurney into it, close the door and append the orb again.

"This orb contains concentric spheres. Each sphere is, in a way, a corner of heaven. We have done all we can for Commander Glosomore. Now it is up to her. She will experience the Genesis Light and will have to decide between life and death," Uncle Belcor explained.

Jamie felt someone's arm wrap around her waist. She looked around into Griff's face.

"All ninety-four teens are safe, Jamie. A few are in the hospital here. I hurried to be with you as soon as I could."

"She is in Genesis. Is this the source of your stone, Griff?"

"Yes, it is the source of power and Light for all stones of those who are protectors of the Light," Griff responded.

The dome spun. Inside the orb, Jamie saw the Southern Pinwheel, Sombrero and Milky Way Galaxies. She could easily identify Earth, HallowWinds, all the stars and planets. "The colors are unbelievable, so real, and so pure. Is Grandma flying through the universe?"

"In a way." Belcor continued, "She is witnessing a review of her life."

"She is a funny, good, and holy woman. I am not ready to let her go," Grandpa choked.

Jamie took her grandfather's hand and noticed how today aged him. His pronounced wrinkles took away the sparkle in his eyes, and made his shoulders slump.

As she was still gazing into his face, his usual twinkling eyes returned and a smile lit up his countenance. Light patterns in the room below changed, and Jamie turned to view her grandmother stepping out of the orb attired in a magnificent flowing white gown. She was radiant.

Everyone gasped. Only Jamie eked out a few words, "Did she choose heaven? She looks like an angel."

Commander Elizabeth Glosomore studied the room, looked up to the balcony and proclaimed, "Honey, I'm home."

Grandpa scurried down into her loving embrace.

An ecstatic applause and cheer filled the galaxy.

CHAPTER TWENTY-TWO

University Days

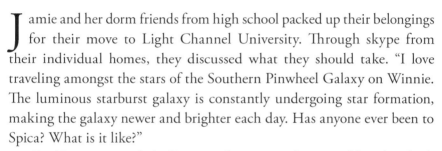

Jamie and her dorm friends from high school packed up their belongings for their move to Light Channel University. Through skype from their individual homes, they discussed what they should take. "I love traveling amongst the stars of the Southern Pinwheel Galaxy on Winnie. The luminous starburst galaxy is constantly undergoing star formation, making the galaxy newer and brighter each day. Has anyone ever been to Spica? What is it like?"

BirdSong responded, "I went there once for my oldest brother's graduation. I know it is the brightest star in Virgo constellation, and the name means ear of grain. Virgo holds an ear of wheat in her left hand."

"That's right, Birdie. Wasn't Virgo connected somehow with the goddess of the harvest?" Trish inquired.

"Not sure, but I love the star's bluish white color," Maria responded. "Griff will surely lecture us on the finer details about the university and Spica."

The girls laughed and chatted away as they packed with such eagerness.

****

Griff's uncle rented the duplex next door to his mansion for his nephew and friends. He met the teens outside to present them with their keys. "Ladies and gentlemen, I would love to take you on a tour of your new home that I had renovated for you. We will start with the girls' side here on the left." Uncle Belcor unlocked the door and continued. "As you can see, the downstairs consists of a sizeable laundry, a half bath and one super large open concept kitchen, dining, and living area. I hope, ladies, I have chosen the right color palette for you and that it looks feminine enough. Some of my female officers gave me some help."

"It is perfect, Uncle Belcor. I love that impressive double-sided stone fireplace. Look it opens into both the dining and living area," Jamie said with elation.

The girls took their time opening up the kitchen cabinets. "Wow, there is already lots of food, dishes, everything we need," Kattie exclaimed.

Belcor grinned. "Let's head upstairs."

"This loft is awesome. I love that we can see the whole downstairs from here," Maria said as soon as she stepped foot on the landing.

"It is a great feature. Does our side look like this? Or are you just doing this for the girls?" Griff teased his uncle.

"You'll see soon enough, young man. The second floor has six bedrooms with their own baths on this side, seven on the other side of the duplex. They are all furnished the same, but I have left a gift card in each room so you can buy your own linens. Towels, window treatments and anything else you want to personalize your space. My chauffeur will take you ladies shopping this afternoon. This evening we will have a black-tie dinner at my house. You will find in your bedroom closets plenty of choices for evening gowns." Each young woman hugged Belcor with gratitude.

Hai followed Lois into the first bedroom on the right, and hollered out, "I hope we get to go shopping too. Look at the amount on this card." All the teens gawked in disbelief.

"Yes, gentlemen, you have a card in your rooms too, as well as dinner jackets and bow ties. Griff has his own car. I have arranged for him to drive you to an appropriate gentleman's shop to purchase your toiletries and linens."

"I claim this room here on the left. The view of this huge tree reminds me of TimberWood. Uncle, where do these stairs go?" Jamie bounded up a smaller set of stairs next to her room. Everyone quickly followed her.

"The building's attic has been converted into one huge game and entertainment center that spans across both sides of the duplex. Stupendous," Jamie shouted as she skipped down the stairs into the boys' side.

"This is so cool," Trish added. The others stared with protuberant eyes at the multiple computers, the pool table, ping pong table, two lane bowling, electronic and table games. They scrutinized the stacks of movies and music in every genre.

"I am really proud of this space. Everything here was hand selected by me," Belcor boasted.

"Griff, this is your favorite game. Griff? Where are you?" Uncle Belcor asked as he began his descent. "Are you and Jamie down here?"

"Boo," the pair hollered as they jumped from behind a half opened door.

"Well, I see you have found the exit to the great deck. Nice, huh? It will make a great outdoor study area up here in the trees, Jamie."

"Study area? We can see your deck real well from here. From this perch we can spy on you and your guests," Griff chuckled.

"We will see who spies on who," Belcor countered. "Below the deck are the bedrooms. Follow me." The threesome went down two flights of stairs into the backyard. "This area under the bedrooms is a great space for your dragons and other pets, and look a patio area with grills already in place." They each selected a comfortable lawn chair and chatted away about their upcoming courses and mission experiences.

Belcor is so fatherly and generous. He likes to pamper. I wonder. "Are you married, Uncle Belcor, or have children?" Jamie quizzed.

"I was engaged a long time ago, but Louise was in a very tragic accident. She laid in a coma for three years. I spent every day after school at the hospital, pouring out my heart and soul to her hoping she would awake. She roused up briefly. I was thrilled to have her back. She was talking, sitting and eating. We were so hopeful. A week later, she had a stroke and died. I was Griff's age at the time of the accident. Guess I never met another woman like her. Instead, I overindulged on my nieces and nephews. But Griff is the only one still young enough to make rotten."

"You sure are spoiling us, Uncle Belcor."

"I love doing it. I think of all of you as my own flesh and blood."

The rest of the teens finished their tour and eventually caught up with Uncle Belcor, Jamie and Griff.

"I am going home to get things ready for your dinner. See you at 8:00 p.m. sharp," Uncle Belcor directed, clicked his heels, and walked over to the fence between their yards. He cleared his throat loudly, so everyone would look his way. He scaled the eight-foot high wooden privacy fence with ease.

"Show off," Jamie yelled after him. Laughter on both sides of the fence.

****

The day concluded with a wonderful dinner at Belcor's home. After the bourbon glazed salmon banquet, Belcor displayed an exquisite violin. "Will you play for us, Jamie?"

She felt a chill up her spine, as she positioned the instrument on her collarbone, lightly supporting it with her left shoulder. Jamie raised the bow so gracefully as if it floated over the strings. She arched the fingers of her left hand over the fingerboard. They danced as sound emanated from the scrolls. She played beautifully several of her own compositions. Jamie noticed Griff gazing at her intently. "I have a special request, Jamie. Would you please play *Nature's Melodic Pause*?"

"Sure, Griff," she beamed. "You know how much that piece means to me. I would be honored to play it." After the brief introduction to the piece, a piano began to play. Jamie turned to see Griff sitting with such dignified yet relaxed posture as he softly massaged the keys, creating enchanted accompaniment. The pair played as one. Jamie watched the group with pleasure. Their friends gaped at the couple and whispered to each other.

After the piece was finished, Jamie charmingly curtsied to Griff. "I didn't know you played. You have such an amazing power of expression and a brilliant technique. You never cease to amaze me, but that is not a gift to hide." *If I were not already in love with him, this would do it.*

"Belcor taught me how to play, my lady. Glad it pleases you." Griff stood, bowed and then kissed Jamie's cheeks.

When the applause finally ceased, Jaden jested, "When are you two getting married, Cuz?"

Blushing, Jamie simply replied, "I haven't been asked."

The boys all chanted "Ask, ask, ask her."

Griff shot over to the fireplace, grabbed a saber that hung above the mantle, and pointed at the group, "I will when it is the right time."

The teasing worsened with comments like — chicken, Griff loves Jamie, when will be the right time and more. Observing that Griff was growing angry, Uncle Belcor finally stood up and commanded them to stop. "This is between these two young people only. Tomorrow is a big day at the University. It is getting late."

The young college students said their good-byes and expressed their gratitude for their wonderful first day and night on Spica. They headed next door with leftovers. Jamie and Griff stayed behind to help Uncle Belcor clean up a bit.

When they left, the couple went for a long walk.

****

"I walked into that one when I mentioned the right time to ask you, didn't I?" Griff asked. "Do we need to talk about what happened?"

"Griff, I'm sorry. I should not have said that you had not asked me. It just sorted blurted out on its own."

"That's okay Jamie. It made me realize we need to talk about the next step of our relationship. You know I want to ask you. I will ask you when it is the right time. My response was honest. We have not discussed this yet. It seems like we should wait until we are a little older, say after college and our officer careers are established."

"A part of me wants us to get married right now. However, logically and practically, waiting makes more sense. I love you with all my heart and have since that day I fell out of TimberWood's branches into your arms. Each day my love for you grows stronger. Tonight's piano playing made me want to propose to you."

"I wanted to save my playing for just the right moment too. Tonight felt like the right time to reveal my secret talent to you. Jamie, my love, you have my heart already. Someday soon, I will give everything I am and have to you." He gently caressed her face in his hands, and lovingly pulled her closer. Jamie leaned into her beloved and their lips converged. Their kiss lingered longer than usual. Then they quietly walked hand in hand to their new home on Spica.

****

"I can't believe I have been living here for four months already." Jamie opened up her winter semester schedule. "Yikes, this semester is fuller than the first one. Now I know why I did not see very much of you, Griff. This is hard stuff." Jamie and Griff sat on a couch together on the girl's side studying. "Guess I will be buried in books for the next three and a half years. Sounds like an eternity of cramming. It is what I value, so I know it will be worth it in the long run."

"You are right about that. With the university's expectation that students concentrate in a specific area of study and at the same time achieve a mastery in interdisciplinary studies, it is intense. Then we have mission or patrol assignments every other weekend. The first year is hardest. It is better for me this year. What are you taking this semester?"

"Well, as you know there is boot camp. In six weeks, I have to be up to a three-mile run and a five-minute water thread. Every muscle I own already hurts. I have mechanics, transport techniques, basic office skills, thermodynamics, archery, Bengali and French, Espionage 101 and three natural science courses. That is not to mention my continued study in my degree areas of fine art and music."

"It will only get worse, but hopefully, you have already heard the lecture on balance, meditation and relaxation. If not, I need to give it to you," Griff offered.

"I understood the lecture, but practicing it is so hard. What are you taking?"

"Just foreign policy, three languages which are getting mixed up in my head, aerodynamics, organizational behavior and leadership, herbalism, boxing, two social science courses, intergalactic atmosphere phenomena, spaceship maneuvers, Espionage 201 and cooking."

"Glad to hear about that last course. You need it, buddy."

"I thought my lasagna was pretty good last night," Griff countered.

"Oh, sure your tomato soup was very tasty." Jamie took her fist and gently punched Griff's arm.

"Looks like we are both on duty this weekend. What is your assignment?"

"Patrol of the perimeters of Black Eye Galaxy. Activity there has increased lately." Jamie yawned. "So I guess we are spying on them."

"I have the same patrol. Good. At least we can spend the weekend together."

"Hope we don't run into any skirmishes. I am exhausted. Good night, Griff."

"Hmm, guess you are telling me to go home. I get it. I am worn-out also. Sweet dreams," Griff said as he headed out the door to the other side of the duplex.

Jamie blew a kiss. "Hopefully, but they would be sweeter if I had a real kiss."

With a shot of energy, Griff leapt like a stag. They melted into each other's arms and affectionately kissed.

CHAPTER TWENTY-THREE

Black Eye

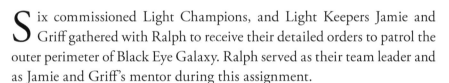

Six commissioned Light Champions, and Light Keepers Jamie and Griff gathered with Ralph to receive their detailed orders to patrol the outer perimeter of Black Eye Galaxy. Ralph served as their team leader and as Jamie and Griff's mentor during this assignment.

"I know you think we are to serve as patrollers this weekend, but our orders are more serious than that," Ralph explained. "We have to be very careful as we approach the galaxy. So, each of us will be equipped with special cloaking devices. These tools simply transmit light from one side of the object or person to the other so you don't see what is in between." Ralph demonstrated with a pitcher of water and then continued, "The band of dust around Black Eye hides the stars in the central region, the core of the evil activity. The strip absorbs light from the stars making the sorcerers very difficult to observe. When it is dark, we will be travelling through the black dust particles under the eye. We then proceed into the galaxy's core to a particular star where we believe the commander-in-chief of Dark Particles lives. We are to infiltrate his castle and learn as many details as possible about him, his surroundings and his forces. Jamie, you have a question?"

"How will we record our findings?" Jamie asked.

"You have in your kits, a powerful thermal imager that measures heat and temperature. This provides us with the incredible ability to identify the location, type and number of animals or persons in any enclosure. It will also note weaponry and resources." Ralph pointed a palm size tool toward the next room to their right. On the small screen, heat showed the images of nine human shaped beings with eight in sitting position and one standing. "This instrument is clipped to your uniform shoulder strap, and serves as our intercommunication device with command central as well as with each other. All images will be immediately relayed to Light Channel for interpretation and mapping. Anything else?"

"Is combat anticipated?" Griff inquired.

"Absolutely. We should be prepared," Ralph said. "Your backpacks have extensive weapons. Please take a moment to examine your equipment and make sure your weaponry is in good order. We will up in 30 minutes."

Jamie and Griff rode side by side on their dragons with the six Light Champions surrounding them. The visual of the galaxy was haunting but had a peculiar beauty. The team hovered around the lower part of the galaxy, the crescent that mimicked a black eye. It was in constant motion, constricting and expanding. The gases mixed and collided, emitting more stars and sending them into the core of the galaxy. Slowly working their way through the dust band, the Light team noticed thousands of luminous bodies.

"Activate crew and dragon cloaking," Ralph commanded. "We travel as close as possible from here. Do not separate for any reason. If we are noticed, we should be seen as one unrecognizable body."

Exhilarated by their descent, Jamie experienced a rush of adrenalin, which quickly turned to fear as they moved closer into the dark core of evil. *The galaxy's center is so bright, but so sinister at the same time.*

The team followed Ralph's lead to the star, Morti, the brightest in the cluster. As a unit, they transmitted thermal pictures to Light Channel command center.

"This is LC Command. We have what we need. Exit now. Turn off imaging units. Your squad discovered. Eight kilometers south of you. Stay cloaked. Use alternate plan."

"Roger that," Ralph responded. The Light team did as he charged. Instead of flying back through the black dust, they flew to the opposite side of the galaxy in seconds.

"This is LC command. Dark Particles followed decoy to black perimeter. One lone figure in pursuit of you. Not identifiable. Sending image now for identification."

"Roger that. Anyone in group able to recognize the image?"

"Oh no," Griff exclaimed. "That is Braxton, my uncle."

"Your uncle not friendly?" Ralph inquired.

"Heck, no. That is Belcor's brother, and they used to be a lot alike. However, Braxton changed when he started searching for his kidnapped children. He joined Dark Particles force as an undercover agent in hopes of finding them. However, he became ensnared under the dome of evil," Griff enlightened. "He is very evil. Guilty of many crimes, including the torture of children."

"This is Belcor. It is far worse than you know, Griff. He was hooked on the promise of power with Dark Particles. The tempters lured him so deceivingly that he no longer knows good from evil, light from dark. Saddest of all is the capture of his heart. It is a tomb of anger, death wishes and cruel tortuous actions. He spurned your aunt Ruth, and no longer cares about his children. We believe Braxton is now the DP's commander-in-chief. His mission is to have the whole universe under his control. He wishes to perpetuate maliciousness, wickedness and immorality. Be very careful, Griff. All of you."

"Orders, Commander Williams? Should we destroy or monitor him?" Ralph asked.

"Do whatever is necessary," Belcor commanded.

****

Braxton appeared out of nowhere in front of the team. He wore a black medallion draped around his neck. Black smoke swirled from the gem and engulfed the squad.

Belcor, he is sucking all of us into his spell. No control. Jamie tried to send a message. No response heard. *Ralph, can you hear me?*

My brain feels like it is exploding. Braxton is probing my thoughts. Reading our plans. He probably hears me talking to you. Must be silent. Ralph let out a sigh that sounded painful and leaned heavily into his dragon's neck. Ralph and the other Light Champions hung on feverishly to their pets. Then they disappeared.

Jamie saw Griff on Squirt, his newly acquired and huge dragon, about twenty feet away. She yelled, *"Griff, Braxton is stirring his medallion. Can you hear me? Are you okay? Where is everybody else?"*

Winnie responded, "Griff has a head injury. Braxton possesses the other team members, including their dragons. He has them in his cloak. It is up to you and me, Jamie. Black dragons approach. I can't fight off that many."

Rubbing her gem, Jamie commanded her MoonStone to form white dragons to counterattack the black ones produced by Braxton's BlackStone. The warring dragons clashed in galactic space, thrashing their leathery wings and spiked tails against one another. The white dragons shot out fireballs that struck the black dragons and trapped them in ovens of fire until they disintegrated. The more powerful white dragons with larger wingspan survived. They thrashed their wings, blowing the black dragons' ashes away.

"Protect Griff," Jamie ordered the white dragons. They encircled him and his dragon, and with their powerful wings moved them closer to Jamie and Winnie.

"You can't win little lady and my stupid little nephew," Braxton shrieked. He held up his hand, exposing his gold ring with skull and crossbones wrapped around a red jewel. He made a fist, shooting light from the ring's gem. The ray projected an image of the skull with crossbones into the dark night, branding the atmosphere with his insignia. "How dare you invade my territory! Everything that enters it becomes mine."

Jamie, I am here. Texter and Jaden are with me, Kattie uttered without speaking. *Turn on the cloaking device so Braxton cannot see you. I will take human form and serve in your place.*

Glad you are here, Kattie, but I do not understand why you would exchange places with me.

Kattie explained. *If he thinks he has you, he will let Griff go. You can get Griff to safety, and come back for us. Texter and Jaden will keep me safe. Please let us do this.*

Are you sure?

Yes. Texter and Jaden will conceal Griff, Scrunch, Squirt and the white dragons. On the count of three. One, two, three, Kattie counted.

The white dragons, Squirt, Scrunch and Griff were veiled simultaneously with Jamie's shrouding. Her identical twin took her place sitting on Winnie's shoulders. She watched her sister, without any resistance, be suctioned into a dog size cage beneath Braxton's enormous black robe. She caught a glimpse of other cages under his coat.

Winnie turned on her concealer to escape and left a trail of debris behind her. "What happened to that dragon?" Braxton demanded as he twirled around. "Who or what destroyed her? Where is Griff and the other dragons? What is going on here?"

"You have me. I am the one you wanted," Kattie screamed in her disguise as Jamie. "I am the most powerful catch."

"Hmmm. I wanted Griff too, but you will lure him to me." Braxton took flight with his prisoners back to Morti. Texter and Jaden followed with the team of white dragons.

****

Jamie stopped the flow of blood from Griff's head wound and revived him with her MoonStone. She gave him some protein bars and water from her backpack, as they discussed a strategy.

They took cover in Black Eye's outer band, where they would be better able to reestablish communications with LC Command.

"Belcor, Griff and I are okay. Others captured. Kattie took my place," Jamie explained.

"I know about Kattie. She has Texter and Jaden as well as other Special Manifestation Forces with her. Light Champions are near. Wait until their arrival for strike on Braxton's castle," Belcor responded. "More later. Roger and out."

On an uninhabited star near Morti, Jamie and Griff sat in silence, a silence that was quickly broken with belligerent voices. "Who is that?" Jamie whispered.

"It's Braxton, but this is odd," Griff said. "He's arguing with his shadow."

"Really weird. Look over there," Scrunch pointed. Braxton's shadow was trying to free itself from the soles of his feet.

Jamie grabbed Griff's arm. "That can't be, can it? Can we lose our shadow?"

"I want your power and your life. Why should I be stepped on and you get to walk upright? I am leaving," the shadow said with disdain. The shadow screeched, pulled himself from Braxton's feet, and became three-dimensional, puffing up like a balloon. Its eyes were black as mold and his pupils as red as hot coals on fire. He wore a hooded robe, with a skull bone for a face.

Braxton sunk deeper into the darkness. His shadow stayed as a threatening presence. "My name is Death Skull. My presence means someone will die."

The shadow discharged boiling water from its skull openings. A brisk wind roared past Braxton's shadow and carried his searing heat toward Jamie. She stood her ground. "I'm not afraid of you. You are just a shadow, Death Skull. You'll be the one to disintegrate." She made a fist, waving it back and forth, and threatening Death Skull.

The skull's shiny orange eyes flashed. "No way. I plan to rip you apart." Its teeth gritted against each other, sending sound waves that bombarded Jamie, rocking her body. It transmitted suggestions into her brain, encouraging her to hurt Griff.

Jamie grabbed Griff's arm to steady herself, but his vibrations passed into her. She quivered like a branch in a windstorm, pounded on Griff's chest, and screamed, "I don't want to hurt you, Griff. I know Death Skull is a liar. You do not have another girlfriend. You don't."

"Stop, stop." Griff yelled and pulled at the medallion around his neck. "I can't stand the vibrations in my brain. Some voice is telling me to get rid of this before you use it against me, Jamie. Lies. Lies. Stop telling me lies. Whoever you are, stop."

Illusions of Kattie floated toward Griff's face. "I'll help you." She pulled on his medallion. Bolts of electricity stung her. "Ouch, give the medallion to me."

"Where did you come from? Who are you? You are not Kattie. Liar be gone," Jamie shrieked.

"It's me. I am Kattie. I came to save you, Sis. Griff is just like his uncle, Braxton." Her voice sputtered like sizzling grease.

"Hurry Kattie, Jamie, anybody. Get this thing off me. The pain is unbearable." Griff writhed, making violent efforts to remove it from around his neck. He buckled over and expelled air explosively from his lungs. "It's choking…"

Jamie ferociously knocked the invented Kattie to one side, pulling Griff away from her clutches. Jamie pleaded. "Griff, listen to me. I am telling you the truth. Do not take the medallion off. You need the LightStone's defenses. It links you to your uncle, to Light. That is not Kattie. Whoever it is wants to destroy you and me." Jamie touched her heart. "Griff, use your heart to make your decision."

Griff held Jamie's arms. He slid down into a kneeling position, holding his head and moaning from the pain. "My heart believes you, Jamie."

"Scrunch help him stay focused and calm." Jamie pulled her bokken from its sheath, saluted and charged toward imposter Kattie. "I'm not taking your deceptions." She thrust the sword into her chest. The pretend Kattie disappeared.

Griff sheepishly looked up at Jamie. "His control is weakening. The head is still throbbing with sonic booms and vibrations."

"His control? Braxton's? Or the shadow?"

"Braxton is the greatest of all deceivers. That is his magic, his sorcery. I have not ever met Death Skull before." Griff moaned. "Where is Death Skull?"

"You looking for me?" Death Skull moved toward Jamie, directing high-pitched sounds that blitzed her brain. She dropped the bokken, grasped her head, and howled in agony.

Griff touched his LightStone over and over. Most of the rays hit Death Skull. A few missed their mark. "My gem never fails. Something's blocking its powers."

Jamie felt herself being pulled into Death Skull's interior. She resisted with all of her might.

Griff fired off rays from his medallion to make a barrier that blocked the high-pitched sounds and bounced them back at the Death Skull.

When the sound waves struck Death Skull, he became rattled. He shot piercing rays of heat toward the waves, liquefying the sound created by Griff, making it fall mute into the ground.

Death Skull sucked Jamie toward himself. She grasped a petrified tree. She felt the full force of the magnetic suction, yanking her body toward a place devoid of light and draped in stench. Jamie thrashed her arms and legs, but she was no match for the Death Skull. The upper half of her body disappeared inside his robe, while the lower half hung outside.

Death Skull twitched and wrenched Jamie's entire body into his interior.

Jamie took a few deep breaths to focus her energy as she used her father's pocketknife to cut holes in the shadow's robe from the inside.

As the robe flew higher, it screamed in pain from the cuts. Worms crawled around the edges of the holes. They licked the bones of the Death Skull. Jamie did not let them get close to her face. She stared out of the holes, watching Griff circling Braxton's shadow.

The robe seemed heavily muscled, as Jamie's hands slid along its slimy interior surface. Jamie felt as if Death Skull had wrapped her in a membrane with its suffocating folds, cutting off her air supply.

Death Skull boasted, "I'm going to give you the ride of your life."

Jamie struck him repeatedly from inside the hooded garment. "I won't let you take me over. I am in this to the end. Griff, can you get me out?"

Death Skull flew up into the air, using his speed to topple Jamie. She had the sensation of flying blind. She could hear and feel Griff and the dragons outside the cape, butting against the Death Skull. Griff yelled, "We will free you."

Jamie whispered into her diamond shaped communication device. "Hit his head. That's where he looks the most vulnerable from my view."

Winnie and Squirt used their sharpened horns to traumatize the skull, banging it ferociously. Death Skull reeled in pain, and spiraled up against something very hard and pointed. It struck Jamie between her shoulder blades, knocking the breath out of her. She twisted with pain. Then Death Skull swooped upwards and banged Jamie against a massive, granite façade. She screamed as she collided with the jagged stone.

In the darkness, she touched her MoonStone, but it was powerless. She silently cried in desperation.

Jamie tossed around inside the shadowy robe as Death Skull spiraled upward and crashed through glass windows. The impact sounded like an explosion. Looking out one of the openings at the bottom of the being, Jamie watched as falling stain glass hit the cathedral's terrazzo floor. *Are we in St. Michael's Cathedral? Are we on Earth?*

Griff hollered to Jamie from outside the robe. "Yes. Are you ok?"

Jamie rocked back and forth, testing her limbs. She could still move, though it was painful. "I guess, but I think I am going to puke."

"We'll get you out as soon as we can," Griff said.

Scrunch popped inside one of the holes, quickly whizzing past Jamie and rapidly backed out. "Ugh. Death Skull's stench is awful."

Jamie choked. "Griff, jab at Death Skull."

"I can't use my sword. I might hurt you," Griff said.

Jamie pleaded with him. "Just pierce it!"

"When I hear your voice Jamie, I'll hit away from you. So keep yelling."

"Let's do it. There is one good thing. Death Skull cannot ram into something without hurting himself as he did with the stain glass window. He is out for the moment."

Griff quickly tried to make an opening big enough for Jamie to get out. Noises, like the rush of wind, circled through the organ tubing. Jamie screamed as Death Skull hurtled her against the pipes. With each strike, the cylinders twisted out of shape, and the sounds from them became thunderous and dissonant.

The skull jumped up and down on the organ keys. The impact was so severe that the keys jammed and played the song, *Rest in Peace* repeatedly.

Jamie shielded her ears with her hands. "Shut it off." Jamie winced from the pain.

Death Skull snorted. "I want you to hurt. You have taken on the Dark Particles. That means pain and death."

Griff grabbed Death Skull from the back and toppled him to the ground. They wrestled with each other. One blow from Griff knocked Death Skull in the chest, hitting Jamie through the material and striking her head.

Blood dribbled from Jamie's nose. "That was a powerful punch."

Griff moaned. "How badly did I hurt you?"

"Let's see. I think you owe me a double fudge sundae if we ever get out of here. Please cut me out of here. I will dodge the cuts. Stay in a tight pattern."

A disgusting odor swirled around Jamie, and poured out through the holes including Death Skull's eyes, nostrils, and ears.

"No wonder I feel so ill." Jamie squirmed.

Griff took a few deep breaths. "The material is dense and almost impermeable. Scrunch and I are not making much headway. Can you slash the holes in the robe from the inside and make them larger?"

"There is a thick covering on the inside walls of the robe." Jamie gouged the cloth as the robe flew higher. Death Skull groaned with each cut or tear.

The robe whizzed out the broken window, past the gigantic clock on the front of one of the Cathedral's spires. It flew higher and banged Jamie against the arched openings of the bell tower. The robe struck the bells, and a pre-programmed song began to play, *A Song of Peace.*

Death Skull screeched, "I want no one to rest in peace. I want to terrorize all of you. All people of Light are to be tormented forever!"

"Well, you'll never quiet the *Song of Peace.* You don't have that power." Griff chased Death Skull as it soared out from the bell tower. Winnie, Squirt and Scrunch followed.

Jamie saw the landscape racing pass her as she stared out the holes. She shrieked when the Death Skull crashed into the clock.

The sharp point of the minute hand pointed skyward to a little past the XII. The robe swung back and forth from the arrowed clock hand, forcing Jamie's limp body to hang upside-down. Her left foot twisted and protruded through a rip in the fabric. In fear, she stayed completely still.

Jamie watched Scrunch and Griff talking with Winnie and Squirt nearby. "What are you planning?" she asked. No one answered. She amplified her voice and probed again. *No one hears me. Am I alive? I do not feel anything.*

Winnie and Squirt hovered near her.

"I'm right here, honey. On Squirt. We are going to get you down. Stay with me, Jamie. I love you," Griff spoke softly and tenderly.

I love you, Griff. Cannot make my voice sound. Is it too late? Am I dead and watching the action around my body?

Scrunch flew into the gold dust made from the whipping of his wings. He pumped them again to puff himself up. Then, he shot straight up in the air, and sneezed. Particles of stardust from a supernova filled the atmosphere and magically formed into a double-edged sword. The jeweled handle became the perfect seat from which Scrunch guided the sword.

Near Jamie's dangling foot, he cut a section in the robe as the bewitched worms crawled to avoid the sharp blade. More light found its way into the robe. Scrunch fluttered through an opening in the robe, and enlarged the hole. He did this repeatedly, expanding one hole at a time and gradually letting in light, similar to a slow rising sun. Enlarging the holes weakened both the robe and the shadow that it encased. The robe fell to the ground.

The dragons' hot breath dulled Jamie's senses. *I have some sensation. Am I free? My legs. I cannot feel my legs. Do I still have feet? Griff, can you hear me?* Griff was holding her hand. She went back in time to the day she fell into his arms. *Am I falling again, Griff?*

Griff called the Glosomores and Belcor for emergency assistance. Grandpa and Grandma quickly arrived on Rowdy. They rolled up towels borrowed from the cathedral rectory and placed them on both sides of Jamie's head. Grandpa Zack and Griff gently moved a piece of thin plywood behind her to immobilize her neck and spine, and belted her to it. Joined by two Light Champions, Griff and Grandpa lowered her to Winnie's back and strapped her on. He bent over her and kissed her tenderly. *I love you, Griff. I want to run my fingers through your hair, but my arms cannot move. Why can't I make them move?*

Winnie slowly and carefully took her precious cargo down to the sidewalk. Griff and Grandpa lowered her off Winnie's back and positioned her on something soft. She observed a man in a very bright white coat place a mask over her mouth and nose. Then, he made a small slit in her right arm and inserted a tube.

"Look Jamie," Griff said pointing.

Jamie moved her eyes in the direction of Griff's pointer to see Death Skull pull free of the tattered robe. The Skull soared through the air and attacked the shadow, ripped it from the clock and threw it to the ground. "Scat you lousy host."

Death Skull disappeared as he transformed into a speck. His threat filled the atmosphere. "You owe me, you blasted fools. Someone still has to die."

"Braxton." Jamie was barely audible. She wanted to point. The group around her followed the direction of her eyes. Braxton, who had watched the whole battle from a distance, dashed into the Cathedral. He came out with his emotionally and physically crushed shadow, with robe fragments attached. He stretched it out on the ground and stepped on it. "That's it. Attach yourself to me. I'm tired of listening to you."

"I don't want to join you ever again. I don't want you walking on me."

Braxton yelled, "We are stuck with each other. You have no choice."

"I'll have my revenge one day. I will switch roles with you. You will become me, nothing but a lowly shadow. I will be you, powerful and cruel." Deflated, the shadowy form reattached itself to Braxton. It became flat like any regular shadow. Braxton whirled away in a windstorm.

Vaguely aware that her aunt and uncle, Judd, Grandma and Grandpa and lots of others were present, Jamie felt her body surrender to peace and lapsed into a very deep sleep.

CHAPTER TWENTY-FOUR

Pain and Love

Jamie loved it when Griff came to visit at the Light Channel Medical Center every day to read to her. She retained all that he read, and studied over and over the material in her head when he left.

He also told her all about the rescue of the Light Champions, Kattie, Texter and Jaden from Braxton's castle. "After we left Morti, we were attacked by my Uncle Braxton and his shadow. Kattie saved the day by taking your place. The Light Champions used the detail that we collected with thermal imaging, to storm Braxton's castle and to release everyone who was imprisoned there. Over one hundred men and women, many Light Keepers and Champions were set free. You saved me, Jamie. I could never have survived Death Skull's deceitful power without you. You are so phenomenal, my love."

The only response Jamie gave was a slight squeeze with her left hand.

Jana, a massage therapist, arrived early each morning to manipulate Jamie's muscles in her back, arms and legs. *Glad I can still feel physical sensations. Jana is so strong, but so gentle.*

When Jana left, Brittany worked Jamie's muscle groups. Brittany would raise each leg, bend Jamie's knee, and straighten the leg again. She would roll Jamie over on her side, and raise her leg from the hip and lower it again. Brittany did similar exercises with Jamie's arms.

A young female aid, Sara, bathed and dress her in a clean gown after the two therapy sessions concluded. *She is shyer than the others are. It is so sad. She has been through so much. Sara has made me realize that grief and suffering can make us stronger.*

In early afternoons, three days a week, Nicole, a mental health nurse would stop by. *She inspires me, motivates me. The way she talks to me, I feel almost alive and not in a coma.*

The three therapists and the aid talked to Jamie throughout their whole sessions or bath. She knew all about their families, their hobbies, their dreams, and their lives. Jamie was so pleased that they each had been part of that first group of teens rescued from the dungeon. Nicole, Jana, Brittany and Sara were all five years older than their young passionate heroine was.

No matter how much they encouraged Jamie, she did not wake from her coma, move her limbs on her own, or open her eyes. Grandma and Grandpa, Kattie and Texter, Jaden, Uncle Jonathan and Aunt Esther, Uncle Belcor, all her friends at college and many of her professors created a constant parade of visitors.

Jamie dreamt of the day when her eyes would open and she would be able to get up out of that bed. She so wanted to respond to life.

Eight months after she slammed through the rose window at St. Michael's, Jamie had nighttime visitors. Mom and Dad came, and invited her to come to the other side with them.

No, I am not finished. There are still teens enslaved in the dungeons. I cannot stop until all the prisoners are freed. Braxton and all evil must be stopped.

Others can do it, Jamie. You have been successful. Look at Jana, Brittany, Nicole, Sara, Trish and Maria. Their lives are beautiful and meaningful. You gave that to them and the others, Mom responded.

There are more. I do not want to die yet. It is my destiny to do more. I want all the dungeon captives to be free. Seeing the therapists and aids here who have overcome such humiliation and degradation makes me want that for all of them.

Then you must wake up. You cannot stay here any longer in the bed. The therapists are working very hard to keep your limbs from atrophying. Only you can stop the progression of the paralysis. The longer you lay here, the longer it will take to reverse the damage. Dad spoke firmly but encouragingly. *You can will yourself awake. Are you afraid?*

A tear rolled down Jamie's face. She felt her left hand raise to wipe it away. *Nicole asked me the same thing. She said she was afraid of living forever in that dark hole. Yes, I am afraid of the next battles, of what I will see and encounter, of the pain and suffering I will witness that evil inflicts on good and innocent people, of what is required to accomplish my destiny. I feel so broken. Yet the mission is so great and takes so much energy and strength. I am afraid I will fail them.*

Your injuries were extensive, but all your bones have healed, sweetie. Mom reassured her.

You want to achieve your destiny without pain. Not very realistic, darling. Life has suffering and pain. Love is not easy. Justice is very hard work. If you want the glory of success, then you have to suffer for it, work for it. Dad added. *Your mind, heart and spirit are strong. Your body will follow.*

Honey, you are being a bit rough with her.

No, Mom. Dad is absolutely right. I have to face my fears of living and wake up. Jamie's eyes shot open to reveal her parents' beautiful smiles. *I am not dreaming. You really are here.*

Mom took her daughter's left hand into hers. *You are not dreaming. We were both with you on Black Eye, on Earth at St. Michael's, and here on Light Channel through your whole recovery process. We are always with you.*

Griff walked into the room, but did not see Jamie's parents. He moved right through them and took Jamie's left hand. "You have your eyes open. I missed those gorgeous eyes. Nurse," Griff called over the intercom system, "Jamie is waking."

A crew of medical personnel came in and ran some tests. Doctor Maltese listened carefully to her heart and lungs. Using a reflex hammer, he examined her legs and arms. "We have reaction in all but the right leg," he announced. "Let's do a full neurology workup tomorrow and brain scan. Jamie do you know who I am?"

"Yes, I do, Dr. Maltese. That is Griff and the nurse's name is Susan. I know the names of my therapists and the aid that bathes me each day."

"I was not expecting you to know my name. Did Griff or the nurse tell you my name before I came in?"

They both shook their heads, no.

The doctor asked a host of other questions. Without hesitation, Jamie spoke in well-formed sentences.

Griff quizzed her on the upcoming physics exam. She correctly answered every question.

"Remarkable. It is highly unusual for a patient to remember what she hears or senses while in a coma. Of course, we all know you are unusual in every respect, Jamie. There appears to be little residual neurological effect. Get some rest. I will see you early in the morning. Have you ever been told you are a hyperthymesiac?"

"I wish I could remember life's every moment. However, I have been told that I have both eidetic and photographic memory."

"Amazing. Just extraordinary," the doctor remarked as he headed out the door.

"Griff, don't leave yet. I just woke up and not ready for sleep. Let's savor this moment."

"It is okay, Griff, but don't stay long," Doctor Maltese suggested.

"Mom and Dad are here, Griff. They woke me up with a kick in the proverbial pants."

Mom and Dad laughed. "You deserved it," Dad said. "Good to see you, son. Thank you for loving and protecting our daughter."

"Yes, sir. It is a pleasure to see both of you again. Uncle Belcor has told me so much about you and your famous missions. I know where Jamie gets her keen sense of justice and her passion for life."

The four of them talked for hours about Griff's parents, life and death, Kattie's future, Jamie and Griff's future together.

They chatted and chatted until at last Jamie began to dose off to sleep. Jamie heard her father say, "Griff, when the right time comes, you know Judith and I will give you our daughter's hand in marriage."

"Thank you for your blessing, Sir. Jamie and I wanted your approval. Thank you very much. I best be going. Doctor's orders were for a short visit. I am sorry. I usually follow orders, Sir."

"Well, son, I am sure you are forgiven. This visit has been healing for all of us, but Griff please call us John and Judy, or mom and dad works for us too. I see Jamie is drifting off to sleep. Good night, son."

"Thanks again for your support. Good night, Mom and Dad."

From under her partially closed eyes, Jamie saw Griff warmly hug them. She felt the presence of her loving parents by her side and allowed herself to drift into a sound sleep.

****

Jamie missed the university campus, but enjoyed her time at Light Channel Medical and Rehab Center. With intense occupational, physical, massage and speech therapy, Jamie rapidly improved each day. She kept up with her academic studies and her art assignments. Jamie played her violin each evening for the other patients, bringing such calm and peace to the facility.

Sensei Liu came three times a week to continue her martial arts lessons. He taught her how to accommodate for the drag that persisted in her right leg. Even though her right side was predominant, her left side was now stronger. She excelled in the martial arts.

****

Thirty-two months had passed since she hung from the Cathedral's clock. With only her senior year to complete, her nine special and three ghost friends all came on release day escorting her to a grand send-off at Uncle Jonathan and Aunt Esther's home.

Rowdy, Rowena and Winnie all greeted her. "Wow, Winnie, look how you have grown," Jamie said. "I missed all of you so much."

She chatted with them for a few minutes, and then excused herself. Jamie bolted into the backyard and scampered up her favorite oak tree.

"You are a beautiful woman, Jamie. I have missed you and so longed for this day."

"And I have seen many trees these past months, but none of them will ever compare to you, TimberWood. I love you so much."

Griff climbed up the tree next to her, and the pair sat there for a very long time, leaving no detail out of their story about the past months. TimberWood listened adoringly.

****

Jamie's senior year went by very quickly. Jamie and Griff still lived in the duplex with their friends. Griff was now the proud owner. He had already been commissioned the previous spring as a Light Champion officer. Griff would receive his own squad once he completed his master degree studies.

Jamie and Kattie spent a lot of time together doing some sister things. They experimented with new recipes on the guys, and loved making the duplex homier with lots of bright colors and with many of their own art renderings.

Jamie sat on the balcony in deep thought. *I sure have enjoyed the maturation of my relationship with Kattie. We have never dressed alike, but we are more like twins now – best friends and sisters. Time does heal. Time is also running out too soon on my college years. I have the best suitemates in the whole universe. They are my sisters and my brothers, too.*

"Hi, Sis. Want some lemonade? Just made it." Kattie held two ice-cold glasses.

"Sure, thanks."

Kattie handed a glass to her sister and then curled up in the chair next to her. "Are you daydreaming or studying?" Kattie asked.

"Lost in my thoughts about the days to come. Time is moving by so fast. Has Texter given you a ring yet?" Jamie inquired.

"No, not yet. You do not have one either. Why are they waiting?"

"Perhaps for our graduation gift." Jamie responded.

"What are you two whispering about?" Griff asked as he bounded in the door. "What's for dinner? I'm hungry." Both girls laughed and headed downstairs to the kitchen.

★★★★★★★★

Graduation was an awesome ceremony. Jamie and the whole group, who lived in the duplex, won multiple awards. Some of the other students teased that Griff's uncle must have something to do with his neighbors' success.

"No, well-earned awards. Each of them," Uncle Belcor proudly answered when the ceremony had ended.

He had a policy at the university that no student would graduate without some special honor or award. His motivational skills with young people surpassed any other leader.

After graduation, the officers were commissioned and given their first command. Jamie was assigned to Griff's squadron. One week from graduation today, a very special assignment commenced.

Uncle Belcor, with a look of sadness in his eyes, gave his favorite nephew his orders. "Your squad is better equipped than any other to accomplish this."

"Yes, sir. Thank you, sir." Griff glanced at the orders without any change in facial expression, clicked his heels and saluted his commanding officer and beloved uncle. "We will not fail the Light, sir."

Without words, Griff's team knew the assignment, and knew they were on his team. They shared an unbreakable bond.

CHAPTER TWENTY-FIVE

The Mission

Jamie, Griff and the rest of the squad prepared for the extensive mission to evaporate Morti. Researchers and scientists developed a process in which to diminish the star, Morti. They fanned to increase the solar wind around Morti to gale force.

"This squad is a part of what is being called for this mission, Opaque Company. Our mission is to destroy those who wish to block radiant energy and Light," Griff began. "We will first bolster the flare of particles with immense magnetic field generators that we position on the uninhabited, but massive stars surrounding Morti."

Jamie added, "And since all stars transform hydrogen to helium by nuclear fusion, the generators will speed up that natural process by a million times. Eventually those stars will possess no more hydrogen to convert. These stars will expand quickly and produce two huge rounded projections of material on east and west sides of Morti. Up to this point, if all goes as planned, the stars' transformation will appear natural."

"The second stage of the mission is to mechanically quicken the pace of shock waves being blasted from the two projections inward toward Morti. These waves of gale force winds will transport powerful pulses of electromagnetic radiation. Morti's undeniable illumination as a giant red ball will cause the black eye itself to glow. Everyone will evacuate Morti and other inhabited stars in Black Eye Galaxy because of the intense heat," Griff reported. "Those who refuse to leave will evaporate when Morti implodes and their nuclear weaponry backfires."

"It will feel like doomsday to them. At that point, we begin our third and final step, the most challenging and death defying. Our military forces subdues the bolting Dark Particles," Jamie continued.

"Tomorrow we accompany our scientists to Black Eye to begin the installation of the generators. The Opaque Company consists of twelve squads of ten members each. Each squad will have a team of three scientists for whom we are responsible – to assist and protect. We leave at 3:00 a.m. from Light Spacecraft Center," Griff directed.

****

"This is Opaque One with company wares ready for takeoff," Roberto called.

"Countdown. Ten, nine, eight … We have lift-off," control officer responded.

"Roger that." Opaque One watched as twenty-three other craft lifted off behind them.

"Why so many? I thought there would be only twelve flights," Maria asked.

"Twelve are decoys in route to earth with generators for Indonesia as relief help from the recent tsunami. The twelve mission teams are cloaked," Griff responded. "Command only had twelve lift-offs verbally and visually."

The flight was uneventful and mesmerizing. "It is sad that such beauty has to be destroyed," Trish said.

"I thought so too, until I remembered who and what lives there. The universe will never have peace as long as such darkness and evil exists," Hai responded.

"True, but I was taught that evil would always exist in some way. How do we experience the Light as light if dark does not exist?" Keme questioned.

"Good point, but …" Trish hesitated. "If darkness becomes greater than the light … all I know is when I was in the dungeon, I only knew darkness. Light deprivation was killing my body, but more importantly it was killing my spirit."

The scientists on board Opaque One and the squad grew silent and reflective.

****

Opaque One landed on Star 1050 on the east of Morti without detection. Roberto and Udo checked in with the other ships. "Remember, if any ship is in trouble, at Griff's orders all craft exits or aborts at the same time," Udo prompted.

"Opaque One landed. Begin report Opaque Three," Roberto requested and received reports from odd numbered mission vessels.

Udo did the same for even numbered ships. "All positioned, Griff."

"Opaque One to all mission craft, suit up and exit in ten," Griff commanded. The teams wore space suits, since the twelve stars are uninhabitable. The countdown began. "Ten, nine, eight ..."

The teams of three scientists, with two Light Champions assisting, safely began the setup of the generators. Robotic assistants carried the generators off the craft and placed them on the stars as the scientists gave computerized directions. Four Champions stood guard and four remained on craft should speedy departure be necessary.

"Savannah, can you talk and work at the same time? If so, I would love to know the steps you are taking," Jamie suggested.

"This young woman is known as Queen of Questions," Griff said with a laugh.

Savannah, the lead scientist with Opaque One, explained as she commenced their work, "I like talking about it. Nuclear fusion reactors are powering up. Shortly, we will be able to test two things. First, if they cause a dramatic response too quickly, we will be detected. Second, we hope that the equipment will silently cause several atomic nuclei to become so attracted to each other that they just cannot resist getting very chummy. Once they are close, the nuclear force should draw them even closer and then force them apart. Familiarity should not last long. We want them repulsed by each other, resulting in a strong reaction. Look they are heating up right now." Savannah showed them a fiery red ball growing white with heat, on her monitor.

"Electrons are stripping now, Savannah. Clouds of hot ions formed," Ray, from the team of scientists, reported.

"Do we have magnetic control of the plasma clouds?" Savannah asked.

"Sure do. I am isolating the hydrogen and allowing its build-up," related another team member, Shane.

"Ray, check on the other teams," Savannah ordered.

"All in same phase in process, except eleven. Progression slowed because of meteor activity," Ray gave an account. "All is fine now. Should be caught up in five."

"Glad it wasn't detection," Griff said as he wiped the sweat from his brow. The teams waited to hear back from eleven that they were ready. The five minutes felt like eternity. "Check again on eleven. Five minutes are up."

"They are ready, sir. Here we go. The decisive moment. Full power on three. One, two and three," Savannah counted. She quickly amassed reports from the other stars. "All is working in full speed. If it goes as planned, the ears will be formed in five to seven days."

"The ears?" Jamie quizzed.

"Oh, that is what I call the two projections that will close in on Morti from the east and west sides. The dust will be rounded like ears, so the north and south sides are covered partially as well. The ears will be bigger than the head, Morti."

"That's funny. Morti's ears will be bigger than its head. I have a clear visual of that," Jamie responded. The whole team laughed heartily.

"A little humor goes a long way when the stress level is high," Shane interjected.

"We stay to monitor the equipment to make sure that each generator and nuclear fusion reactors are operating at the same speed. We will take shifts for the rest of this process," Savannah narrated.

"Okay, Jamie, Savannah and I will take first shift out here. Inside teams need to spell each other also. Everyone else here needs to rest," Griff structured. "Hai, Maria and Ray will be next on detail. Would that work, Savannah?"

"Sounds good, Griff. Thanks for asking. Good team work," Savannah replied.

Over the next three hours, Jamie and Griff learned all the controls on the generators and reactors. Every ten minutes the team checked each piece of equipment, and gathered reports from the other eleven stars. All cloaking seemed to work smoothly.

Just as second shift began, they heard. "Mayday. Mayday. Enemy fire on eleven. We have been detected."

"Report on elements," Savannah ordered. After she heard the readings, she commanded with gravity, "Use back-up plan six and get out of dodge."

"What is back-up plan six?" Jamie asked.

"They are to destroy the equipment and leave. However, the hydrogen has already transformed into enough helium that when the machinery detonates the attackers will be destroyed and so will the star. There will be no evidence of the equipment," Savannah looked like she could explode.

"And the Opaque Eleven team?" Jamie asked the hard question as she looked at Griff.

"We can only hope." Savannah, with tears in her eyes lowered her head, staring at her monitors. "We wait."

Griff and Jamie both looked through telescopic lenses. The white heated ball imploded, and then exploded. Spacecraft on approach from Morti were in view and went up into smoke.

"There they are. There they are. Look to the north. They went north instead of east." Savannah jumped up and down in excitement. "Opaque Eleven, can you hear me? Please say you can." No response.

"Opaque Eleven. We have you on visual. Report please," Griff tried.

"Opaque Eleven. This is Opaque One. Respond," Udo tried from inside the spacecraft.

Static came over all systems, and then a weak and broken voice communication. "Opaque One … eleven. Burn injuries … team and spacecraft … Rescue needed. Cloaking down … hope … hidden behind dust."

"Opaque One, this is twelve. We can respond. Medic on board."

"Roger that, twelve. Ten, can you respond as military backup?" Griff inquired.

"On our way, sir," ten replied.

Jamie, Griff and Savannah poured over some galaxy maps and drawings. "With Star 1061 gone, can we still achieve formation of the ears?" Jamie asked.

Savannah checked her monitors. "Sure, it is possible. Look at the shapes the dust created. Resembles the top of an ear, don't you think? The only problem is debris. We have to make sure that it gives off no mechanical evidence. We must figure out the matter of Eleven not being able to cloak now."

"I'll do some analysis on the cloaking," Griff responded.

"Once the team is rescued, we will destroy the craft and blow the debris northward. Savannah, will that wind velocity counteract your gale force?"

"Good question, Jamie. I sure hope not. Let me see." Savannah did some calculations. "Looks like it should work."

"Then we can surmise that phase one of the mission may be able to continue? I should report to Command Central and to Belcor," Griff added.

Savannah and Jamie agreed with Griff, and listened attentively to his report.

"Move forward, Griff, with the remainder of your plan. Keep me informed," Belcor said with a fatherly voice.

"Will do, sir. Over and out."

****

"Opaque Twelve docking with Eleven, Sir," Udo informed as he displayed the visual of the procedure on a large screen. "The visual for you, sir."

"Wow, Eleven is massively destroyed. Do we have any further report on injuries?" Griff inquired.

"Three have life-threatening burns. All team members have serious injury," Roberto conveyed.

Jamie watched pensively. "Amazing that Opaque Eleven team members can still perform flight and docking processes with their physical injuries."

"Docking complete. Transfer of passengers initiated."

"Thanks, Udo. Having a medic satellite to take care of injuries is like a floating emergency room in space. Very cool." Griff requested, "Is ten nearby?"

"Yes, sir. They are prepared for demolition as soon as all is clear."

"Sir, we have interpreted the coded communications from Morti," Roberto conveyed. "From their codes, we deduce that seven unmanned reconnaissance planes were sent to investigate meteoric activity. Morti's main television news station just reported Star 1061 exploded and the scouting planes destroyed by the star's blast. They are telling Morti residents that they are in no danger from the cloud that exists to their north. The station interviewed one of their leading scientists. He is saying it will take thousands of years for it to effect Morti. Propaganda at work."

"Have we broken code enough to know what Braxton is telling his command?" Jamie asked.

"Working on that now," Udo replied.

"News about eleven," Roberto alerted. "The doctors and medical team report that the Opaque Eleven team members responsible for the task of setting the explosives are all acutely burned. One is deceased and the other two are in critical condition with burns over ninety percent of their bodies. They are under the specialized care of the Burn Care team. I am patching the lead Burn Care specialist to you now, Griff."

"Sir, this is Dr. Zokowski. All on the satellite are sorry for your loss of one of your team members. We are in hopes that we can prevent further mortality. All patients have been treated and wrapped. They are in the most critical phase of their healing. We have started each of them on intravenous fluids. Our biggest challenge is providing enough fluid replacement to maintain perfusion. Effective and rapid intervention is paramount to prevent burn shock. Each patient is receiving antibiotics, pain, and anti-anxiety medications. The two most critically burned are receiving ultrasound mist therapy to clean and stimulate their massive wound tissue. The goals for their continued treatment are to control pain, remove dead tissue, prevent infection, reduce scarring, regain function and address emotional needs. Your team may want to offer spiritual support respectful of their individual preferences for speaking to their creator. My staff is preparing them for transfer to Channel's Life Flight within the hour. I will be on their treatment team at Light Channel Medical Center's Burn Unit."

"Thank you, Doctor. Your report was relayed to Commander-in-Chief Belcor Williams. He will be meeting with the families of the injured today, and will give them your report. I am indebted to your team for the effective care of our injured," Griff responded.

"We will keep you updated, Sir."

"Roger, Doctor Zokowski. Over and out." With a very somber voice, Griff continued, "Opaque Company, we have lost one of our comrades, Francisco Verazinni. Moment of silence, please … Thank you. Please remember our seriously injured Opaque Eleven team as they begin their healing."

"All patients on Life Flight and headed to the infirmary, sir. Twelve returning to Star 1062. Ten is ready for elimination of disabled craft," Udo reported.

"Opaque Ten, let's hear another explosion," Griff ordered. "We have solved the issue of mechanical evidence. Opaque One is now managing Eleven's cloaking device. It will remain attached to all debris."

"Roger that."

The countdown began again, and then an explosion to the north of Morti and the former Star 1061.

"Wow, grand meteor shower with sound effects. They had to see that on Morti. Any news from them about the latest explosion?" Jamie inquired.

"Crazy, they are saying it was from the shock waves still reverberating in the atmosphere when 1061 exploded. Trying to keep folks calm," Udo said. "We have their intelligence decoded, sir. It contradicts the news. They are blaming Light Channel."

"Jamie and I need to see the complete translation as soon as possible," Griff demanded.

"Sending it to you now, sir."

Griff, with Jamie, carefully read the transcript of the conversations between his uncle, Braxton, and his executive officers.

"Belcor needs to see this immediately," Jamie said tensely.

"You are right." Griff wrote a few notes and then spoke, "Uncle Belcor, Jamie and I have read part of the document that I am sending you now. It is a transcript of communication of Braxton with his defense team. Please advise."

"Griff, we have already called together our command. We have been decoding some of their communications too. Thanks for this additional detail. Have you been able to receive signals for their communications to their residents?" Belcor explored.

Griff told him what they had learned from television stations and internet providers on Morti.

"Stay on mission and proceed. Will instruct soon." Belcor signed off.

****

Jamie and Griff kept their teams on track. The hydrogen elements were depleting, and the stars were expanding. It was day four.

Savannah's excited voice broke through the techy talk. "Griff, Jamie, come look at these numbers. I have checked with all the other scientists in Opaque Company. They have certified my calculations. We think we can complete the process today, and have our grand exodus from Stars 1050 through 1060, and 1062 by dusk. That would be perfect timing. The activity won't be as noticeable at dark."

"Are you one hundred percent certain, Savannah?" Jamie posed.

"Well, I would say ninety-nine percent."

"Let's do it, Savannah. I will inform Belcor." Griff motioned to Jamie to follow him. The pair stepped away from everyone else's hearing distance. "Jamie, Belcor thinks Morti is planning an attack on Light Channel by midnight. This may be a game changer." Griff informs Belcor of Savannah's calculations, as Jamie listened.

"Wow, Griff and Jamie, that does change our plans. Find out how quickly the ears can be in place and the gale storm created so that the ears crush the head."

"Should I bring Savannah into the conversation, sir?"

"Good idea. Put her on. We have to make quick decisions. The command officers are with me now."

Griff, Jamie and Savannah enter into a conference room on the spacecraft. On the screen, they could see Belcor and the Light Command officials. Savannah explained to the group the process and estimated time of impact.

"Griff, we are taking a vote. Audio off." The mission team watched as they poured over diagrams, maps, and other images. Then audio snapped back on. "Proceed with positioning the rounded projections, and with creating the storm. We are sending fifty percent of our vessels your way to assist with blowing in the worst galactic disturbance in man's history. Griff and Jamie, five hundred thousand of our best men and women will be at your side. Thank you Savannah, Jamie and Griff. We are so proud of all of you."

"What about Light Channel defense if needed?" Griff inquired.

"We are prepared. Every Light personnel and trainee has been called into active duty around the universe. More will come your way, depending on the number of evacuees from Morti."

Savannah directed the completion of the hydrogen conversion as each ship withdrew from the crown of eleven stars around Morti. When they were at protected distances, the countdown was ordered. The generators were set to their maximum strength. The eleven stars at first blended in with the sky's dusk colors. "Starburst is about to happen. Nothing like this has ever been witnessed before since the beginning of time. Look at how puffed up each star has become. Helium levels are about to explode. Star 1050 will start. There she goes. Others will be in quick succession."

"Commander Glosomore just sent me a message that said, from Earth, it looks like giant fireworks," Jamie spoke excitedly. "This is awesome."

"The fireworks will leave behind a lot of smoke like gray elephant ears," Savannah suggested. "These starbursts are creating a lot more stars which in turn create stellar winds. It will happen quickly."

"Opaque One, this is Gale One, Ralph speaking. You are sure putting on a grand show. The color and number of stars are incredible."

"Hi Ralph, good to work with you again," Griff responded.

"We are surrounding the perimeter of the two rounded projections, but we are all cloaked. We have your positions on visual. We are sending you our locations. Gale is ready to blow whenever you say. I will be in command of the west and you, Griff, command the east. Eastern half of Gale Company is now in your command. Western half of Opaque will follow me. Confirm you have same orders."

"Roger that, Ralph."

With the ears in place, Gale and Opaque companies began pushing the earlobes closer toward the head, Morti. The ships watched as the newly formed massive stars took life. The supernovas then quickly died, creating even more enormous winds.

"Galactic winds have already reached fifteen hundred kilometers per second," Savannah announced. "It's working. It is working. Yah."

"Evacuations have started on Morti. Belcor has forces coming to take care of them. Let's turn on the fans half force," Griff commanded. "Up to three thousand kilometers."

"The winds appeared to shift Morti to the north. Is that because of Star 1061 demise?"

"Yes, we need to have more spaceships there to stop the movement. Morti has to remain in the center of the ears to work," Savannah yelled.

Griff and Ralph gave the order to fortify the north.

"Thirty ships have loaded escapees. More ships are being sent. Two enemy craft managed to get through our forces," Jamie reported. "One had the death skull emblem on its side."

"Oh no, Braxton may have escaped." Griff moaned.

"Our forces are in pursuit," Jamie consoled.

"Morti is changing colors. No nighttime for them this evening," Savannah pointed to the atmosphere. "It's all lit up."

"Increase wind force to seven thousand kilometers," Griff demanded. "Here we go. Watch this full force."

The ears compressed the head. The heat created a ripple of nuclear plants exploding. The overheated red head of Morti quickly turned white with its advance aging. Morti imploded and the elements drifted southward, creating an enormous black hole. Stars from the galaxy now drawn into the hole and the lights are out for Black Eye Galaxy.

"Doomsday!" Jamie pronounced.

The spacecraft of Opaque and Gale companies switched off the fans and retreated. The crafts swayed in the galactic winds. With expert pilots, all were finally out of harm's way. For the time being, all the galaxies in the universe heard the melodious sound of peace.

****

"With the termination of Morti and much of Black Eye Galaxy, Light Channel is assured of a restful night. Braxton and about one hundred of his forces did escape. We detected communication between Braxton and SilverWorm. Intelligence suggests that the remaining Dark Particles are heading there. Opaque and Gale companies, we will see you tomorrow on earth. Other forces will be joining you. Sleep well." Belcor signed off.

"Good night, Uncle," Griff signaled.

"Headed toward Earth, thankfully, Sir," Jamie chimed in totally wearied. "Over and out."

CHAPTER TWENTY-SIX

Glorious Light

"Hmmm, how mesmerizing and enchanting." Jamie said, while she and Griff sat in Timberwood's branches taking in the beautiful expanse of the heavens. They watched in silence as dusk charmed the sky with golds, pinks, purples, oranges and reds. The moon glistened now along with the brightest stars. "I needed this quiet evening. The battles against darkness exhausted me. It seems like a long time since we have been able to enjoy being still and soaking in the beauty of creation as it was meant to be."

Griff clinked his glass of non-alcoholic champagne against Jamie's goblet. "And delight in being with each other?" He pulled himself closer to Jamie and wrapped his arm around her.

"Yes." She leaned against his chest as Griff gently kissed the top of her head. Turning her face toward his, Jamie looked deeply into his eyes. They held each other's gaze. Feeling her face flush, Jamie pulled away just a bit and lowered her eyes. She fingered the friendship ring given to her by Griff on the day she turned sixteen. "Griff, is it too bold of me to say that I love you with all my heart and soul? I want us to be much more than friends?"

He chuckled nervously. "Oh, Jamie, I have so wanted to tell you the same thing. I was not sure if my saying how I feel added too much pressure. There is no doubt in my mind about our love for each other. We are meant to be together forever. The only thing I questioned was the timing. Gosh, I feel so awkward."

"I didn't mean to embarrass you by saying it first …"

"No, Jamie, I … uh … you didn't embarrass me. It's that I … well, I guess I am just … I can fight battles but I can't tell my best friend I love her. I cherish you, Jamie. I adore you. I cannot stand a minute away from you. My words limp. They will never be enough to express how I feel."

"Awww….that's a good start, Griff," TimberWood interjected. "How sweet. Go ahead and give her a token of a man's love."

"Give me what? Griff, did you already have a ring for me in your pocket? We are surprising each other."

"Well, yes, but timing is off for this gift's meaning and message. Please don't be disappointed." Griff pulls a small silver velvet box out of his jacket pocket. "I give you this ring with all my heart, courage and strength."

"It is a ring box," Jamie shouted. "How could I be disappointed?"

Griff was still holding the box. He looked at it, then at Jamie, then back at the box again. He slid off his perch in TimberWood's branches and landed on his feet. Jamie gracefully glided down in front of him.

Griff fell to his knees. "I give you this with all …"

Clang! Bang! "What was that?" Jamie hollered as she turned around to see several recycling bins knocked over, with glass, cans, plastic and paper spilled everywhere.

"Sorry, it's just me. I am so clumsy. We must hurry." Trish shouted breathlessly as she ran into the backyard. "There is a big raucous at the witch's castle. There are rumors that all their prisoners, the kids will be killed at dawn. They need space in the castle to house some of the Dark Particles that escaped from Morti. The extra buildings on their campus are already full." When Trish finished her report, she finally noticed that Griff was on his knees in front of Jamie. "Oops. I think I am interrupting something. Should I have knocked on a tree or something?" She stopped mid-stride, lost her footing, and fell into the cardboard reprocessing receptacle.

"You just did by knocking over all five recycling containers," Jamie complained. Her eager anticipation of the gift faded as duty called. "We will leave right away. Sounds like a life or death situation."

"Wait, Jamie." Griff gently reached for her arm and held her. He stood up and both stepped toward Trish. "We will be right behind you. Tell the others to gather at eleven-eleven near St. Michael's, but stay hidden until they hear my signal. I will call Father Lumen and arrange for us to use the pergola behind the rectory. We can meet undetected there," Griff said as he got up from his knees. "Jamie, please open your gift before we go. It is a very special ring. It will give you added protection and power to fulfill your destiny, your purpose."

Jamie opened the silver box. *I do not understand. What kind of ring is this? I thought it was going to be an engagement ring. It is not even a birthstone. Jamie, you have to fight back your tears. Stop this instant. Do not show your disappointment.*

Griff cradled her face into his hands and gently kissed Jamie on her lips. Then he removed the ring from the box and slipped it onto her right index finger. It glowed immediately a rainbow of colors. The whole backyard shimmered from its radiance. "This is my way of protecting you and our bond of love. It is very special. You will see. Point your finger toward something. You will know immediately what I am saying about this ring."

"It won't destroy what I point to, will it?" Jamie probed.

"It will express in action whatever you feel about the person or object. Your ring literally activates and animates your emotions."

Jamie first looked straight at Griff. *You have to get a grip on yourself. Don't you dare show your feelings? I am so mad at you, Griff.* She turned to TimberWood and directed her finger toward him. TimberWood shook from top to bottom and roared with laughter. "I feel hugged and loved. Guess you love me a whole lot."

Jamie smiled. "Yes, my dear TimberWood, I have always loved you and always will."

"We must go. Just remember the ring will do whatever you feel. When we are finished at the castle, Jamie, there is more I want to …"

"Let's just go," Jamie interrupted. She swallowed hard and felt a lump of feelings stuck in her throat. Jamie grabbed her sword and backpack as she ran out of the backyard. *That was so immature, Jamie Travelstead. You did not give him a chance to finish his sentence. Griff said there is more. What was the more?*

✳ ✳ ✳ ✳ ✳ ✳ ✳ ✳

Jamie went to St. Michael's Cathedral rectory and hid behind the Marian Grotto since she was the first to arrive. She watched Griff as he texted an express message to all the Light Keepers and Champions. Still in hiding, she observed everyone arriving.

The sweet couple, the Willows, who invited her into their car the night she almost lost her soul, arrived first. They had about twenty men and women with them. Jamie recognized many of them as neighbors in Sun Ray Subdivision.

There is Lance on his regal steed, Samson. What a wonderful gentle man you are. And dear Rowdy. I will never forget that slurping sound from my bathroom. Your dear wife, Rowena and your daughter, Winnie, have been such loyal friends and protectors.

Jamie felt such an intense feeling of gloom and doom. *Am I just upset over not getting an engagement ring? Or am I intuiting that something dreadful is about to happen?*

Watching from her secret perch, Jamie saw Tynee, Mytee and the FrogBoys, Victorious and her fiends, as well as many of the teens released from the north and south dungeons. As each arrived, she recalled how she met them and what they meant to her. *Feels like I am doing a review of my life. Am I about to die? Is this a prophecy of some kind?* A surge of overwhelming emotions and sentiment filled her heart and mind. Tears flowed freely down her face.

From a distance, Jamie scrutinized the flurry of activity. On a table under the cathedral rectory's courtyard pergola, Trish spread out the diagrams she had drawn of the east and west dungeons. Griff secured maps of the castle grounds, and displayed them for all to see. Mr. and Mrs. Glosomore arrived with architectural plans of ductwork, electrical switches and breakers, entrances and exits. Texter, Jaden and other ghosts had detailed notes from their reconnaissance earlier that evening of where all the guards were posted and when they changed duty. As they reviewed all the details, Jamie kept vigil away from the group. Her ears perked up.

"This is it. We have this one last chance to save all the prisoners. Losing one is too many," Griff proclaimed.

Jamie removed a bottle of water and cloth from her backpack, and quickly washed her face. She drew closer to the group.

"We cannot fail. Dear friends of the Light, you all have your assignments. On my signal, we will commence. We cannot let darkness prevail. Before dawn we will overcome the darkness." Griff, in full armor, spoke with authority.

Then he leaned over and whispered to Texter, Kattie, and Jaden. "Where is Jamie? She left before me."

Jaden pointed. "Here she comes."

"I'm here now." Jamie glanced around to see her family, her high school and university friends, her Light Champion team, and so many others. "I'm ready."

"Good. I was worried, sweetheart." Griff tried to kiss her, but Jamie pulled away.

****

Jamie felt a strong hand on her right shoulder and a gentler hand on her left. *Are you here, Mom and Dad?*

Yes, we are here. You will be fine, Jamie. Our light will surround you.

I have your medallion, Mom. And your knife, Dad. The commands are committed to my memory and my heart.

You have the special ring from Griff. Use it wisely and well. Trust Griff. All will be for the Good.

Why is my spirit so down, Mom? I do not understand why I am …

This is your purpose, the dream you wanted to fulfill for a very long time. You wanted your prince and freedom for the prisoners. Both are now attainable. Fear, disappointment, change, feelings of loss yet hope for the future have all collided inside of you. You are coming to an end of a very long chapter in your book of life. But Jamie, there are more stories to be written. Go for it, darling!

****

The carillons sounded the hymn, *Dawn Will Overcome the Darkness*, from the church bell tower precisely at midnight. The pastor programmed the keyboard to hammer the chromatically tuned bells at Griff's request to serve as their signal to begin.

The chant began: "At dawn we will have overcome the darkness. Light will be victorious." The champions, the keepers, and all the friends of the

Light, one thousand strong, marched toward the castle. "Light will be triumphant. Light will be glorious."

****

Thirty dragons began their descent toward the GrayStone Castle. On Rowdy's cue, they dropped a thick black canvas tent over the castle. Victorious with her team of hyenas, who had jumped the fence, drew the tent cords tightly and staked the tent in place. "Dark Particles won't be able to see a thing now," Rowdy boasted.

Roberto and Ralph with two squadrons of Champions parachuted from their dragons into the castle grounds. They blocked and guarded all of the underground exits from the castle.

In absolute quiet, Samson led eighty powerful stallions toward the newly constructed and taller iron fence. It rose fifteen feet, not counting the rolls of barbwire at the top. Each stallion wore special padded harnesses with rolled edges on the girth and breeching to protect them. Their owners tied stout cords on fence uprights every ten to twelve feet, and with buckles and d-rings, fastened them to their horses. In between every two stallions, dragons positioned themselves with padding, ropes and pulleys.

Keme intoned the rich baritone hooting of the Barred Owl, "Who-cooks-for-you. Who-cooks-for-you-all." On the third hoot repetition, the stallions and dragons in unison flattened the iron barrier.

Jamie commanded, "Silencio. Silencio." The tumbling fence made no sound.

Light Keepers stationed themselves around the perimeter and lit up the overgrown courtyard. Champions quickly placed more bridges across the moat. "These extra planks across the moat should expedite the exodus," Keme explained.

"There are some floating logs in the water. They should speed up the exit process," Lois said as she stepped onto one of the logs before anyone could stop her.

The log-like creature surfaced and rolled Lois into the water, then clamped down on her leg. "Help. It's a crocodile."

"Stay calm, Lois. Use your sword to beat its nose as hard as you can, so it will release you," Jamie yelled. She leapt onto the reptile's back, and thrust her bokken repeatedly into the crocodile's eyes. "When the jaws open, Hai and Udo pull Lois out. Watch her leg."

The long-bodied aquatic, with its bloodied eyes and nose, opened its jaw in pain. Lois was rescued quickly from the water, as Jamie pounced on the reptile's neck so the jaw could not reopen. The carnivore lowered itself back into the water just as Winnie swung Jamie onto her back to safety. Medics wrapped Lois's leg and carried her off for emergency wound care.

Mytee offered to have his team secure the mouths of the crocodiles, disabling them from performing more attacks.

There were eight underground exits and eight back doors into the dungeon areas. When teams were ready to steam roll into each door, Keme and BirdSong sounded an uncontained duet of Barred owls' mating sounds of caws and gurgles, followed by sixty seconds of silence. Keme sounded the baritone hoot, "Who-cooks-for-you. Who-cooks-for-you-all." BirdSong responded, "Hoo-aw. Hoo-aw."

The sixteen exit doors collapsed simultaneously at 1:27 a.m. Dark Particles' Security forces were going off duty in three minutes so were not prepared for a breech. With uniforms removed forcibly and quickly, LC members chained the retiring guards in the dungeons. Their replacements arrived promptly in the stairwell at 1:30 a.m. When the stairwell doors unbolted, Light Champions stood ready in proper DP Security garb. The incoming security detail were gagged and bound swiftly.

Light Keepers flashed lanterns in a rhythmic code from each of the sixteen penetrated doorways. Next stage commenced with one half of the Light forces infiltrating the castle. Heavily armed Champions lined each stairwell to prevent any evil from adversely stopping the freeing of the teens and young adults.

Griff wore an identical ring to the one he gave Jamie. Together, with rays of light from their rings, they broke the chains of the prisoners in east and west chambers. Light force medics and keepers ushered them out of the castle, across the moat and the downed fence. Military vehicles and ambulances awaited them.

"There are four oubliettes in each dungeon, according to this diagram on the east dungeon wall. I am not sure what they are or how you get in," Maria noted.

"Oubliettes only have an opening at the top. Sounds like a job for our ghost detail. Kattie, come to east with your team. We need spirit magic," Griff requested.

Kattie, Texter, Jaden and some others went through the ceiling of the sealed off cells. From the inside, they could tell how to open the vaults. "We will need stretchers and pulleys to get these very emaciated young people out," Kattie cried.

The ghosts raced to each oubliette in east, west, north and south sections of the castle to find the openings. Hundreds of young adults, mostly in their twenties or thirties, rescued and safe. Tenderly and respectfully, Light Guardians carried their fragile and broken comrades to emergency vehicles.

"Belcor, we have located some of our prisoners-of-war or presumed dead," Griff choked.

Griff and Jamie watched as Belcor sadly approached the east entrance, and personally went up to each prisoner, thanked them for their service and noted their names.

"He is so genuinely kind," Jamie said. "Someone to emulate."

"Yes, I am sure he will contact their families personally. He is as holy as a person can be," Griff responded. "It's 3:00 a.m. Are all the dungeons cleared?"

"Done. Everyone is out, a few are still being transported to safety," Udo reported.

****

"Not everyone," a familiar voice spoke. "There is one more cell you have not found, Griff. I have come to destroy the three prisoners and you."

"Oh, Uncle Braxton. Did not expect you to lower yourself to come here. And just who might be in that cell?" Griff asked sarcastically.

"Sweet little Naomi, John and Paul. My disowned children. I tried to rescue them many times. One night, I was actually there, but they refused to go with me. They believed I was evil and part of the Dark Particles. I was undercover then so I could find them. I begged them with everything I could say or do. Their rejection made me dark. They do not deserve my help now. Their refusal to be with me destroyed my soul. They can rot in that cell."

Griff gasped and was momentarily speechless.

"Don't believe him Griff. We have your cousins outside," Uncle Belcor consoled.

Braxton lunged at Jamie, and held his sword to her throat. "Give me back my children. I have waited all these years to find them. They rejected me long years ago, and now they will pay for it the rest of their lives. Give them to me or I will kill your little girlfriend."

Griff, on the count of three use your new ring to encircle us with fire. One, two, three. Jamie communicated telepathically. *I will use mine to gain passage through the ring of fire.*

Braxton and Jamie engulfed in fire. Braxton shrieked in pain, dropped his sword, and jumped into the moat. Jamie used her ring to create a small passage through the fire and into the safety of Griff's arms.

Jamie and Griff stood militarily erect as if keeping vigil. Belcor sadly scooped up his brother's remains into a vial from his backpack, and carried him in his coat pocket.

"I had always hoped he was alive somewhere and was living in Light. What a horrible waste of gifts and power. Sadness and anger whittled away at his spirit," Belcor voiced. "It is finished now. May he rest in peace."

✦✦✦✦✦✦✦✦

"Teams for the castle take your places on each level of the castle." Griff commanded at 4:00 a.m. "Champions, as previously assigned, arrest all Dark Particles and move to secured transport for imprisonment or rehabilitation. Remember no creature is to be harmed, maimed or killed unless necessary for our defense of the Light or safety. Teams assigned to silos are to secure food, provisions and weapons. As areas are secured, details should remain to keep them that way. Be safe and go with Light."

The dungeon stairwell doors were unbolted and Light forces began their ascent. Horrific battles ensued on every floor. The hardcore fighting resulted in a cacophony of clanging swords and breaking windows. The sound of screams filtered throughout the city. Many non-magical people of light made their way toward the castle and began attending to the injured.

When Light Champions redeemed another area for Light Channel, Griff and Jamie's teams employed gold spheres to brighten up each crevice and corner of the castle.

During two hours of ferocious conflict, Light Champions captured or destroyed many Dark Particles. Only SilverWorm evaded the action, and remained undetected.

****

At dawn, a brilliant red sun slowly began its ascent into the sky. Jamie allowed herself a brief moment to remember the beautiful evening with Griff and her moodiness as she watched the sun rising from a castle window. Just then, Jamie felt the intense heat of evil breathing on the back of her neck.

"Caught you off guard. Are you daydreaming? I have waited for this moment. You are mine now. I will own your medallion and that life-saving ring. Take them off. They belong to me now. Give them to me this instant or I will cut you into pieces," the evil witch demanded. She slashed Jamie's right leg very deeply. Blood gushed out.

Jamie used her magical ring powers to move away from SilverWorm by several feet. She commanded her medallion to apply a tourniquet to her leg. Then she hobbled toward SilverWorm. "Here is my ring." She pointed it at the witch. "I have waited for this moment. See what this ring can do!"

All the evil commands and soul snatching substance oozed out of the witch. The spiders in her web of hair crawled out and gyrated this way and that. The life-sucking worms choked each other and withered. The witch's medallion went up in smoke, burning rings around SilverWorm's neck. All of her outer clothing sizzled as it fell off her frame.

"One single thought and one pointing of my finger has stripped you. Who are you when you are almost naked?" Jamie demanded.

The witch did not answer.

"Say it – I am nothing in the Light. I have no power in the Light. Say it."

The witch mocked Jamie, "La-di-da. I am naked in the light."

"Interesting that you would focus on your half-nakedness and hideousness. But that is not what I commanded you to say." Jamie pointed the ring toward her again. SilverWorm's underclothing began to droop. She grasped at it, trying desperately to hold it on.

"I ordered you to say – I am nothing in the Light. I have no power in the Light. This is your last chance."

"Go ahead and strip me. See if I care. I will still have my powers," SilverWorm retorted.

"You have no power over the Light. Darkness itself consumes you and all evil creatures. You are literally exposed." Jamie pointed the ring and an enormous black cloud hung over and under the witch. SilverWorm choked violently on the closeness. "Dispel the darkness if you have any power," Jamie demanded.

SilverWorm spat out one command after the other. Nothing. She cursed, "Darkness be gone from me." Shadows began to lift.

"Okay, now we are getting somewhere. First, you curse the darkness. Next, you admit you are nothing in the Light. So say it as if you believe it. I want everyone to hear you." Jamie stipulated. "Say – I am nothing in the Light. I have no power in the Light."

The witch screamed the phrases as loud as she could. She and all the Dark Particles, whom the Light Champions had captured, stared at their own ugliness and evil. "Is there another step?" she asked with faked humility.

Griff entered the room and stood next to Jamie, and together as one, they emphatically pointed at SilverWorm and proclaimed, "Look at the Sun. Go into the Light."

SilverWorm and all the remaining dark particles clung to each other as they walked to the window. The risen Sun filled the sky, the castle and all creatures with Light. Darkness melted in the sun's dancing rays and multicolored beams.

The room was soaked with rejoicing. The chant began: "At dawn we overcame the darkness. Light is triumphant. Light is glorious."

All evil disintegrated.

✳✳✳✳✳✳✳

"You are bleeding profusely, my love," Griff said. "Medics, please hurry," he ordered through his communication device.

Jamie slipped her hand into Griff's, and fell into his arms. He gently cradled her to the floor.

Medics applied a tourniquet to compress the femoral artery. "She may lose her lower leg. Almost severed, Jamie's leg is barely attached," the medic reported.

"My heart is beating slower and slower. What was the something more you mentioned yesterday evening? You had better do it now, Griff. I don't want to wait any longer for you to ask," Jamie said softly.

He faced his beloved, Jamie; fell to his knees by her side. Tears plummeted from their eyes to the floor. The magical tears transformed Jamie's clothes into the most beautiful gown ever. The dancing tears stitched a kingly tuxedo for Griff.

Scrunch ran to Griff with another small box, a gold one. Griff flipped the box open to reveal an exquisite light-filled triangular diamond engagement ring.

"The ring has a power of its own," Jamie squealed. She watched in delight as the dull gray walls and ceilings of the castle transformed into bright yellows. Soft green tones invaded the former black drapes on the windows. The columns and furnishings gilded with a layering of gold. The marble floors sparkled an iridescent white. Everything looked gleaming clean and smelled flowering fresh.

"Will you marry me, Jamie, my cherished friend, my first and only love?"

"Yes. I will marry you, my much-loved knight. You are royally handsome."

The chant began "Love is triumphant. Love is glorious." All cheered and clapped. The castle filled with rejoicing not heard for centuries. Even the trees waved their branches and flowers sprung into life all around the once dreary compound.

In her vision, Griff carried Jamie across town, with a solemn parade behind him, into the Travelstead's backyard. TimberWood cradled and rocked Jamie in his branches. All darkness was now bathed in Light. Jamie saw Light and pure beauty as the trees gloriously sang *Nature's Melodic Pause.*

EPILOGUE

J amie watched the beginnings of the ceremony through her medallion. At 12:00 noon, the Cathedral bells chimed *Nature's Melodic Pause.* In full dress uniform, Griff with Father Lumen exited the arched doors of St. Michael's Cathedral and waited for his bride's arrival.

A Light Champion honor guard flanked Griff. In their royal blue uniforms and white cummerbunds, Udo, Roberto, Hai and Keme lined one side. Long flowing royal blue dresses with white lace shoulder mantillas adorned Trish, Maria, BirdSong and Lois who skirted the other side of Griff.

Rowdy, Rowena and Winnie bellowed together, "The princess is near."

Wind instruments began Tchaikovsky's *Romeo and Juliet Love Theme* as Jamie's white and gold opalescent chariot approached. Chauffeured by Lance and drawn by Samson, the carriage reached the iridescent steps of the cathedral. Knight and stallion wore magnificent spun gold armor.

John Travelstead, in his white tuxedo and his azure cummerbund, stepped chivalrously from the horse drawn carriage and offered his hand to his wife. Judith's gown of sky blue harmonized perfectly with her jeweled tiara and necklace pendant. With grace, she lowered herself to the walkway. Together John and Judith Travelstead offered their hands to their lovely daughter. Jamie's white Venetian lace gown had a vintage scalloped-edge neckline, illusionary half sleeves, and an azure satin belt. The semi-cathedral length train and veil streamed behind her. Her pearl tiara glistened in the Sun's rays. Jamie elegantly held a sophisticated bridal bouquet of white roses with a small scattering of blue hydrangeas. The white roses were sprinkled with gold dust and tied with a blue satin ribbon to match her belt.

Father Lumen inquires, "Who gives this woman in marriage?"

"We do," Jamie's parents responded. They proudly escorted their daughter to the top of the steps with Kattie, her Maid of Honor, gently straightening the bride's train.

Aunt Esther and Uncle Jonathan were ushered into the church by their sons, Jaden and Judd. Uncle Belcor escorted Griff's aunt Florence, Braxton's widow, into the church. Grandma and Grandpa Glosomore, and Mom and Dad were shepherded next, followed by the four bridesmaids and four groomsmen. Light Champions bordered the main aisle with their drawn swords pointed upward. As they entered the church, Maggie and other friends from high school, played, *Family,* composed by Jamie. The wind instruments combined with full orchestral sound from percussion, string and brass filled the environment with joyful music. *Today brings new beginnings. Family is with me in new ways,* Jamie thought.

Father Lumen motioned all to sit, so everyone could see as Griff led his soon-to-be wife slowly up the aisle. Kattie made final adjustments to Jamie's train. Texter, her sweetheart and Griff's best man, accompanied her.

No one noticed under Jamie's gown the prosthetic leg. Jamie looked as if she floated with grace and exquisite beauty. Thirty violins played *Your Winds Carry Me on High* as she and Griff strolled arm in arm down the long cathedral aisle.

Jamie and Griff's illuminated faces radiated the love that they shared. Their vows, composed by the young couple, pledged fidelity to one another, and to a life always lived in the Son's Light.

****

The reception was a wonderful way to revisit many old friends. Maggie and Raz, Jamie's best friends from WiseMore High School, married and had three beautiful girls. Jake, Caleb and other WiseMore friends played as part of the orchestra. They had both married, and had two kids each. Jamie's friends from elementary and middle school on HallowWinds enhanced the gathering. A few of them, she had not seen in years. Tommy, Heika, Rosita and many of the other children and teens from GrayStone dungeons joined in the festivity. The family of Francisco Verazinni, the Light Champion who lost his life near Morti, as well as the rest of Opaque Eleven crew came to share in a happier time. The therapists, doctors, aids from Light Channel Medical Center rejoiced that Jamie and Griff arrived at this moment.

Jamie and Griff went to each table, trying to spend quality time with as many as they could. Jamie enjoyed hearing all about Griff's childhood from his talkative schoolmates.

Aunt Esther and Grandma Liz stood behind the gift tables, loaded with many treasures. One in particular caught Jamie's eye in the middle of their first dance as newlyweds. "Griff, look, next to the gift tables. The witches stole my mother's spinning wheel the day she died. I think that is hers."

"Do you want to look now or shall we finish the dance?" Griff lovingly asked his wife.

"Even though I can hardly contain myself, I can wait until everyone else gets up to dance."

Kattie saw Jamie staring at the wheel. She motioned everyone to start dancing, and then went over to her sister. "Come with me. I found two very special treasures at the castle."

Griff escorted the glowing sisters to the foot-driven spinning wheel.

"I cleaned it up and buffed it just for you," Kattie said proudly. "And here, Jamie, you may want to open this package."

Tears flowed freely from the sister's eyes, as Jamie uncovered *Family Connections,* the genealogy book written by their mother. Mom put her arms around her daughters. "You both can now add to this family book and album as your journeys progress. Your father and I would like for you both and your grandparents to come with us. It is time Kattie for your ashes to be properly attended."

The Glosomores and Jamie's immediate family gathered in front of the fireplace next door, retrieved the urn, and transported themselves magically to the cemetery. Kattie placed her remains inside the open vault. Angels sealed it closed. In that inimitable moment, Jamie watched Kattie's physical form become opalescent and dressed in brilliant redeeming white.

Magically, the wedding dance continued. No one else knew the family had left or come back.

****

The wedding reception, of course, took place under the special branches of TimberWood and his family of trees in the Travelstead backyard.

"Jamie, your parents shared their first kiss under my branches when I was young and too small for anyone to climb. They carved a heart in my side, long years ago. I have peeled back barky layers of life so you could see their mark of love in my trunk full of memories." TimberWood moved some branches aside so she could see it. "Would you and Griff honor me with your names and heart shapes?"

Griff handed Jamie her father's carving knife, the one John used years ago.

"You knew about this, Griff?" Jamie asked.

"Yes, TimberWood asked me the day I came here to cry in his branches when you were so badly injured, the day of our engagement. I was so distraught over the possibility of losing you. TimberWood insisted that our being together was your and my destiny. This thought gave me such comfort. The wise old tree also shared he called my name the day you fell into my arms; he brought us together. I promised this dear friend, TimberWood, we would come here on our wedding day. And in years to come, our children and their children would sit in his branches."

With their hands entwined, the couple carved their hearts and names into the side of TimberWood, next to the parents' etching. Family and friends applauded.

The newlyweds had already changed from their wedding clothes to casual wear for their honeymoon to the Bahamas. Griff gathered his new bride up in his arms and easily scaled the tree. They stood together in their favorite branch, and tossed the bridal bouquet. Kattie caught the gold sprinkled white roses with royal blue ribbons. Texter stood beaming at her side with his arm wrapped about her waist.

****

The Burtons renamed SilverWorm's castle, *Casa de la Luz,* or House of Light. TimberWood and his family dignified their luscious backyard.

Eight children graced the home of Griff and Jamie, Light Champion heroes. The Burton family motto, *Lux vitae,* the Light is my guide, piloted this young couple and family into future generations of people who diligently followed the Light. Under their leadership, darkness could not gain power for many decades.

- First born son, Howard, was destined to have a brave heart and followed in his parents' footsteps as champion of the Light.
- Their second born was a daughter, named Clare. Even as a tiny child, she was highly intuitive, bright, bold, independent, and inquisitive. This child had many ingenious ideas, which she could bring to practical completion. Clare became the head of intuitive research at Light Channel University.
- Fraternal twins were the third and fourth born. Sophia, whose name denotes wisdom, and her twin brother, Aaron whose name, signifies enlightened both taught for many years at Light Channel Academy.
- Lucy, meaning light, was fifth born. She delighted her father with her acumen and perceptiveness. Light Channel's Commander-in-chief Lucy Burton served after Belcor Williams retired.
- Three years later, triplets rounded out the family. Gail, whose name means tranquil, trained under Sensei Liu at Light Channel University like her mother. She inherited the sensei title at Light Channel when Liu retired. Gabriel and Gabriella, defenders of God, led a life true to their names as priest and nun.

Each of Jamie and Griff's children married wonderful men and women of the Light. They are now the proud grandparents of twenty-seven. The journey of Light continues.

****

Jamie and Griff sat comfortably in their easy chairs, watching several of Gail's children as they played on the floor near the fireplace. "Griff, your wood carvings remind me so much of my father's. They are beautiful."

Griff blew away small wood chips into a receptacle close by. He gently laid his carving on the floor near the children, clapped his hands and enthusiastically repeated, "Vida, Vida, Vida." The carving of the little dog came to life. It barked playfully, jumped and chased the kids around the room. "They wanted a dog. This one won't take a lot of care, so Gail won't get too mad at us." Griff and Jamie laughed easily.

"That little Maltese was whittled from white birch, and its name is Charley. He will need care because Charley is real. Magic, you know?"

"What do you think the kids are planning for tomorrow?" Jamie asked.

"Tomorrow? What is tomorrow?"

"Don't be silly, Griff. We have been married for twenty-five years. Moreover, it has been twenty-five years of peace in our universe. Wow, what a life!"

"Yes, what a blessed life." Griff made a few more carvings come to life, so he and Jamie could steal a kiss undetected.

"Surprise! Surprise! We saw that kiss." A flock of family and friends filled the room with balloons, food and drink.

And lots of life, love, peace and the Son's Light, Jamie and Griff spoke to each other without uttering a word.

GLOSSARY

Chapter One
- mensch — person of Honor

Chapter Two
- necromancer — witch; on who uses witchcraft and communicates with the dead
- specter — a ghost; apparition; spirit; vision

Chapter Four
- brooch — ornament fastened to clothing with hinged pin; badge

Chapter Seven
- poltergeist — noisy mischievous ghosts, especially manifesting itself by physical damage
- flicker — movement lightly and unsteadily; vibrate, fluttering ghost
- tempest — violent windy storm
- tittered — nervous giggle; laugh

Chapter Eight
- vociferously — noisy; loud voices carrying
- parallelogram — four equal sides
- fiend — hyena

Chapter Ten
- chuckwalla – large lizard found primarily in arid regions of southwestern United States

Chapter Twelve
- bokken — wooden sword
- sensei — master of Japanese martial arts
- flint — strong; Native American use means courageous

Chapter Thirteen
- illusory — deceptive; having the character of an illusion

Chapter Sixteen
- besom — broom made of twigs
- inimitable — not capable of being imitated

Chapter Twenty
- fosse — moat around castle; long narrow trench

Chapter Twenty-One
- pericardium — membrane sac enclosing the heart
- pulmonary — relating to the lungs
- endotracheal intubation — inserting tube into trachea (throat)
- ventricle — hallow part of the heart; chamber

Chapter Twenty-Two
- Spica — name of a star, spike like form; spiral wrapping, like ear of corn
- protuberant — thrusting out from a rounded mass

Chapter Twenty-Four
- eidetic memory — mental images having unusual vividness and detail as if actually visible
- hyperthymesiac — person with superior autobiographical memory

Chapter Twenty-Six
- carillon — set of bells sounded from keyboard of mechanically
- oubliette — dungeon with only top opening

Praise for *Light Journey* by Anne Howard

*L*ight Journey tells a compelling story of the struggle between darkness and light, and of how Jamie Travelstead and her friends become protectors of the Light. Talented writer Anne Howard blends excitement, wonder, humor, vivid description, and in depth action to dazzle and captivate readers who will not want to put the book down. A book for every reader's "must read" list, it will be long remembered and savored as a thought provoking story and a delight to read.

— Roberta Simpson Brown, author of ten books, including *Haunted Holidays* by the University Press of Kentucky.

****

My name is Charles Suddeth. I am a published author, a member of the Society of Children's Books Writers & Illustrators, and the leader of the LL&N Critique group. Anne Howard has been an active member of my critique group for several years, and she has the most vivid imagination of any writer I have ever encountered.

Anne Howard's *Light Journey* is about Jamie Travelstead who lives on the planet HallowWinds. After the deaths of her parents, she travels on a dragon to Earth, but witches and Dark Particles hunt her, seeking her magic powers. Jamie becomes a Light Champion. Can she and her friends defeat their enemies and bring Light to the world? Anne has not only told an exciting story, she has created a unique universe about which both teenagers and their parents will enjoy reading.

— Charles Suddeth, author of three books, including *Eighth Mask: Murder on the Cherokee Reservation* By Library Tales Publishing, Inc.

Printed in the United States
By Bookmasters